Waking in Time

Published by Curious Fox,
an imprint of Capstone Global Library Limited,
264 Banbury Road, Oxford, OX2 7DY
Registered company number: 6695582
www.curious-fox.com

All characters in this publication are fictitious and any resemblance to real
persons, living or dead, is purely coincidental.

ISBN 978-1-78202-593-1

20 19 18 17 16
10 9 8 7 6 5 4 3 2 1

A CIP catalogue for this book is available from the British Library.

Printed and bound by CPI Group (UK) Ltd, Croydon, CR0 4YY

Cover photo credit: Shutterstock/lassedesignen, sheff

Waking in Time

by Angie Stanton

Curious Fox
a capstone company-publishers for children

For Margo.

Your friendship is timeless.

CHAPTER 1

Grandma used to say, "When one door closes, a window opens. And if that doesn't happen, throw a rock and break in." She could always make me laugh, but the door has closed, and there is no window or rock I can use to reach her now.

It's barely been a month, and the mound over her grave hasn't settled yet. Mom and I stand on the thick carpet of damp grass and stare at her name etched beside my grandfather's on grey marble, cold and final. Sharon R Bailey. How is it possible that I'll never see her again?

"Today's the day, Mom," my mother says. "I'm driving Abbi to Madison, just like you both wanted." Her voice breaks and I squeeze her hand.

My mom wanted me to stay close to home for college, in Ohio, but I always knew that the University of Wisconsin was where I belonged. I don't know how Mom will do with both Grandma and me gone, but it's too late to change my plans now.

"I miss you, Gram." The words slip out as a whisper in the hope she can somehow hear me, but I don't feel her presence. She's not here. Maybe I'll feel closer to her when I get to campus, a place I haven't even seen yet. Gram's sudden cancer diagnosis caused us to cancel our first visit, and when we tried to make the trip a few months later, she'd taken a turn for the worse. So, I'm going in blind to my new world. My hands twitch with anxiety.

We stand over her grave and try not to cry, missing the woman who could turn an average day into a grand adventure. After a while Mom sighs. "I suppose we should hit the road."

"I love you, Grandma," I whisper, sniffing back tears. I climb into Mom's Murano, stuffed to the top with every can't-live-without item we could think of, and we're on our way to my new life.

***

After sharing driving duties, we pull into Madison that afternoon. The GPS guides us onto campus and we're suddenly surrounded by students. I feel swallowed up by the massive buildings, some modern and new with gleaming windows and steel framing, others ancient with stone pillars and grand facades.

Mom creeps along in the car as students dart across the street in front of us and bikers whiz past. "This campus is huge. A private college would have offered a more personal experience," Mom murmurs, biting her lip nervously.

"It's a little late for that argument now." My stomach jumbles with excited nerves at the prospect of how different my life will be here after growing up in a small town.

"I know, but I'm still allowed to worry. Don't listen to

me, though. Everything will be great. I'm sure Grandma was right – this is where you belong." Mom squeezes my knee as she turns onto Observatory Drive. The road is steep and has tight turns that reveal a breathtaking view of shimmering Lake Mendota.

I roll down my window and the scent of fresh water reminds me of summer camp. A warm breeze blows through my hair. "I can get used to this…"

We continue on, taking in every detail of the campus from the thick woods on one side of the car to the numerous old buildings on the other. Mom suddenly points. "There's that bell tower Grandma used to talk about."

An impressive stone structure crowns the top of the hill. "The Carillon Tower," I say, remembering Gram's stories of how the bells could be heard all across campus. The tall square building towers high above the treetops with its decorative cornice and parapets.

The road dips down a hill and up another. We pull in front of a massive stone building, named Elizabeth Waters, with wings jutting out from the centre core like stacked Legos. We look at each other and then at the imposing building that will be my new home. My nerves bubble over again.

"Ready?" Mom asks, barely masking her own anxiety.

I've lived in the same house since I was four. This is going to take time to get used to, but I'm never one to shy away from a challenge. "Yup. Let's do this."

Inside the airy foyer, a curved wrought iron balustrade leads up to the main landing and office. There is a half-circle nook on either side, each containing a crescent-shaped upholstered bench.

Mom sits and rubs her hand over the fabric. "Look at these old benches – I think they're covered in horse hair. If I didn't know better, I'd say they were original…"

"Mom." I wave her over to help me with the check-in paperwork. After collecting my room key and lanyard, which holds an ID that gets me into the building, we follow the corridor to the next wing, looking for room 4418. We pass bulletin boards bursting with social event notices, club sign-ups and floor meetings. Each dorm room door has the names of its residents written in thick black Sharpie on a bright orange star.

Students come and go, sidestepping past us to avoid bumping the two pillows in my arms, the oversized back-pack on my shoulder and the giant suitcase Mom is pull-ing. Some say hi, others avoid eye contact. I try to appear friendly, but not overeager.

"There are so many boys," Mom whispers, smiling at each one as they pass.

"Mom! Stop staring!"

"I can't help it. They're all so adorable. Oh, don't forget the condoms. I put them in your purse – not that I'm con-doning what you might do with these…"

I stop and turn on her. "Seriously, Mom. Please stop talking."

She shrugs and feigns innocence but stays quiet.

We continue on until I find my room. "Abbi" is printed on one orange star alongside one that says "Jada" – the roommate I've only chatted with online a couple of times.

I slide my key into the solid old lock and turn. The door clicks, then swings open as if caught by an unseen breeze, and I'm drawn into my new home. One side of the room is fully moved in and the shelves are overflowing with snacks, mugs, framed photos and books. Star-shaped string lights are draped from the ceiling and posters of Beyoncé and Jay Z hang on the wall over the bed. There's a coffeemaker and makeup mirror crowded onto the small desk, and a small TV on top of the microwave. A corkboard above holds pictures and necklaces secured with push pins.

My side of the room mirrors the layout but is in stark contrast with its sad blank walls, empty shelves and bare mattress.

"Home, sweet home," Mom announces, bringing my monstrous rolling suitcase to a halt.

A minute later, a group of student volunteers appear with a luggage cart containing the rest of my belongings, and I'm soon surrounded by the chaos of unpacking.

Mom's making my bed with new sheets, and I'm unloading notebooks and a reading lamp when Jada walks in.

"Abbi, you made it!" Jada has gorgeous corkscrew hair, wears a tank top and shorts and has toenails painted bright purple.

"Jada!"

"Hey, roomie!" She pulls me into a hug. "I hope you don't mind that I took this side." She tosses her keys onto her desk.

"Not at all. I love your twinkle lights."

"Look at your cool stuff! All your accessories match. I love the teal and grey theme."

"Hi, I'm Abbi's mom," my mother says.

"Nice to meet you, Mrs. Thorp."

Mom smiles as Jada and I make our first impressions with each other. As an only child, I've always had my own room growing up, so sharing with a complete stranger is going to be new for me.

With Jada's help, I'm unpacked in no time. I've left behind all my high school keepsakes. I'm starting a new chapter of life, and there isn't really any need for pictures of me and my friends cheerleading on our senior trip to Florida. I pin up a pic of me and Grandma at the Grand Canyon a couple of years ago. Other than a handful of family pictures, I'm starting fresh. Looking at how everything fits in, I can see myself spending a lot of time in this cosy little room.

Mom shakes open my quilt, an intricate design made up of old clothing scraps. It lands on top of the sheets like a layer of colourful icing.

"Your bedspread is beautiful. Did you make this?" Jada asks my mom.

"Abbi's grandmother made it." Mom smiles at me.

Jada turns to me with a sympathetic face. "I'm sorry, I forgot that your grandma recently passed." She examines the square patterns. "Some of these look really old."

Mom leans forward and points to a square. "This is from Abbi's baby blanket. And this one's from her grandmother's wedding dress."

A swell of pride fills me. Grandma was hardly the traditionally sweet old lady who knitted and sewed. She was much more comfortable at a dusty dig site in the middle of some remote desert wearing her favourite Peruvian sweater and Birkenstocks, or trudging through mud when she'd take me geocaching in state parks. So when she decided to make this quilt for me, it was a true labor of love that included pricked fingers and colourful swearwords.

"She also gave me this Badger calendar. What do you think? Is it too much?" I ask, hanging it up.

"It's just enough to show school pride without going overboard," Jada says with a laugh. "Wait till you see Erin and Anna's room down the hall. It's like someone hurled Badger red and white all over."

Mom dusts her hands off on her jeans. "I think that'll about do it. Jada, do you want to join us for a soda and a snack? I'm sure there's got to be dozens of good places to eat around here."

"Thanks, but I've gotta take off for the boathouse. They're giving a rowing demonstration today, but Abbi, later we can explore campus if you want."

"Yeah, I'd love to." I'm grateful that the roommate lottery gave me Jada and not some boring stick in the mud.

Jada collects her ID and keys. "You guys should check out the Memorial Union Terrace. My parents and I had lunch there earlier. It's attached to the student union and overlooks the lake. Amazing view."

"Thanks. We will!" Mom calls after her.

After loading all the empty boxes back into the car for Mom to haul home, we explore the building. We follow the steps down from the main entrance of the dormitory. It's like one of the grand staircases from *Gone with the Wind* or something. At the base of the stairs is a large carpeted sitting room filled with outdated furniture. "Antiques," Mom corrects me. Along one wall is a fireplace framed by couches and a large coffee table. There are wall sconces and old-fashioned radiators. Heavy beige drapes hang at the large picture windows that overlook a patio below.

"I bet this was the date parlour," Mom says, soaking it all in.

"What the heck is a date parlour?"

"Gram used to tell stories about how the gentlemen callers would wait for their dates here in the date parlour. Back in her day, guys weren't allowed in the dorm rooms. The boys dressed up in suit jackets and waited for their dates to make their entrance. Isn't that romantic?"

"Let's go and eat," I say, trying not to roll my eyes.

* * *

The Terrace is packed with people gathered at brightly coloured tables with a spectacular view of the lake, and a dozen or so students are catching rays out on the pier. Boats bob in the water, and birds flit near the shore. Cooks at an outside concession area are grilling up burgers, brats and hotdogs. I still can't believe this is my new home. It all seems too good to be true.

"Oh, honey. You're going to love it here. You were right to pick Madison over a small school," Mom says as we wander through the crowd and find a table with orange sunburst chairs under the shade of an old oak.

"It's like an awesome club I don't belong to," I murmur.

"Give it a few days and you'll be as comfortable as those kids over there." She gestures to a table of girls laughing and talking over sodas and nachos, as if they don't have a care in the world. I want to be those girls, and someday I will be. I tell myself that I've got plenty of time.

Mom and I nibble at our food, stretching out our last

hour together, until she reluctantly lays her napkin on her plate. "I hate to say this, but I'd better head off and let you settle in."

I clutch her arm as reality hits. "You don't have to go yet," I say to stall the inevitable.

"The longer I stay, the longer you aren't meeting new friends." She squeezes my hand. "I won't lie. I'm going to miss you like crazy, kiddo, but it's time. Plus I need to get some miles behind me if I'm going to get back for my staff meeting tomorrow."

My nervousness cranks back up. When she leaves, yet another door will be closing on my life. Sure, the giant window of college is opening up before me, but what if I'm not ready? Leaving Mom and home so soon after losing Grandma feels like a roller coaster that won't ever stop dropping.

We walk back to the car in silence.

"Now don't do anything dumb like I did and dye your hair blue. Oh, and no more tattoos. The one is plenty." Mom brushes my hair aside and touches the tiny star on my neck that I got in honour of Grandma. She pulls me in for one last hug. "I love you so much, Abbi. You'll have the time of your life – I promise," she says in my ear.

"I love you too," I whisper, my throat tightening. I know I'll love it here, but it feels as if I'm on the precipice of something huge, and I'm scared. I look around at other students, chatting and horsing around. Either this is harder for me than for them, or they're just hiding it really well.

"I'll see you at Thanksgiving." Mom forces a smile as she buckles her seatbelt.

I nod, not trusting my voice.

"And you can plan on me calling every day, at least for a while."

"Okay," I squeak out.

Mom blows a kiss and pulls away, and my new life begins.

CHAPTER 2

So this is college life. I've only been on campus for two days. It's still odd not to wake in my own room back home. Yet somehow, even though everything here at the UW is new and different, I feel closer to Grandma. I like thinking about her attending classes here so many years ago. Did she walk on the same paths I'm learning to take? Did she take the same stairways, or sit at the same place in the cafeteria that Jada and I have staked out? I smooth my hand over her old quilt. My heart warms as I recall the excited look in her eyes when I told her I would be living in Liz Waters, just like she did.

I stretch my legs over the side of my bed, and the ancient wooden frame gives a creak. Someone carved a symbol into the headboard years before. It looks like hands on a clock without the numbers or face. I touch the marred wood and wonder who did this and how long ago. I stand and look out of the window at the swaying treetops and Lake Mendota beyond.

The door opens and Jada carries in a shipping box and a steaming cup of coffee.

"Oh good, you're up. You got mail," she says.

"Already?" Mom promised she'd send care packages from home. I never imagined she'd start so soon. "I hope it's chocolate chip cookies and the pair of Sperrys I forgot."

Jada sets the box down. "My vote is for cookies. Save some for me – I'll be right back."

While she's gone, I rip into the package, but it's not cookies or shoes. It's Grandma's old hatbox.

I pause and lift out the vintage container covered in a faded floral damask fabric with a fraying rose-coloured cord. Tied to the top is a sealed envelope with a yellow sticky note from Mom.

Abbi,

I found this old hatbox of your grandmother's. She told me a long time ago she was saving it for you.

Miss you!

Love,

Mom

I tear away the Post-it. Grandma had scrawled "Abbi" on the envelope in her flowing handwriting.

Running my hand over the beautiful, aged hatbox, I remember being little and staring up at it high on a shelf in Grandma's wardrobe. When I asked what it was, she told me it was a hatbox from her younger days. I begged to try on the hats that I thought must be inside, but she laughed and said there were only old papers in it.

My heart pounds against my chest. "Oh, Grandma, what have you given me?" I whisper.

I remove the envelope from under the ribbon, carefully slit it open and slip out a single sheet. A waft of Grandma's perfume scents the air. My hands begin to shake when I see her familiar script filling the page.

My sweet Abbi,

You have been the gem of my life, and just when this darn cancer came calling, I realized who you are.

Here are a few mementos from the past. I hope they guide you and help you find the answers that I never could. Remember, you promised. I won't say more, lest you think I've gone batty.

All my love,

Grandma

I turn the page over, but there's nothing more. Maybe she actually *had* gone batty at the end. In and out of a medicated haze, she had said a lot of crazy things. She had asked me to promise to "find the baby," and I said that of course I promised, even though she wasn't making any sense. I just knew I had to reassure her.

I sigh, remembering those awful last days, and open the box. Inside I discover old pictures, keepsakes from Grandma's time at college, a faded birth certificate with a torn corner and names I don't recognize, a frilly handkerchief and letters from her mother. I lay them on the bed one by one and then lift out a framed picture of Grandma as a smiling teenager, standing with her parents. I've seen the photo many times before on her dresser. It occurs to me that I never asked Grandma about her parents, and now it's too late. My throat tightens as fresh grief rises inside me.

The door opens and Jada's back. "What's the matter?"

I wipe away a tear. "Oh, nothing. My mom sent a box of stuff that was my grandma's." Jada eyes the contents strewn across my bed.

"I'm sorry. It must be hard to go through her things." She perches next to me and looks through the items.

"It's awful … but also kind of good, you know?" I gather the clippings and pictures and return them to the box. A picture slips out and drops to the floor.

Jada picks it up. "Oh my God! You look exactly like your grandma!"

"Where? Let me see." I lean over and peer at the black-and-white photo. Smiling back at me is Grandma wearing a wool skirt and sweater, her short hair curled. But that's not who Jada is looking at. It's the grinning girl next to Grandma, who really does look just like me. She has my same long, brown hair, but it's curled under, with the front swirled into a round roll and styled like Grandma's. My look-alike wears a plaid skirt and a shirt with a rounded collar. An icy cold tingle runs down my spine.

"You and your grandmother could be twins," Jada continues, hovering over my shoulder.

"But that girl's not my grandma. That is." I point to my lighter-haired grandmother. "I don't know who the other girl is."

Jada gives me a quizzical look and flips the picture over. "'Best friends, 1951.' That could seriously be you. That is freaky!" She shakes her head. "Well, now you know you had a doppelganger back in ancient times."

Jada hands back the photo, and I study the face of the girl who eerily resembles me. "Grandma always told me how much she loved college and her friends. But after graduation she moved away and lost touch with everyone."

"I hate to interrupt your reminiscing, but don't you have a lecture soon?" Jada says as she checks the time on her phone.

"Oh shoot. I'm going to be late for my first physics class!" I slide the lid onto the box and leap out of bed.

"Physics, pfft. Overachiever!" Jada teases, slipping her laptop into her backpack.

"Not really. It was the only lesson left that fit my schedule."

After throwing on clothes and quickly brushing my teeth, I grab my lanyard and backpack, then rush through the halls and past the security-locked front doors.

Outside I take a left onto Observatory Drive and walk up towards Bascom Hill. The early September sun shines brightly, the lush grass smells fresh with dew and the lake glistens in the distance. Within minutes, I'm at the top of Bascom Hill, gazing towards the state capitol, majestic at the other end of State Street.

Inside Bascom Hall, I check my schedule again for the room number, then take a flight of steps to an old lecture hall laid out theater style. Its wooden seats are intricately adorned with iron frames. The floor is an aged, sealed concrete, but the elevated stage is state of the art, with speakers, lighting and a projection screen. I'm amazed at every turn to see how the university has kept traces of the early years mixed in with modern improvements. Like the present is overlapping history, with some of the edges still showing.

I find an aisle seat halfway down. About a hundred other students are scattered throughout the room. There is the occasional group of students sitting together, but mostly everyone is staring at their phones. I'm about to text Mom about receiving the hatbox, but the professor enters, so I stash my phone away.

"Good morning, I'm Professor Jones. Welcome to Quantum Physics. This semester we'll be studying string theory, quantum chromodynamics and M theory."

I stifle my groan.

He continues, "If you stick with me, at the end of the semester we'll even discuss the theory of time travel as written up by Professor Emeritus WC Smith."

I roll my eyes at the mention of time travel, but at least it sounds interesting. Maybe there's hope for this class after all.

"If the name Smith sounds familiar, it may be because of the new physics library that bears Professor Smith's name, or perhaps because of his groundbreaking work in holographic principle that has made this university a leader in the field of physics. But for now, let's get started on the basics."

* * *

After class, my head swimming with complicated formulas, I head off to the bookshop in search of a book for my English Lit class. I know the indie bookshop is close, but I'm not exactly sure where. I stop to check my phone in a small pedestrian mall area filled with metal benches, and trees just beginning to change colour. Nearby a guy in a navy T-shirt and cargo shorts is taking a picture of a building. A closer look reveals that he is actually focusing in on a dedication plaque on Smith Physics Library – the library my professor just mentioned.

I step closer to read the plaque.

"Embrace the impossible, for it will lead you to the answers you seek." ~WC Smith

"That's vague," I say.

The guy laughs. "Sounds like a philosopher, doesn't it?" He's tall, well over six feet, rail thin, with short brown hair.

"Why are you taking a picture of it?"

"For my grandpa. He used to work on campus. I thought I'd send him some pictures to cheer him up."

"Want me to take a picture of you next to the plaque?"

"Sure." He hands me his phone and stands next to it. He points at the plaque and makes a goofy face that makes me laugh. He's kind of cute, despite his high forehead and prominent nose.

I take two shots and hand back his phone.

"Thanks." He looks at the pictures and smiles. "Gramps is going to love this. He's a feisty old fella. I like to send him stuff to keep him entertained. He's not been doing too well lately."

"I'm sorry to hear that. My grandma died a few weeks ago." I immediately wish I hadn't blabbed that personal factoid. It's probably not what someone with a sick grandparent wants to hear, but he doesn't seem to mind.

"I'm sorry. That must be hard."

I nod. "Thanks. It is. My grandma went to school here in the fifties." I glance around at all the campus buildings. "She was so excited when I told her I was coming to Madison." I wish so badly that I could be sending silly pictures to her too.

"That must make it even harder." He shakes his head sympathetically. "By the way, I'm Colton."

"Abbi," I say. "This campus is huge. I'm still trying to find my way around."

"Give it time, you'll master it. I'm in Tripp Hall, by the lake. What about you?"

"Liz Waters."

He smiles. "Hey, we're practically neighbours. If you need any help, I know campus pretty well."

"Actually, I'm trying to find a used bookshop near here."

"What's the address?"

I show him my phone.

"It's the next street over, so you're close." He points me in the right direction.

I tell him thanks and head for the bookshop. Even though I've just met a nice guy, I've got a weird, uneasy feeling that I can't put my finger on. Maybe it's homesickness? Or thinking about Grandma? I try to snap out of it but instead feel myself being pulled into a funk that insists on following me for the rest of the day.

* * *

Later that night I still can't shake the feeling. I'm in college – I should be having the time of my life! I stare at my UW calendar and try to imagine Grandma on her first few days here. If only I could call her and talk about it. She always had a knack for cheering me up.

Plopping down on my bed, I hold the hatbox. What answers did Grandma want me to find? What did she mean when she said she realized who I was? And what exactly did I unknowingly promise her?

Jada rushes in, tosses her handbag onto her desk, then halts when she sees me. "What's the matter?"

"Nothing." I shrug, a little embarrassed that every time she walks in I seem to be in bed, sulking.

"Okay, I see what's happening, and you are not hiding in here all night. I met a guy at the Union today. He and his friends are having a bonfire out on Picnic Point. And you and I are going."

"Thanks, but I don't feel much like a party tonight." I shuffle through the pile of old photos.

"You want to stay here and curl up with your sad memories? Is that what your Grandma would have wanted you to do?"

A smile sneaks onto my lips. "No." I realize that *I am*

turning out to be the stick-in-the-mud roommate I was worried about getting.

"Exactly. You need to get out and have some fun. It's a gorgeous night. Let's go."

I slowly get up. "All right."

"Good girl!" Jada cheers.

The night is mild, as if September is trying to hang on to summer. We walk the mile or so along the lakeshore, but the walk goes quickly as Jada shares stories from her time on her high school volleyball team and her decision to go into communications. I tell her about my embarrassing attempt to run hurdles in track and how I'm still undecided on a major.

We pass several dorms with lights glowing from the windows. The massive University Hospital buildings loom in the distance like a small city dropped on the edge of campus. Students fly past on bikes, forcing us to cling to the edge of the paved path.

Finally we arrive at a stone wall entrance to Picnic Point. "How did you know how to find this place?" I ask. A full moon creates shadows from the trees and brush and offers a welcome bit of light as we take a narrow path through the woods.

"Dan, that guy I met, told me how to get here," Jada says, seemingly unaffected by the spooky trail.

"Are you sure this isn't one of those pranks they pull on freshmen, luring us into the woods to freak us out?" I say, wishing I had a flashlight.

"Even if it is, who cares?" she laughs. "It's a lot better than staying in! Did you know there are Native American effigy mounds around here?"

"Now you're telling me the place is haunted?"

Jada snorts. "Probably. At a campus this old, there's bound to be tons of interesting history."

Pea gravel crunches under our feet, loud above the sound of the chirping cicadas. The path narrows as trees close in around us, and just when I'm ready to chicken out and turn back, it opens back up to a moonlit clearing. I smell the scent of burning wood, reminding me of campfires with Mom and Grandma where I'd roast marshmallows for everyone. Then I hear laughter in the distance.

"See, I told you it's real," Jada says.

I sigh in relief as a bonfire comes into view, a festive array of flickering flames. Two dozen students are clustered around a huge bonfire, some sitting on built-in ledges ringing the pit.

Most carry a red plastic cup, which is either a party cliché or maybe a nod to the Wisconsin Badgers. My first official college party.

"Hey, I see Dan. Come on." Jada points and I follow her around the perimeter until she stops in front of a guy with a Badger Hockey T-shirt and a buzz cut.

"You came," he calls out and hugs Jada.

"I told you I would, and I brought my friend Abbi."

"Hey, Abbi, how ya doing?"

"She needs serious cheering up," Jada answers for me.

"Let me get you guys a beer," he says and pumps us each a cup from a half keg in the back of a large wagon.

"Cheers!" The three of us tap our cups.

I take a foamy sip and try not to wince as I swallow the bitter liquid. It's not my first beer ... but nearly.

I check out the area and see that we're at the end of

a long, narrow peninsula. The lake surrounds us on three sides with a spectacular view of the state capitol and downtown. I nudge Jada. "Check out the view."

"Isn't it the most amazing place ever?" she squeals.

I wonder if Grandma ever came to Picnic Point, but I can't let myself get all sad again. Not tonight. So I down the nasty beer and go for a refill, hoping campus security doesn't show up.

A few beers later, music blasts and the party has exploded in size. I mingle and answer the questions "what's your major?" and "where are you from?" a dozen times. Jada is laughing with Dan and his friends.

Some guy named Mitch with thick lips, bushy eyebrows and no sense of personal space parks himself next to me on the ledge. He launches into the getting-to-know-you routine, and my subtle efforts to brush him off fail.

"Well, you're not in Ohio any more," he slurs, his hot breath on my face. "Now you're in Madison. You're a Badger. You've got to *be* a Badger. You've got to give up all that Buckeye crap."

"I know, right," I mumble, just to shut him up, but he keeps blathering on. I focus on the bonfire, where the wood crackles and sparks fly.

"You've got to go to every football game. Please tell me you've got season tickets, because if you don't, I might have to walk away right now."

"Actually, I don't have tickets." I hope he'll follow through on his threat to leave. At least the beer is numbing my senses.

"Unbelievable!" he yells, spilling beer on my sandals and sopping my toes.

"Hey!" I flick my feet to get rid of the pooling beer, but he doesn't seem to notice.

"Well, I'll have to drum up an extra ticket, and you can come with me. In fact, there's a game tomorrow..." He moves in closer.

I lean away. "Really, that's okay. I'm not much of a football person."

"What? Now see. It's a good thing you met me, because I can fix that." Mitch puts his meaty hand on my thigh. I shove it off.

"There you are! I've been searching all over for you," a voice says.

I glance up and see Colton, the guy I met in front of the physics library. He towers over Mitch.

"Hi!" I get up quickly but then feel the ground tilt under me. Colton puts his arm around me, and I lean into him, grateful for the escape.

"I thought you said to meet here at ten," he says, the light from the bonfire dancing in his brown eyes.

"I did?"

"You did," he lies. "Who's your friend?"

I turn to Mitch, who now looks as if someone has stolen a ball from him on the playground. "This is Mitch. He likes football. A lot."

"How ya doing, Mitch? I'm Colton."

"Hey," Mitch says without enthusiasm. "I gotta get another beer." He frowns and wobbles off.

"Thank you! I could not get rid of him."

Colton releases me. "Yeah, I noticed. I've been watching you for the last ten minutes. I've never seen anyone look so uncomfortable."

I swat his arm. "You could have come over sooner." So he was watching me? He is kind of adorable.

"I thought maybe you liked him." He smirks.

"Ew. He's built like a box, smells like Deep Heat and loves to hear himself talk."

"Is that what that smell was?" Colton laughs. "So, hey, do you want to get out of here?"

I've had enough party for one night, and he seems pretty trustworthy. "Sure, just let me tell my roommate first." We push through the crowd until I spot Jada perched on Dan's lap. "Jada, I'm going to head back. Do you want to come?" But I can see she's happy right where she is.

Jada gives me a meaningful look. "No. I'm good. I'll go back with Erin and Anna."

"Have fun." I grin, knowing she will, and I return to Colton. "We can go."

He leads us out of the growing mass of people. Once we're away from the crowd, the stillness of the night surrounds us like a dark fog as the air cools.

"Did you have a good time?" he asks.

"Not especially. I didn't really even want to come." I burp and taste beer. "'Scuse me."

Colton pretends not to notice, but the corner of his mouth curls. "Then why did you?"

"Jada made me. She says I needed cheering up. I figured if I drank enough, I'd get happier."

"And why did you need cheering up?"

I hate to be a big downer, but he did ask. "My mom sent me this old hatbox filled with stuff from my grandma. Seeing her things made me sad."

He gestures to a bench just off the path, overlooking a view of the city, and we sit. "I can see how that would bum you out, but would you prefer she hadn't given them to you?"

I shrug. "I guess it's all still so fresh." I pause for a minute, then say, "I thought coming to Madison would be a fresh start, get my mind off everything. But … I just have this nagging feeling. It's weird, but it's almost like I forgot something, or, I don't know, left my iron on or something. Does that make any sense?"

Colton looks at me kindly, and my skin tingles. "Sounds like a bad case of freshman nerves, that's all," he says. "Things will fall into place for you here, you'll see. Give it time."

I gaze into his eyes, so dark and mysterious in the moonlight. Apparently the beer has really relaxed me, because before I realize what I'm doing, I ask him, "Are you going to kiss me?"

Colton smiles and leans in. Suddenly a group of guys bursts onto the path and spot us on the bench. We spring apart before we've even touched.

"Go for it, man," one says, and they all laugh.

"Seriously, don't let us stop you," says another.

"Got any friends?" They make obnoxious kissing sounds and other lewd noises as they pass.

"On second thought, maybe the universe is trying to tell me not to," Colton says.

I stare back out over the water. What kind of answer is that? I sort of thought we had a connection. "Do I smell like Deep Heat too?" I shiver in the cool air.

"No." He laughs and puts his arm around me.

"Then why are you here?" And why did he put his arm around me?

I rest my head on his shoulder, suddenly very tired.

"I really like you. But I have this feeling that we're better off friends. You see, if I kiss you, eventually I'll start acting like a jerk, and then you'll hate me, and then I won't get to hang out with you any more."

I lift my head to protest. "But you've barely hung out with me now."

"Exactly. And I think that you could use a friend right now more than some drunk guy slurping at your neck."

I look him in the eye and realize that he's actually been listening to what I've said tonight. Unlike meat-hands Mitch.

"Abbi, I gotta tell you, I date – a lot. But I don't have many girls that are just friends. You know? I should introduce you to my roommate. He's a really nice guy, and I think you two might hit it off."

"You realize that is the ultimate rejection." I frown and kick a rock away. "No thanks, I'd rather meet someone by chance than through a cheesy set up."

Colton laughs again. "I meant it as a compliment."

I stand and start walking again, needing to get away from my embarrassment. My foot catches on a crack in the path. I trip, but Colton is already at my side, catching my arm to keep me upright. "How come you're not drunk?" I ask, my head swimming.

"I hide it well. You, on the other hand, are a rookie."

An owl calls eerily nearby. "Did you know there are effigy mounds around here?" I ask to change the subject.

"You read that in a guide book or something?" he asks with a smile. "I can show you one. Do you want to see it?"

"Of course!"

"Legend has it there's buried treasure on Picnic Point too."

"Did you read that in the guidebook?" I parrot back sarcastically.

"No, it's true! I always heard the story growing up, but someone actually posted online today that a couple of grad students doing soil research discovered a time capsule or something."

"Seriously?"

"Yup."

"So, how do you know so much about this place?"

"My family used to come here a lot when I was a kid. We'd feed the ducks at the Union Terrace and eat Babcock Hall ice cream."

I sink my hands into my pockets to stay warm in the cooling night air. "I only have my mom. Everyone else is gone."

"Your dad too?" he asks softly.

"He died when I was little. Mom never remarried." I think of my tiny family and how this summer it got smaller still with the loss of Grandma.

"I'm sorry. I can't imagine that. My family is huge."

"That sounds nice. I've always wanted a big, crazy family."

"Yeah, it's pretty fun. Maybe I'll have to bring you home with me sometime to meet them." He comes to a sudden stop. "Here it is."

"What?" I look around but don't really see anything.

"The effigy mound." He points.

There's a huge grassy bump in the ground, but I can't see much else in the dim light.

"Impressive, isn't it?" he says.

"Not really."

"I'm kidding. They really aren't much to look at. There's an obvious one outside my dorm and another up near the Carillon Tower."

We walk back to Liz Waters, my head really buzzing now from too much beer. Colton escorts me to the front door. "It was nice to run into you again."

"Thanks for saving me earlier. I owe you one," I say.

"Good. I'm sure I'll figure a way to collect. I'll see you around."

I make my way to my room, toss my lanyard and phone onto the besdide table and fall into bed. I push Grandma's hatbox to the side, too tired to even set it on the floor. Tonight was an epic fail. The one guy I attracted was an obnoxious drunk. Colton sort of acted as if he liked me, but only sees me as friend material. Story of my life. I burp again.

I know I should get up and take an ibuprofen and drink some water, but I'm tired, my head is all floaty and it would take too much effort. As I lie in bed, staring blankly at the dark ceiling, my fingers travel along the quilt. They graze over the patchwork of textures that took a lifetime to create. I feel something else and realize I didn't put all the pictures back in the hatbox. I drop them onto my bedside table so they don't get crushed.

Rolling over into the softness of my pillow, I hear the gong of bells like in a cathedral. They sound so near.

I can't remember any church this close to Liz Waters. And then I remember the Carillon Tower, that imposing structure that caught my attention when Mom and I arrived on campus. That must be where the ringing comes from, but why would it be playing so late at night?

The tune is nice, soothing and a little bit haunting. The notes repeat. I close my eyes and let the bells lull me to sleep.

As I'm drifting off, one of the bells rings off key.

CHAPTER 3

The next morning I blink awake. The bright sun makes my head throb, or maybe it's last night's drinking. My mouth is dry and sleep gums up my eyes. Turning my head towards Jada's side of the room, my eyes land on a poster of Michael Jackson surrounded by ghoulish zombies. I squint. *"Thriller?"*

I'm about to ask Jada when she had time to redecorate when I realize that it isn't her in the other bed. Instead it's a girl with a mass of strawberry blond hair. I glance around my room and do a double take. Everything is different, from the neon curtains on the windows, to the blue shag carpeting on the floor.

I jerk up. What the hell? My heart pounds. Whose room am I in?

Then I realize Grandma's quilt is on my bed, and I give a small sigh of relief. This must be some kind of epic prank.

The hatbox is wedged between the wall and the bottom corner of the bed, but on the bedside table my cell phone is missing, as is my lanyard and ID. Instead, a key on a plain key chain sits in its place along with some bills and loose change. Where's my stuff? My wooden hairbrush is replaced with a purple plastic one, and there's an old digital clock radio with weird knobs and dials next to it.

Panic creeps back in. I've never seen these things before in my life. Did someone come while I was sleeping and switch everything around? An anxious scan of my open wardrobe shows all my clothes are replaced with items I don't recognize.

I tiptoe across the room and crack open the door to the hall to see if a group of girls are waiting outside to yell "Surprise!" or something.

"What are you doing?" the strawberry blond stranger moans sleepily from Jada's bed.

I jump and shut the door louder than I meant to.

"Go back to bed, Abigail. It's too early."

I freeze. How does she know my name? And then I notice the Badger wall calendar hanging next to a retro touch-tone phone on the wall.

It reads OCTOBER 1983.

My jaw drops and the tiny hairs on my neck stand up. Okay, this has to be some extreme hoax that someone went to a lot of trouble to pull off. Or a dream? I need to calm down and figure out what the hell is happening. I quietly open the door again and sneak out. The hallway is the same, except the walls are now painted yellow instead of blue. The bulletin board is there, but the announcements pinned to it are all different. A girl appears from across the hall in a pink terry cloth bathrobe, wearing fuzzy slippers and glasses with lenses so big around they cover half her face.

"Hi, Abigail." She smiles and hurries past.

This girl knows me, but I'm pretty darn sure I've never seen her before, and why is everyone calling me Abigail instead of Abbi? I follow her. "Excuse me. Have we met?"

She stares at me with wide eyes as if I'm an idiot. "You're pulling my leg, right?"

"Actually, no. I think I got roofied or something last night. My head is really messed up."

"Roofied?" Her face is screwed up in confusion.

"You know, drugged," I say.

She looks aghast. "That's terrible! Who would do that?"

"I have no idea. Do you know where I was last night?"

"We all went to Headliners. It was totally rad. You don't remember? Is Linda okay?" She looks down the hall towards my room with concern.

"Linda?"

"Your roommate?" she says slowly as if I'm a foreigner who doesn't understand the language, which is exactly how I feel.

"Right! Yeah. Linda's still asleep," I say, thinking of the girl in Jada's bed. This is all wrong. This girl thinks I was at Headliners, and I've never heard of the place. I'm either still dreaming or have accidentally fallen asleep in the wrong dorm room.

I trudge back to "my" room, and notice that each door has an orange pumpkin cutout bearing the roommates' names. Yesterday our names were printed on bright orange stars, as if we were celebrities instead of kinder-garteners celebrating harvest.

"Abigail" is on one of the pumpkins, but instead of Jada's name, the other pumpkin says "Linda." Something is very out of place. I'm beginning to realize that the something is me.

I wonder if maybe someone moved my bed to another floor while I was passed out, but it's still 4418 – the same room number.

Back in the room, I stare at the unfamiliar clothes in my wardrobe. Putting any of these on would make me feel like a thief. Not one of these items is mine, but I can't go out in public in the extra-large UW T-shirt I wore to bed last night. I rifle through the unfamiliar items in the dresser, finally settling on a pair of super-short jean shorts that come all the way up above my belly button. To my surprise, they fit perfectly. I settle on a T-shirt with an image of some cartoon character named Ziggy. Whatever that is.

As I grab the key ring, Linda stirs. "Where are you going so early?" she mumbles, her face smooshed to her pillow.

Away from here, because waking up in this twilight zone is freaking me out. I open the door. "Breakfast."

"Abigail?"

I swallow. "Yeah?"

"Grab me a Pop-Tart, would ya?"

I glance at the two pumpkin-shaped name tags on our door. "Sure … Linda."

"Thanks," she says as I sneak away, desperate to get out of there.

I take the back steps located right outside my room to avoid the main staircase and the rest of the residents. I can't handle any more surprises. I push out the rarely used ground-level security door that faces the lake.

Everything outside looks normal. Thank God. The trees, the lake, the Social Sciences Building. I heave a breath of relief and lean against the stone wall of the building to ground myself. Goose bumps prick my arms – I assume from the cold morning air and not the stark fear that I'm trying to keep under control.

What the hell is happening? Why is everything screwed up? This has got to be some elaborate joke. It's the only thing that makes sense. But how did they pull it off? And why me? I expect Jada to jump out with a hidden camera … but nothing.

I stumble down the hill through the damp grass to the lake, needing to find clarity and to replay last night. Did someone slip something in my drink? I don't think so, but I know I drank too much. I remember Colton walking me home, me asking if he would kiss me and then him not kissing me. I groan and knock my head against a tree. Solid oak. I'm definitely awake now.

A few guys jog by. Their hair is a little long and their running shorts are way too short for guys, but otherwise, they look normal. Maybe I just had some sort of temporary breakdown, and if I go back up to the room everything will be normal? But I'm not ready to go back there.

On a hunch, I follow the path towards Picnic Point. That's the last place I was before going to bed. When I pass Tripp and Adams Hall and then the playing fields, I can't put my finger on it, but something is eerily off. It's as if the trees are trying to speak to me. At the entrance to Picnic Point, I notice the gravel car park. I could have sworn it was tarmac yesterday. And the sign looks different too. Then again it was dark out, so I can't know for sure. Still, something's not right.

I jog down the path to the end of Picnic Point, racking my brain for details from last night. The scent of pine trees and the decay of fallen leaves surround me. The path opens up, revealing small sandy beach areas that I couldn't see in the dark last night.

Out of breath, I reach the end of the path and start. The huge gathering circle and fire ring are gone. All of it.

There is a large grassy clearing, but that's all. Not even a bench. No sign of the bonfire. But this is definitely Picnic Point. Across the water I spot the Union Terrace and the state capitol jutting into the sky, but this isn't the place I visited last night. And yet it has to be. Is there more than one Picnic Point? I break out in a sweat.

I think about the calendar back in the room. It said 1983, but that can't be possible. I stare at my surroundings, not sure what I'm looking for, but searching for answers. I'm not about to look like a lunatic and ask someone, "Hey, can you tell me what time it is? Oh, and also the year?"

I head back down the path, trying to shake off the panic that is screaming at the edge of my mind. This time I search for clues from each person I pass, which isn't too many this early in the day. But I do notice that two guys I pass wear their shirts tucked into high-waisted jeans. It'd be funny if it weren't so terrifying. The cars in the car park are old. Not old as in rusted out, but old as in large, unfamiliar models.

I don't know what to do except to go back to the dorm. Girls pour out of the front doors in a steady stream on their way to lectures. Inside, a stack of the *Daily Cardinal*, the school newspaper, fills a rack, and I grab one. A jolt goes through me when I see the date.

OCTOBER 21, 1983.

I stagger back. No hoax could be this elaborate.

No! I wasn't even born in 1983. My mom, I calculate the years in my head, would be a teenager. My grandma is … alive! I can call her! Pushing the rest of the chaos out of my head, I rush through the halls to my room.

"Where've you been? I thought you were bringing me a Pop-Tart?" Linda says. She's dressed for the day and lifting a yellow backpack onto her shoulder.

"Huh? Oh, sorry." I search through my desk for my missing phone, but I can't find it.

"If you tell someone you're going to bring them breakfast, you should really do it," Linda complains.

"What?" I look up. "I totally forgot. I'll bring you one tomorrow." I move to my cluttered dresser and see a wallet I don't recognize, a wide-toothed comb, a large purple tube that reads Bonne Bell Lip Smackers and a printed class schedule. "Have you seen my phone?"

"What are you talking about?"

"My phone. I left it on my bedside table."

Linda's looking at me as if I've lost my mind. "Uh, duh. It's on the wall."

And then it hits me. Cell phones don't exist in 1983. So my phone evaporated into thin air along with the rest of my stuff? I drop onto my bed, trying to digest this realization.

Linda combs her bangs back and then sprays them with a stifling quantity of hairspray. "Do you want me to wait so we can walk to physics together?"

"No. I'm not going." My mind darts at rapid-fire speed.

I can fix this. I'm sure of it. I just need to get a grip on reality first, and then I'll be able to figure out how to get out of the wrong century.

"Are you sure? Today's lecture is supposed to be really interesting."

"Positive. I have something I have to do."

"Suit yourself." Linda rolls her eyes and heads out, leaving the door open.

Thank God she's gone. Now I can think straight. Grandma lived in the same house in Ohio since Mom was a kid, and she never got rid of her landline. I lift the handset off the cradle of the wall phone. I'm about to talk to Grandma! I suddenly get the jitters. What will I say? I hang up the phone and step away.

I've called Grandma a zillion times over the years, but I've just come to terms with the idea that I'll never talk to her again. With a deep bracing breath, I approach the phone again, lift the handset and press the buttons for the number that I know by heart.

The ringing on the other end sounds strange. I grip the receiver, praying for a connection to reality.

"Hello," a familiar voice answers. It is strong and youthful in comparison to the last days of her life, when it was weak and throaty. A flood of relief washes over me.

"Grandma," I whisper, tears springing to my eyes. I picture her grey hair styled in an efficient bob and the cubic zirconia earrings she never took off. A gift from my grandfather. She always said she'd rather travel than get fine jewelry, so he gave her the faux diamonds along with airline tickets.

"I'm sorry. You have the wrong number," she says with predictable kindness.

"No. Grandma, it's me, Abbi!" But then I remember there is no way she'd know me in 1983, and my gut clenches in despair.

"I wish I could help you, but I'm afraid you must have dialed wrong."

"You're right. I must have," I squeeze my eyes shut and focus, desperate to keep her on the line. The fact that Grandma exists, that I'm hearing her voice, is proof that I'm in a different time, that I'm not going crazy. Or that I've gone extremely crazy.

"My daughter is only fifteen, so having a granddaughter would be quite a shock," she laughs, and my heart aches, knowing that in my world, that laugh is gone.

Tears run down my cheeks. "I guess it would." I try to imagine Mom at fifteen, probably immersed in school and working towards the straight As that will lead her to a successful career in software programming. I'd like to talk to her, hear her confident voice and beg her to help me. But she'd think I was nuts.

"You have a nice day," Grandma says. I'm losing her again.

"I'll try. Thank you."

I hang up and lean my head against the wall, the coiled phone cord swinging next to me. I wipe away my tears. All I want to do is call Grandma back and tell her everything, that I really am her granddaughter, that her own daughter will marry late, become a widow early and move into a house just down the block from her. That she and I are like best friends who share a love of natural disaster movies, blue nail polish and Cheetos. I could tell Grandma everything about her life, but it would be cruel to scare her that way.

"Abigail? Are you all right?"

I look up to find another girl wearing ginormous glasses standing in the doorway. She looks like an owl with shoulder-length dark hair and feathered bangs. "You know me?" I ask.

"No duh," she says. It takes me a second to realize she means yes.

"How long?"

"Since welcome week...? You're freaking me out. What's going on?" She steps into the room.

"And we're friends? You and me?"

The girl nods, but she's looking at me strangely. I have no idea who she is.

"What the hell, Abigail? It's me, Margo. You know that. What's wrong?"

I shake my head and try to get a grip. "I don't know. Nothing. I had a strange dream. Were we together last night?"

"Yeah, at Headliners. We went with half the floor to hear a band."

Same answer as the girl in the pink robe. "That's right," I say, pretending to remember.

"You sure you're all right?" She narrows her eyes in concern.

"I'm fine. Really. I must have hit my head or something. Can we go back again tonight?"

"I guess. Why?"

Because maybe that would jog my memory. Or, since

it's where I apparently was last night in 1983, it might have something to do with why I travelled back in time.

* * *

That night, along with Linda, Margo and some other girls from the floor, we go to Headliners. I'm wearing Guess jeans, a cheesy graphic top with an Esprit label and a pair of ankle boots that I actually kind of like.

As we cross Library Mall to State Street, I struggle not to stare and point out how all the shops are different. The Walgreens is gone and a Rennebohms stands in its place. Traffic crowds State Street, but just yesterday State Street was closed to all but city buses and bikes. When we turn onto University Avenue, I'm shocked to find the entire University Square four-storey building and the parking ramp across the street gone. In its place is a small one-storey building with a car park across from it. Every time I turn a corner, I blink to digest the staggering changes. But I can't let myself fall into a heap of despair. I have to figure this out so I can go home.

Once inside Headliners, everyone starts pulling out their IDs.

I pull Margo aside. "I don't have a fake ID."

Her brows narrow in confusion. "I thought you were eighteen."

"I am."

"Yeah, so you don't need a fake. Duh! Don't you have yours with you?"

I dig through the bag I found in my room and pull out the wallet. Sure enough there's a photo ID with my face, my name and my date of birth. But the year is different.

1962.

Holy crap.

I show it to Margo.

"Not me, ya goof. Him." She pushes me towards the guy checking IDs.

He glances at my ID then smears the back of my hand with an ink stamp. I'm pushed inside the dark nightclub and engulfed by the thumping bass of vaguely familiar music.

We crowd the bar for a drink. Our IDs aren't needed since our hands are stamped. Apparently the drinking age is eighteen in 1983 – the only improvement I've noticed so far. Margo pushes a bottle into my hands, but it's not a beer. I check out the label. Bartles & Jaymes black cherry wine cooler. Seriously? But everyone's drinking them so ... bottom's up.

After downing my second disgustingly sweet fruity bottle, the burning fear inside me eases. This is better. If I have truly travelled through time, why not make the best of it? Or maybe if this all turns out to be some bizarre dream, I'll kick myself later for not taking advantage of the situation.

The club is packed with students, and there's a general wild party vibe. Some guys are wearing jeans, but others are wearing ridiculous snug-fitting pants with lots of zips. A lot of people sport mullets, an unfortunate look if you ask me.

The band plays classic rock. I recognize several of the songs from my mom's oldies playlist, such as "Surrender" and "Dream Police." I take a moment to check out the band. The drum kit reads Cheap Trick. I am listening to the actual band Cheap Trick! My mom loved them back in the day and still has their original vinyl albums. The lead singer has long blond hair and is wearing an open vest with no shirt, and parachute pants. I grin. He's appropriately hot. What I wouldn't give for Mom to see this.

The night is a blur of pounding music, pulsing lights and a dance floor sticky from spilled drinks. A bunch of guys have infiltrated our group. Everyone is flirting and yelling to be heard over the loud music. Everyone except Margo, who keeps watching me, still weirded out from my oddball questions earlier. I lift my bottle to hers. At this point, who cares how much I drink? I'll pay the price tomorrow with a hangover, but maybe I'll wake up back in the present, where I belong.

A long-faced guy named Jim wearing a Members Only jacket has been hitting on me for the past half hour. He gives me a drunken smile that comes off as more of a leer. I turn to ignore him, but he grabs me by the hips and pulls me in for the sloppiest, most disgusting kiss ever.

I shove him away. "What the hell! Back off!"

Before I realize what's happening, some guy with sandy-coloured hair appears out of nowhere and slugs Jim, sending him falling back into the crowd. Jim quickly recovers his wits and tackles my heroic defender before I can see his face. They go down in a violent tangle, knocking into other people.

In a flash the two guys fighting multiplies into more and more until there's a fully fledged brawl. Linda screams and Margo grabs my arm as people push in our direction to escape the fight. I'm about to follow when I hear someone yell my name. I glance around, but it's wall-to-wall people, and I see no familiar faces. Not that I know anyone in 1983 anyway. I'm familiar to these people (because in their world I've apparently been here all along?), but I don't recognize a soul.

I hear it again. It's a guy's voice and he sounds desperate. I whip around but can't spot anyone familiar in the mass of hysteria.

"Let's get out of here," Margo yells over the music.

"Abbi, over here!" the voice calls again, and it's urgent. It occurs to me that everyone else in this time has called me Abigail, so why is this person saying "Abbi?"

I spin around and search the crowd. Guys are shoving each other and some throw punches. In the panic, the whole crowd surges forward. Margo drags me outside.

"Wait! Someone is calling my name. I have to go back." Is it the guy who hit Jim?

"Are you bonkers? You'll get trampled."

But that voice knows me. I don't know how, or who he is, but my gut says it means something. I try to go back, but squad cars with flashing lights line the curb and more sirens blare in the distance. Campus police push the crowd back, and students scatter like ants.

"I need to get in. My friend is in there," I lie.

"Miss, unless you'd like a drunk and disorderly, I suggest you go home."

"Abigail, we have to go!" Margo hauls me away, but I keep looking back, wondering what or who I've just missed.

We stagger back to Liz Waters, most of the group giggling and talking about the hot singer in the band and the excitement of the fight I caused. We climb Bascom Hill, which is exhausting when sober and near impossible when you've drunk enough alcohol to block out a shift in time.

Back in my room I down an aspirin, change into my own baggy T-shirt and fall into my messy bed. It occurs to me that I was drunk last night, drunker than I've ever been, and I time travelled. Let's see if it happens again and sends me home.

I'm trying to stop the room from spinning when my leg bumps Grandma's hatbox. I heard her voice today. It reminds me of one of our last conversations before she died and that bizarre promise she asked me to make. She was confused and kept saying I had to help her find the baby, and that I should keep searching. She got herself all worked up and started to cry, and the nurse had to give her a sedative. I blink my watery eyes and run my hands over the familiar patches of her quilt.

The full moon shines through the window, illuminating Linda's Michael Jackson poster. I pray that when I wake up I'll be back where I belong. In my hazy stupor, I yawn and close my eyes. Sleep tugs at me like a familiar friend.

Just as I'm at the edge of sleep, I hear bells playing and wonder again why they play so late at night. Before I can come up with a reason, I drift off.

* * *

I wake in a hangover fog. For a minute I'm confused and don't know where I am. Then yesterday comes crashing back. Somehow I was transported to 1983. Looking around, the room is totally different from yesterday. Gone is the "Thriller" poster. In its place is a poster of a yellow smiley face. The bedspread is tie-dyed, clothes litter the bed and floor on the other side of the room and something stinks.

No! This can't be happening again. I've got to be hallucinating or in some deep REM state that won't allow me to wake. I sit up and dangle my legs from the bed. My bed, with my quilt and Grandma's hatbox. It's all mine, except what's on the bedside table. Everything from yesterday is gone, replaced by a new array of retro items.

I look around for the bad smell. My roommate's desk has sticks of burned-out incense in an old amber-coloured ashtray, the kind Grandma saved from when my pipe-smoking grandpa was still around.

At the end of my roommate's bed is a huge orange beanbag chair next to an ancient stereo and a stack of vinyl albums. My pulse begins to rev towards full-blown panic as I grasp my new reality. I've travelled again. And in the wrong direction.

My wardrobe door is covered with strings of beads, hanging like a curtain. I spy a calendar on the wall. I can already tell it's different from yesterday. I rise slowly, afraid of what I'll find. And then I'm close enough to see it.

August 1970.

I gasp and quickly cover my mouth so as not to wake my hippie, incense-burning roommate. She stirs, so I grab a towel from a hook and run for the bathroom. The bathroom is familiar – the only difference is the white painted walls. I take the last shower stall and blast the water. Why am I trapped in time? Under the hot, stinging spray, I let myself cry.

I hide in that stall for nearly an hour. Is this really

happening? And why? Girls come and go, and I'm grateful that no one yells at me for hogging one of the showers. I can't bear to face these strange girls who might say they know me.

When all is quiet, I sneak back to my room. Thankfully my roommate is gone, her bedding heaped as if a mole just crawled out.

What should I do? I can hide out here and hope that tonight I go back to my own time. But I'm not sure I can drink myself into a stupor three nights in a row. Also I can't just stare at the walls of this room all day, breathing in the stench of that incense. Maybe I should try to blend in and pretend to be a normal college student. In 1970. Yeah, right.

I pick up the timetable lying on the desk. According to the days checked off the calendar, today is August twenty-third. That means I have physics. What is with all the physics? I don't even like the subject. After dressing in jeans with obscenely wide flares and a peasant shirt, I stuff the timetable and a pen into a funky macramé bag I find on my dresser and head off to Bascom Hall, feeling like an imposter.

I take a seat near the back. The lecture hall looks the same, with the old wooden seats and cement floor. But the high-tech stage is replaced by a plain podium and chalkboard. A distinguished-looking man with greying hair at his temples and wearing glasses and a tweed jacket gives a stack of papers to a student in the front row to hand out.

"Good morning. I'm Professor Smith. Welcome to Physics 101."

Colton took pictures in front of the brand-new Smith

Physics Library two days ago. Is this the same Professor Smith? He must be dead in my time. Poor guy. I wonder how he'd react if I sprang that little tidbit on him.

The professor gives an overview of the course and how we will be discussing laws of thermodynamics, string theory and quantum mechanics. I glaze over as he speaks. I've got my own scientific conundrum to figure out. Two days ago I was in present day, yesterday in 1983, and today in 1970. I desperately want to go home but have no idea how. I need to think about this logically.

I list off the things in my head that happened both nights and that might be relevant: Getting drunk? Obnoxious guys trying to kiss me? Those ringing bells?

As I search my memory, I notice the professor surveying the crowded lecture hall while he speaks. When his eyes land on me, he starts and breaks off mid-sentence.

A huge smile spreads across his face. I turn back to see who he's looking at, but when I turn forward again, he's still focused on me.

"I think that's enough for today," he says, abruptly dismissing everyone. "See you all back here on Wednesday."

The students, thrilled to have a short class, gather their books and herd towards the door. I stay glued to my seat as they pass. Something is up and I'm not sure what. The professor approaches with eagerness in his brown eyes.

"Abbi, I've been waiting a very long time to see you again."

CHAPTER 4

The last of the students file out, and it's just the two of us in the empty lecture hall. My heart takes off like a shot. "You know me?"

The professor stands over me and grins, his eyes bright with excitement as I shrink down in my seat. "Yes. We've become good friends over the years."

I don't know if it's relief or dread I'm feeling, but it's more information than I had before. "Over what years? How is that possible? How is *this* possible?" I whisper, gesturing to the room – and the fact I shouldn't be here. He's the first person who seems to know that I'm not from this time, so I decide my only option is to trust him.

"It's a scientific anomaly, Abbi. Your unusual capacity to move through time has been my life's work for the past two decades. May I sit?"

I nod, stunned, and he lowers himself into the creaky seat next to me. Up close I notice the crow's-feet at his eyes and that his hair is peppered with grey throughout, but he doesn't seem terribly old.

"I have several theories that prove promising. A great many things are coming together right now." He smiles, apparently happy about all this and not at all concerned that I've travelled through time.

"If you know me, but I don't know you, then I must have met you in the past – or, your past." I stop short, realizing what that means. "Oh, God. I travel *further* back in time!"

My face flushes with panic, and I can't catch my breath. Why is this happening? I grip the wooden armrests as if they can hold me in one place. "I can't keep doing this. I need to go home," I say with pleading eyes.

Professor Smith lays his hand on my arm for a moment and reassures me in a patient voice. "It's all right. I'm working as quickly as I can to help restore you to where you belong."

My mouth goes dry. "How many times do I travel back?" I ask softly, terrified of the answer.

His forehead wrinkles as he considers my question. "Abbi, it's not a good idea for me to relay anything to you about your future."

I want to scream that my *future* should not occur in the past. "You've got to be kidding me!" It appears he's the only person who knows what's going on, and he's not going to tell me?

The professor forms a steeple with his fingers and pauses, deep in thought. His eyes are steady and his jaw is set when he says, "I'm trying to untangle how this is happening, and I fear anything you do to change the natural course of events could jeopardize my zeroing in on the solution."

I can't believe it. He's going to leave me in the dark, floundering on my own. "Please, Professor, you have to help me," I beg in desperation. "I can't keep bouncing through time."

He looks me in the eye, reminding me of my grandfather when I was a little girl. "I shouldn't say this, but I promise you'll be fine. You actually become quite adept at acclimatizing to new times. And trust me, I've dedicated my career to trying to solve your time travelling. Honestly, if this can be solved, I will do it."

His whole career? He says all this as if it's great news. If I hadn't already cried myself out in the shower this morning, I'd start bawling right now.

I slump in my seat. "You don't know how to help me."

He changes the subject, which depresses me even more.

"I do have questions for you. Since it's fresh in your mind, tell me everything you can about who you interacted with here on campus before you travelled the first time."

Pulling myself together, I look into his confident, steady eyes. It's clear he wants to help, and if there's anything at all he can do, then I want to help him help me. Heck, he has a library named after him in the future, so he must be brilliant. He holds my gaze. I smile weakly. "I can't believe we've talked before. This is so weird."

"Yes, it is. What's even more odd is that you look exactly the same as you did when I first met you, back when I was a young man." He smiles and his eyes crinkle.

I gulp, realizing that means I must travel *a lot* further back, which I can't stomach the thought of. A sheen of perspiration covers my forehead.

"Tell me, who are the people you interacted with on

campus before you time travelled?" he asks again. He pulls a pen and a small notebook from his inside jacket pocket.

Determined to stay focused and not fall apart at my uncertain future, I answer. "I was in my dorm room, alone. It was around midnight."

"Before that? What did you do that first night?"

I think back. Was it only two nights ago? By years it's several decades. In some ways it seems like long ago and in others, only a blink of time.

"I was with my roommate, Jada, at a bonfire on Picnic Point. There were a lot of people there." The sight of the crackling fire comes back to me. Did something happen there that set all this in motion?

"Anyone specific you spoke to?"

I cringe remembering Mitch blithering on. "One guy who kept hitting on me. He was really drunk."

"What was his name?"

"Mitch. Why? It's not like you know anyone in the future."

He jots down notes. "Every detail helps. You never know when one small detail will fit into a bigger picture. Anyone else?"

"A ton of kids I'd never met before, some freshmen, but mostly upperclassmen. I didn't talk to anyone for very long. Oh, there was this other guy. I met him earlier that day outside the physics library." I wonder if I should tell him about the name of the library, but decide maybe I shouldn't. "I saw him again at the party," I continue. "He walked me home after getting rid of the drunk guy."

"He was the last person you saw before going to bed and time travelling?"

"Yes." And that was the last time anything in my life was normal. I'd do anything to get that normal feeling back again.

"And you live in Elizabeth Waters?"

I nod.

"Room 4418?"

I startle. "How'd you know that?"

"You told me a long time ago." His amused smile says we really are old friends, something I still can't fathom. "Did the boy go to your room with you?"

"No! And why would it matter?" And what if he had? Did the professor really think I was going to reveal every personal thing of my life? He may say he knows me, but to me – at least right now – he's pretty much a total stranger.

He must read the frustration on my face. "I'm trying to consider every minute detail to see if there is anything specific you did, or some peculiarity that someone else did, that might have triggered your time travel. Please, tell me more about this boy."

"You think he has something to do with it?"

"Anything's possible." The professor averts his eyes, acting evasive. I want to know why, but it's becoming painfully clear he isn't going to tell me anything. I sigh.

"He's tall, he's from somewhere near Madison, he has brown hair…"

"Are you sure it was brown?" He seems perplexed.

"Positive. Why?"

The professor shakes his head as if disappointed and ignores my question. "What else? What's this boy's name?"

"Colton."

The professor creases his brow but doesn't look up. "And his last name?"

"I don't know. He never mentioned it."

The professor leans closer. "Are you sure? Think back to that time very carefully."

His intensity is starting to freak me out. "It happened two days ago. I'm positive. He just said Colton."

"Tell me more about him. What does he look like?"

"His hair was pretty short. He maybe had brown eyes, I'm not positive. Is that what you want to know?" The professor nods as he records all of this into his notebook.

"What else?" I say to myself, trying to remember our conversation. I was pretty drunk. "He was friendly, easy to like. He mentioned he has a big family with lots of siblings and cousins." I can't imagine how any of this can help.

"Yes, yes," Professor Smith mumbles, scribbling notes in his notebook.

"Does it mean something?"

He looks up, peering at me through the thick lenses of his glasses. "Honestly, I have no idea."

I sigh. This is a waste of time. Colton had done nothing more than walk me home. He hadn't even come into the building. Other than being incredibly likable and kind of cute, I can't imagine how he had anything to do with me flying through time.

The professor and I talk about each and every person I came in contact with at my dorm, from Jada to the students working at the front desk. We discuss all the places I'd gone, my timetable, everything.

Students begin filing into the room for the next class.

The professor frowns at their interruption. "I'm afraid we have to end our talk for now." He stands.

"What? You're the only person here who really knows me. I need your help." Does he seriously think he can just walk away? I don't think so.

The professor gathers his briefcase. "Walk with me." I follow him out of the lecture hall and down the stairs. "Abbi, you're understandably frightened, and all of this is overwhelming, but maybe these words will help."

He pauses near the doors. "A wise girl once told me that no matter how bad things seem, they will work out, so never lose hope. Believe in yourself. And she was right. Have faith. Stay strong." He smiles thoughtfully, opens the door and we exit into the bright daylight.

"There is so much promise in this field of research. I have every reason to believe that the answers are within reach." He says the words with such confidence, but he's leaving out a critical issue.

At the corner, I stop, forcing him to face me. "You don't know if I ever make it home, do you?"

The light in his eyes dims, and the hope in my heart is crushed. The professor looks away to avoid acknowledging my fears, then glances at his watch.

"Darn it. I have a faculty meeting with the head of my department. I'd skip it, but I've been working on a grant proposal to fund my research. Your research," he says pointedly. "Ironic timing."

We continue, me trudging reluctantly along, ignoring the people we pass as I imagine myself floating through time for the rest of my life.

"If I'm not at the meeting, the funding could all fall

apart, and we can't have that, especially now that you're here again. Abbi, I know your situation is difficult, but you must believe that I am working hard to rectify it. You are the reason for my entire field of study. To think – I almost went into what was then the new field of computing instead. I'd just received a job offer in New York when you appeared in my life, but I was so inspired by your plight, I knew I had to pursue physics instead."

While it's nice that he's so dedicated to helping me, that's of little help at the moment. I'm stuck in a foreign time and don't know what to do. I don't want to be left alone, and he's my only hope. "What should I do now? When will I see you again?"

"I'm afraid it must wait until later this evening."

A stab of fear hits me in the gut.

"I'm sorry to leave you like this, but this meeting really is crucial. I wouldn't put you off if it were anything else. I want to show you the theories I'm working on. I'm close to proving how we can tie this phenomenon to string theory."

"And then you'll be able to send me back?" I ask, imagining myself back where I belong.

"Slow down. It's much more complicated than that. I'll explain it all tonight, say, in my office at eight o'clock? That should give me time to have everything ready for you."

We turn the corner and there are student protesters picketing in front of a large grey building. They chant, "Smash Army Math!"

I turn to him. "What is Army Math, and what's so bad about it?"

"Abbi, the Vietnam War is going on. I assume you've learned about that in your history lessons."

"Yes, but honestly, I don't remember much about it other than that there was a lot of controversy about the US being involved."

"That's putting it lightly. Many believe the federally funded Army Mathematics Research Center is doing work in support of the military operations in Vietnam." The professor frowns at their chanting, then turns to me and takes my hand. "I'm sorry, but right now I've got to run. We're at a huge turning point, Abbi. Don't give up." He pats my hand, then steps away.

"But what should I do until tonight?" I call out.

He turns back. "Experience 1970. You've been given a rare gift. Not many people can move through time, but I caution you to be careful and avoid interacting with others as much as possible. We don't want to take a chance that you alter the future."

"Not *many*? Don't you mean I'm the *only* person who moves through time?"

An odd expression colours his face, and he steps back to me. He's about to say something, then hesitates.

"What?" I ask. He'd better not pull his big secretive act again.

He looks into my eyes and must see something that convinces him. "Abbi, you aren't the only person I know of who moves through time. There is one other."

I swear my world stops on its axis. "Who?"

The professor pauses. He glances at me, then at the picketers and then at his watch. "I'm incredibly late, and this is one meeting I can't miss. But here, take this." He pulls a red bandana out of his jacket pocket and pushes it into my hands. "Be wary of the picketers. You never know when the police will throw tear gas to clear them away. Keep the bandana handy. I'll see you at eight o'clock."

Professor Smith turns and crosses through the picket line as students yell, "Down with Vietnam!" He disappears into a building. Above the door, engraved into the stone, is the name STERLING HALL.

* * *

The rest of the afternoon and evening I try to follow the professor's advice. I explore campus, discovering changes. The enormous Helen C White Library that was perched on the edge of the lake a few days ago is still under construction. The trees appear smaller, there seem to be fewer car parks and the cars in them are models I've only seen in old movies.

But the biggest difference is the presence of Vietnam protestors. These long-haired students, many of the guys with thick mustaches, chant, "We won't fight another rich man's war!", "Down with Nixon!" and "Make love, not war!" I skirt around them.

In contrast, I spy other students studying under the shade of giant oaks, girls wearing suede fringed vests leisurely strolling to class and guys with shaggy hair playing Frisbee on the Bascom Hill lawn. Now that I look more closely, nearly all of the students have a bandana tied loosely around their neck or hanging from the pocket of their hip-hugging, flared jeans. Apparently the tear gas threat is real. I pat my pocket to make sure the professor's bandana is still there.

For dinner, I head to the Student Union and grab a burger, which seems puny compared to the size of the burgers served in my time. Instead of sitting inside the dimly lit Rathskeller dining room with its arched entryways, German murals and shelves of beer steins, I take my tray outside to the Union Terrace and sit by myself.

The late-afternoon sun hangs low in the sky, warming my skin and sending ripples of light off the water. I don't want to mix with the girls from my dorm. They know me, but I don't know them. How can that be? It's my creepy reality now, and it's lonely. The colourful green, orange and yellow chairs that I'd sat in a few days ago are now a similar sunburst style, but different enough to remind me I'm an outsider in this time. I eat my burger and a bag of Cheetos while staring out over the lake, but my food is tasteless.

The sun sinks lower in the sky, turning the thin clouds to warm pinks and oranges. Small waves wash to shore as an evening boater speeds by. Ducks bob easily over the turbulence, some looking like gawky teenagers ready to fly the nest and the safety of Mom and Dad. And here I am, desperate to fly *back* to my family. I toss bits of bread from my bun into the water, and the ducks motor towards me as if propelled by underwater engines.

I still have time before meeting up with the professor, so I cut through Library Mall to Lake Street with thoughts of checking out Headliners to see if it exists yet in this time. Maybe there's something there that will give me some answers. But when I hook a right onto Lake Street, I see a mob of protestors. An air of anger marches with them.

I rush around the group, set on my mission. I'm halfway to the end of the block when three police cars squeal to a stop across the middle of the street, effectively blocking it. I attempt to sneak around on the pavement, but then a mass of police officers appears around the cars in riot gear. I halt in my tracks, pretty sure this is a sign they don't want to be approached. I turn to see the protestors coming closer and their numbers growing.

"Halt where you are and clear the street," an officer demands over a megaphone, but the crowd surges forward. I'm stuck between the two warring factions with nowhere to go.

There are two guys and another girl on the pavement with me, and they're as startled as I am. The guy wearing a tie-dyed T-shirt moves quickly, dodging inside the McDonald's. "Come on!" he says, and the rest of us follow, not sure what else to do.

We watch out of the windows as the chanting grows louder and the protestors push closer, challenging the police. I'm relieved to be safely away from them, even though I'm sort of stuck. If I have to be stranded during a Vietnam protest, at least there are french fries available.

Feeling nervous about being too close to the windows, I duck behind the others pushing to see out and take a seat in one of the booths. I wonder if this is what the professor had in mind when he said I should experience 1970. It's then that I realize I'm going to be late for my meeting with him. I can't let that happen. I approach the door, considering the repercussions of trying to sneak through the standoff. I'm just an innocent bystander, right?

I'm about to push the door open and take my chances

when several loud pops explode and smoke fills the air. The protesting students scream and back away, and the officers advance, gaining ground. Inside the McDonald's, the people holing up with me all gasp and move further into the restaurant.

"Don't even think of opening that door!" a girl wearing a peace sign medallion yells at me.

I'm about to ask why, when an overwhelming burning sensation reaches my nose and throat. Like an invisible hand has pushed us, we all back away from the door and in unison begin coughing up the awful chemical.

"Quick, block the door," another yells. A worker from the kitchen runs forward with damp cloths and presses them against the bottom of the door where the gas is seeping inside. He locks it to ensure no one opens the door and lets more of it in.

My eyes burn and I blink to clear away the tears. I see others tying bandanas over their faces, and I reach for mine.

"Come on, the bathroom has got to be better than this," a woman yells, and a few people squeeze into the ladies' toilets.

"What's going on?" I choke out.

"You must be new here," a woman in a McDonald's uniform says.

I nod. She has no idea.

"The police shot pepper spray at the protestors. We're going to be stuck here until the air clears and the police have broken up the crowd."

I look around the cramped, tiled room. "How long will that take?"

"Depends," she says. "I'd say at least an hour."

Great. I'm stuck hiding out in a dingy bathroom when I should be meeting with the one man who can possibly help me.

The minutes tick by like slow, drawn-out water torture. The lingering scent of pepper permeates the air and we all take turns running our bandanas under the tap to soothe our burning noses and eyes.

Two hours later we're finally released from our fast food refuge. The street is empty except for a pair of officers keeping the peace with their stoic presence. I'm incredibly late for my meeting with Professor Smith. I hope he doesn't think I stood him up on purpose or, worse, travelled again before we could talk.

The quickest route to his office is up and over Bascom Hill, and it's like conquering the harshest StairMaster ever created. I finally reach Sterling Hall and locate his name on the staff directory in the lobby. I climb the stairs only to discover his office dark and locked. A note is taped to the door with my name on it.

I rip it off, panting for breath.

Abbi,

Perhaps our lines got crossed. I've gone to Liz Waters dorm to wait for you.

Professor Smith

Great. I jog the two blocks to my dorm expecting to find the professor in the lobby, but he's not there – just a couple of girls working in the office as others come and go. I realize I haven't seen a single guy in the dorm. Apparently it's girls only in this time.

With no sign of the professor, I head to my room to see if somehow he's there. Without air conditioning, the girls have propped open the doors and windows, allowing the warm air to flow through the building. Girls gossip and giggle while Otis Redding's "Sittin' on the Dock of the Bay" fills the air, unaware and unaffected by the pepper spray event I just endured across campus. Does this sort of thing happen all the time in the seventies?

When I reach my hallway, there is no professor waiting, no note on the door. I let myself into my room, my last hope to find him waiting for me. No luck. Shit. Where can he be?

I head back to the lobby and the chatting office girls. I take a chance and ask, "Did you happen to see a professor waiting in the lobby tonight?"

"Oh yeah. Are you Abbi Thorp?"

"Yeah!" I say, hoping they have some message for me like, *"Oh, by the way, here's your pass back to the twenty-first century. Thanks for visiting!"*

"He left a note for you." She hands over a pink message slip with my name on it.

"Thanks." I take the paper, sit on one of the crescent-shaped benches my mom coveted and read.

Abbi,

I'm concerned to have missed you twice. I must head home for a bit but will be back at my office late tonight as there's much to accomplish while you're here.

Unfortunately, with your dorm curfew, our meeting will have to wait until morning. Please meet at my office at 8 a.m.

Smith

Blowing out a long sigh of frustration, I drag myself back to my room. This night has been the biggest disaster. I dump my macramé bag on the bed and plop down beside it. I touch the carving on the corner of my headboard. If I don't look beyond my bed, I can almost pretend I'm back in my own time.

Exhausted from an awful day, I crawl under my quilt. I'm a time traveller. The fact that I'll keep travelling is too big a problem to wrap my mind around. I clutch Grandma's hatbox and wish for home. If only sheer longing could send me back.

Hours later, in the deep of the night, a deafening noise rocks the building, causing the windows to rattle and the room to shake. I'm thrown from bed and land on the cold tiles along with my roommate's incense ashtray, which shatters on impact.

"What was that?" my roommate cries out beside me.

"It felt like an earthquake."

We crawl to our feet, and I slip on sandals to protect against the broken glass. She beats me to the door and whips it open. Already the hallway is filling with girls. No one could possibly sleep through a noise that loud.

"What was that?" someone cries.

"It sounded like an explosion," says a girl wrapped in a terry cloth bathrobe.

"Quiet. I hear something," another says.

We crowd around the windows facing Observatory Drive, but our wing of the building is too low to see more than the neighbouring Social Sciences Building.

Within minutes, sirens howl in the distance and flashing lights are seen from every direction. I pull on a pair of shorts and sandals and join the others running outside for a better look. Flames shoot into the sky on the other side of the hill. We cut across the lawn towards Charter Street. The windows of Van Hise Hall are blown out. Parked cars with their windows shattered make it look as if we're in a war zone. Some cars are even tipped to one side, two tyres jutting into the air. A thick layer of grey debris covers everything, but what I see next is even more devastating – the horrific scene of Sterling Hall ablaze in the distance.

Professor Smith! He was going back to his office to work late. But he couldn't possibly have worked until three in the morning. Could he? God, no.

Soon fire trucks, police cars and ambulances surround the smoking building. Rescue personnel roam everywhere, looking for anyone to save. I rush forwards, but a police officer holds up his hand and blocks my way.

"What happened?" I cry.

"Stay back. There's broken glass everywhere," he says, his face pinched in stress.

I crane my neck to look past him. "But Professor Smith was going to work late. Someone needs to check and see if he was inside, if he's okay." Flames lick through the blasted-out windows as firemen attach their hoses to a hydrant.

"Miss, we don't know anything yet. Go back to your dorm. This area isn't safe."

Helpless, I watch the chaos from a distance as swarms of emergency workers hustle around the devastation. Professor Smith is my only hope. If he dies, who will help me get home? And then I think of his family – assuming he has a family. I offer a prayer that the professor is okay and that his loved ones are spared that heartbreak.

More official vehicles arrive, and the crowd of students I'm standing with is pushed back over the hill so far that we can't see anything but the flashing lights bouncing off the taller buildings. The stench from the blast of the burning building stays with me as I return to Liz Waters, and a sickening bile rises in my stomach. My nightmare keeps getting worse.

No one can sleep. Rumours fly about who would do such a thing. Some say it's the protesters, but all I can think of is September 11 and that it was terrorists. But I say nothing, of course. Another girl says that the Army Mathematics Department housed in Sterling Hall was the target. I don't understand why anyone would bomb a building on a college campus. I cling to every word of speculation, desperate for answers and fearing for the professor.

Professor Smith said to meet him at eight a.m. As the time nears, I dress and go as close as possible to the scene, but it's blocked off to Charter Street. I wait for an hour but see no sign of him.

So I return to the dorm and wait on the steps all day, pacing, then sitting, then pacing again. The professor knows I'm here. He might try to get a message to me or come and find me. But he never does. The phone lines are down, and power isn't restored until late in the day. Did he live or die last night?

I have never wished for technology more than at this moment. It's so frustrating that I can't go online and research the bombing. I can't log on to get an update from CNN. I hate 1970.

Around four o'clock, *The Capital Times* newspaper is delivered with the headline BOMB RUINS U MATHEMATICS UNIT; RESEARCHER DIES, 4 HURT.

My hands tremble, shaking the newspaper. A researcher has died. I scan the article. His identity has not yet been released. Others were injured but are expected to survive. What if it was the professor who died? Is that why there's a library named after him?

That night, exhausted from lack of sleep and desperate with worry for Professor Smith and for my own powerless situation, I collapse into sleep. On the edge of consciousness, the bells of the Carillon Tower begin to play.

One bell rings off key.

CHAPTER 5

The next morning, I wake slowly. My eyes are drawn to the cracks in the ceiling above my bed. Yesterday's bombing flashes in my mind. Is Professor Smith alive?

I jerk upright and swing my legs over the side of the bed. I'm startled by a red and white Wisconsin pennant on the wall over my roommate's bed and bouncy, cheerful music playing.

My heart lurches, and reality sucker punches me in the gut. I've travelled again.

I check my bed. Thank God – Grandma's hatbox is still at the foot. What have I left behind that I might need? I straighten the blanket and find the red bandana Professor Smith gave me; I snatch it up, clenching it like a lifeline. It's now a souvenir from my time in the seventies, along with the hippy macramé handbag.

My roommate has her back to me. She is dressing and singing along to the radio, *"Who put bomp in the bomp, bomp, bomp."* She has pin curls bobby-pinned all over her head like little snails. Not a pretty sight. I run my hand through my long hair and already know I won't fit in here.

The room is a mess of pants and bras hanging to dry

from the bookshelves and curtain rods, bath towels on the floor and discarded clothes and shoes heaped in a pile.

The clock on my bedside table is a beige box with numbers around the dial and a second hand ticking softly. The Bucky the Badger wall calendar confirms the year.

1961.

An icy cold fear jolts through my veins like a poison. I try to calm the catapulting of my heart. Why did this happen again? And how far back am I going to go?

The last thing I recall from before I fell asleep are the chimes of the Carillon Tower, and how it played out of tune. Did it always ring off key or was that the first time?

Oh my God. Professor Smith! It's 1961. He's alive! But is he even on campus in this year? I shoot out of bed.

"Oh! You startled me!" My roommate jumps at my unexpected motion. She's wearing dark-rimmed glasses on her pointy nose and a brown cotton dress. She turns back to the mirror to finish removing the bobby pins from her hair, leaving her short hair in a mass of tight curls.

"Sorry, I just realized I'm late for something." I ignore her and rummage through the wardrobe, finding ugly plaid cotton dresses. I settle on a blue-checkered number with a rounded collar and grab a pair of leather shoes from the pile on the floor. After pulling my hair back in a messy ponytail, I slip out of the door. I peek back to see that the nameplates are now simple construction paper smiling suns and discover that my new roommate's name is Janice. I file that away and race off in search of the professor.

But the moment I step outside, my new reality crashes in. Van Hise Hall, which normally towers across the street, is gone. I take a step back. In its place is a tree-covered hill. The Social Sciences Building, which yesterday stood next to Liz Waters, has disappeared too. I stare at a thick cluster of woods where the enormous building once stood. I now have a clear view of the Carillon Tower. It seems to wink down at me. I shudder.

As I pause to pull myself together, an enormous green car with fin-like fenders roars down Observatory Drive. It's as if I've stepped onto an old movie set.

Going back in time is one thing, but this world … I barely recognize it.

And then I realize that Sterling Hall might not exist yet either.

I run to the corner in my stiff leather shoes and crest the hill. The building is fully intact. I heave a sigh of relief. Not one sign of the lethal bomb that will gut it in the future.

Dashing down the hill, I push through the front doors into the marble foyer. Scanning the directory, I nearly cry in relief when I spot his name. Professor WC Smith. His office is still in Room 304. I've got to see him.

I climb the stairs two at a time, then round the bend and run down the hall. I reach for the door handle, barely registering that I have no idea what I'll say. The professor must know me in 1961, right? I turn the handle, but the door is locked. I jiggle it again, but nothing. Dejected, I pound my fist on the door.

"Professor Smith is teaching a class. His office hours begin at eleven o'clock," says a woman carrying an armful of files. Her hair is a jumble of short curls, and she's sporting cat-eye glasses.

"Where?" I bark, probably looking like a rabid dog the way I turn on her.

"His schedule is there on the door," she snips, stepping forwards. "He's in Bascom Hall. His lecture finishes up in about twenty minutes."

"Thank you!" I rush off, and by the time I reach Bascom, a cramp has me bent over in pain and gasping to catch my breath. I pause outside the familiar lecture room and try to collect myself. With a sweaty hand, I open the door and step into the same room where I met him two days ago ... which was 1970.

Scanning the lecture hall full of students, I get the world's worst case of déjà vu, but there's no sign of the professor. On the stage, a trim, dark-haired man scribbles some complex maths equation on a blackboard.

And then he turns and speaks to the class in a voice I recognize. I stagger back, catch my foot on a step and fall on my butt. The cold floor chills me through the thin fabric of my dress.

Professor Smith, minus the greying hair and stout frame he had the last time I saw him, glances in my direction. He starts, and then his face lights up as if I'm the best surprise ever.

This is real. He told me in 1970 that we'd met before, and now, in 1961, he clearly knows me. So this is not the first time we meet ... which means I have further back to go. A prickly fear creeps up my back.

The students turn to see what caused the distraction. I force an uneasy smile as all eyes land on me. I'm at a loss for what to do next.

Professor Smith quickly sets down the chalk and

wipes his hands together. "That concludes today's lecture. Today's office hours are cancelled due to an unexpected scheduling issue," he says in a rush as he gathers his papers, all while keeping an eye on me as if he's afraid I'll slip away.

The students collect their books and murmur to each other as they shuffle past. I avoid eye contact, not sure how to act. The students look so different. The guys' hair is slicked back with a greasy product, some wear thick-rimmed glasses and some wear T-shirts with cigarette packs rolled in their sleeves. I assumed that was a greaser stereotype, but apparently it's actual history. The girls all wear skirts or dresses, and penny loafers or leather saddle shoes with dainty white ankle socks. I stand and tug the edge of my dress down, uncomfortable in the latest style.

As soon as the hall empties, Professor Smith bounds forwards. It's weird to see someone get nine years younger overnight.

"Abbi. It's you!" He says with an eager smile. "It's wonderful to see you again after so many years. You have no idea!" He reaches out his hand to me, his face brimming with excitement.

I can't help myself. I step back.

"It's okay," he reassures, dropping his hand to his side, his expression now etched with concern. "Don't be frightened. You're safe."

But I don't feel safe. I don't understand anything, and I'm bouncing through time. It's possible that he died yesterday, and I don't know what to say or do. My eyes dart around the lecture hall, from the tall windows to the stage to the wooden seats, as if I'm caged in.

"Why don't we walk?" he suggests, holding the door. I pass through, noticing the trim angle of his chin and the brightness in his eyes. Gone are the crow's-feet he had just two days ago, as if some miracle serum cured them overnight.

We take the steps and exit Bascom Hall in silence, me picking at my thumbnail and trying to fend off a panic attack. Professor Smith politely gives me time to pull myself together.

Finally, I speak, peeking at him in a sideways glance. "This isn't the first time you've met me?"

He's about to speak, then hesitates.

"What?" I ask.

He pauses on the pavement, rubs his chin with his fingers and considers his words. My question wasn't that difficult, and I'm pretty sure I know the answer anyway.

Professor Smith sighs and looks at me. "I hesitate to reveal too much about your future, or my past, in case something is altered and irrevocably changes the outcome."

"Come on! I sprang here from 1970 ... where I just met you. I'm freaking out!" Two guys with books carried at their side amble down the pavement towards us, eyeing me curiously. "You've gotta help me," I whisper.

He nods and waits for the students to pass. "I'm trying. If we're to get to the bottom of this and find answers, I need you to tell me everything you know that may have anything to do with your time travel."

"Seriously? We just did that two days ago!" I don't want to regurgitate all this again. I want help. I want an actual explanation of what the hell is happening to me.

"Yes, for you it was two days ago, but 1970 is nearly a decade away for me and I haven't seen you for many years. By reviewing all the particulars again, perhaps I'll pick up on some minute detail you neglected to mention before." He raises a thick, all-knowing eyebrow and smiles.

I sigh. Of course, he's right.

We round the corner. "This is so strange," I say quietly, taking in my surroundings.

"What's that?" Professor Smith asks.

"I haven't gotten used to the fact that so many of the buildings are gone."

He looks around. "What buildings?"

"There, by the Carillon Tower. There's supposed to be a huge building." I point. "And Van Hise is gone. It's got to be a dozen stories high."

"Are you sure?" He stares at the wooded hill where a decade later a tall building will stand.

"Positive. Yesterday they were here, and today they aren't."

"If your yesterday was 1970, then it makes perfect sense that there would be many changes now."

No kidding, like a much younger professor.

"How about we go to the Union Terrace? That should be a familiar place," he says. "Is it still there in the future? Wait – never mind. Don't tell me." He grins and I know he's teasing.

"It is." I smile and begin to relax.

I tell him about the bells chiming off key and speculate it might have also been a full moon, but I'm not sure. I forgot to mention that tidbit when I talked to him before.

On the way to the Union, we pass the spot where the

massive Helen C White Library had nearly been finished in 1970. Today in its place is a grand old home that looks as if it's been resting on the hillside for a hundred years. I shake my head in awe, but think better of mentioning it to the professor.

But the Union isn't reassuring either. Students mill around looking like a scene out of the movie *Grease*. The guys wear high-waisted trousers that show off their white socks. Nearly all the girls wear their hair short with tight curls. Not the most flattering of looks, in my opinion. I half expect movie cameras to roll in and for the whole group to break into the song, "Summer Lovin'".

A cluster of guys in military dress walk by, and I see a few more ahead of us. "What's up with the guys wearing uniforms?" I ask, wondering what war might be going on. It's too early for Vietnam, and World War II is long over.

"Students don't wear uniforms in the future?"

"Not at school, and only if they're enlisted."

"Every male student is required to join the ROTC and train two days a week. After World War II, we need to be prepared. Don't you study the war in the future?"

"Yeah, not that I paid a lot of attention. It's ancient history in my day."

The professor's jaw tightens, and I feel that I'm about to be scolded. "Well, it's fresh in the minds of all of us now," he says. "Many people lost brothers, fathers, friends and neighbours to the war."

"Sorry. I didn't mean to offend you. Did you lose a family member?"

"No. At least not that I know of, but I lost friends."

"What do you mean, not that you know of?"

"I was raised in an orphanage," he says, matter-of-factly. "I don't know anything about my family."

"Seriously?" I'm not sure orphanages even exist in my time.

"Yes. In Chicago. But not to worry. I have a family of my own now." He guides us to the food queue at the Rathskeller.

"Are your parents, ah … dead?"

He shrugs. "I don't know." He orders two lemonades. "It used to bother me, but I don't dwell on it any more."

"Wow." I'm not sure how to respond. Growing up without my dad was really hard, but at least I had Mom and Grandma. Professor Smith lived his whole childhood without any family at all.

He collects our glasses, hands me one and guides us out onto the terrace, to a table in the shade of a large tree to ward off the heat. While not quite as large as the expanded Union Terrace I know, it still holds the charm and festive atmosphere. There's no outdoor food stall, but a different version of the sunburst chairs are still here. Gone are the tiered stairs to the water, but there's a pier with a few brave souls showing off their pale skin in hideous swimsuits with thick straps and low-cut legs. There's a huge beautiful boathouse set between the Red Gym and the lake. It has a round turret on the corner, and piers that stretch far out over the water.

"So, tell me more details that might give me clues to your" – the professor pauses. He glances around at the people nearby and seems to change his wording – "strange situation." He reaches into his briefcase and pulls out a notebook and pen.

"After we met in 1970, you said—"

The professor frowns and holds up his hand to stop me from going on.

"What?"

"It's best if you don't tell me about our interactions in the future. Stick to the facts related to your skips in time," he says quietly so his words aren't overheard.

I huff. "Fine. But maybe you get Alzheimer's in the future." I stare out at the lake and see a couple of long skinny boats being rowed by a bunch of guys.

"What is Alzheimer's?" he asks, then quickly catches himself. "Never mind. Better that I don't know." He drinks his lemonade, downing half the glass as if it's hard liquor and he needs to numb his senses.

"I've travelled three times in the past few days and this is the second time I've met you. What do you think that means?"

"I've given that a great deal of thought over the years. My best theory is that you're travelling in a parallel universe with magnetic pulls that have drawn us together."

"English, please."

"I believe that I'm supposed to help you manage your, er, talent."

"It's hardly a talent. I have no control over it. I don't get to choose where I go, and I have no idea how to get home." I pause, looking out at the shimmering lake. "Do I ever travel forward? Because, so far, I never have."

A flicker of something – resignation? – colours his eyes, and I have my answer. I sigh. "So it's only backwards. I can't keep..." I break off, not trusting my voice. I focus on stirring my lemonade and doing everything in my power to contain the white-hot tears burning behind my eyes.

"Tell me this," I say, struggling to keep my composure. "How are you supposed to help me if you only know me in the past? When I met you before, I didn't know what I should tell you that would help your search. If you haven't solved my problem by then, how are you going to solve it now?"

Now it's the professor's turn to mask his emotions. If I were him, that would be extremely bad news. He deflects my question. "Perhaps that's what this visit in time is about – for you to give me some pertinent information that will help my future research."

I take a deep breath and tell him everything I can think of, leaving no stone unturned. Tables fill and empty around us as students come and go, and Professor Smith scribbles notes furiously, asking for clarifications, and nodding thoughtfully as the wheels spin in his mind.

"Everything in my room is totally different, except my bed. Whatever's on it seems to travel with me, but anything on the floor or on my bedside table is gone. I wake up and find new things from whatever year I've landed in. And everyone around me seems to think nothing of it. It's as if to them, I was always there."

"Parallel universes," Professor Smith murmurs softly as he keeps writing.

"Maybe I need to ask my roommates more questions?"

He considers the idea, then shakes his head. "Tread carefully. You don't want to tamper with the phenomena of time travel or cause mass hysteria. Not that anyone would believe you anyway. They might send you to the loony bin."

"I guess you're right. So that makes you my only friend." I smile weakly and draw patterns in the condensation on the side of my glass, watching as it collects and rolls down, creating a puddle on the table.

He looks at me kindly. "You have other friends, but I need you to promise you won't tell anyone about your ... situation. I can't stress this enough." He pats my hand.

Now my curiosity is sparked. "Why? Does something bad happen?"

"Not at all and I want to keep it that way." Professor Smith smiles again and says, "You'll understand why when the time comes." He's keeping too much information from me again.

"But what if I don't? Why don't you just tell me when that time might be?"

He pinches his lips together and adjusts his glasses. "I can't."

"That's bull. Of course you can," I snap, tired of his secrets.

"No, Abbi. You're going to have to trust me," he says firmly, then glances at his wristwatch. "Darn it. I need to be going. I'm subbing in for the department chair's graduate level class. We'll have to meet this evening."

"No!" I grab his arm. The professor looks at me in surprise.

"I'm sorry," I say, releasing him. "It's just that yesterday, you had to go and then I never saw you again. I shot back in time. If you leave now, what if I travel back before I can talk to you again? Wait! Do you know how long I'm here? Did I tell you?" My worries come out in a jumbled heap.

"Abbi," he replies calmly, "from what I know, you've never travelled during the light of day. If you travel before I see you again, then it's meant to be, and possibly part of this phenomenon," he says like a sage old prophet.

"Now you're leaving it all up to fate? That's the stupidest thing I've ever heard!" I throw my hands in the air. "I thought you were a scientist! You don't really care." The sting of tears builds behind my eyes again.

"I care far more than you know," he says in a fatherly tone that breaks through my fears.

I want to trust him. I want to know he will help me, so I pull myself together and ask calmly, "When can I see you again?"

"Soon." He stands and pushes in his chair. "I'm going to request approval to see your dorm room. I think the secret must lie there."

"Let's go now. I'll show you myself." I jump up and join him.

"No, no." He gestures me back to my seat. "That wouldn't be appropriate or permitted. I must go through proper channels and contact the head of student housing."

I plop back into my chair. "That's ridiculous."

"Perhaps to you, but this is how things work in 1961. It should only take me a couple of hours. I'll rush the request as soon as I'm out of class. When I know something, I'll leave a message for you at the front desk." He drains his glass of lemonade. "In the meantime, why don't you enjoy the terrace and take a walk. Perhaps it'll help you recall something else."

I don't want him to leave me alone. Also, I need to warn him about the Sterling Hall bombing.

"Professor?"

"Yes?"

"In August of 1970, promise me you'll never work past midnight at Sterling Hall."

He frowns and shakes his head. "Abbi! I told you–"

"I don't care. You have to promise me."

A warm smile covers his face. "And you need to promise me to stop trying to meddle with time."

"But–"

He holds out his hand. "Ut-ut."

"Fine," I sigh, and he walks away.

Finishing my lemonade alone on the terrace, I watch the activity over at the boathouse as the narrow rowing boats glide up to the dock and a team of boisterous rowers climbs out. After unhooking oars that seem impossibly long, they work together to lift and carry the boat into the building. Their camaraderie is unmistakable even from this distance, further driving home just how alone I am.

Miserable, I collect my empty glass and return to the Rathskeller dining room. The automatic doors are gone, but inside, not much has changed – the dim light of the room, the rich, dark wood and the murals featuring German quotations and beer steins.

But the students look so different. Some gather in groups, others are solo, leaning over thick textbooks. There are no mobile phones, headphones or laptops. Many of the guys part their hair sharply, others have squared-off crew cuts. The girls with their red lipstick and colourful neck scarves clutch their books, giggling and whispering.

I wish I could tell my friends about this day, but even in my own time, I'm not sure who my friends are. There's

Jada, who seems great, but I barely know her. Will I ever see her again? And there's Colton. Would we have become friends if I had stayed? Most eighteen-year-olds don't consider their grandma their friend, but I did. She would be alive now, probably living in Ohio. But calling her on the phone again is certainly out.

I pull at my tight collar and loosen the top button.

"Abbi!" an excited voice calls out.

I turn to find a guy with scruffy, sandy-coloured hair and a brilliant smile coming straight for me, and fast. I look around to see if he is talking to someone else, but there's only me.

Should I be glad or scared to discover that someone else in 1961 seems excited to see me? Maybe he's like all the girls in my dorm, who seem to think I've always been here? Maybe we have classes together?

Without warning, he scoops me into a hug, swings me around and plants a long, passionate kiss on my lips.

He-llo!

CHAPTER 6

The stranger grins, revealing an adorable dimple. "Abbi! I never thought it would happen. I mean I hoped so, I prayed for it and you were right. Here you are, exactly when you said you'd be." He flicks his head so a lock of hair sweeps to the side, and he can't contain his infectious smile.

I'm relieved that this tall, handsome guy seems to know me, but I'm stunned at his familiarity. Even so, I find myself smiling into deep blue eyes. His strong arms are wrapped comfortably around me as if that's where they belong. My hands rest against his chest, where I feel his heart racing beneath his button-down shirt.

"You look exactly the same." He gazes at me as if I'm the most precious person on the planet.

I don't know how to respond, but as crazy as it sounds, I kind of like the feel of him. He's lean and smells good, like the outdoors. He has a straight, narrow nose and feathery eyebrows that frame his expressive eyes. After a few awkward seconds, to which he seems totally oblivious, I find my voice. "I'm sorry, but how exactly do we know each other?"

He immediately releases me. "Oh rats! Abbi, forgive

me. I had it all planned out how I was going to approach you, but then got swept up in the moment and forgot that you haven't met me yet."

My heart nearly ricochets out of my chest. Does this mean he knows I time travel?

"Let's get out of here." Without asking, he takes my hand and leads me out of the Rathskeller. He obviously knows more about what's going on than I do, so I follow, allowing myself a glimmer of hope.

He takes me outside and down a narrow dirt path by the lakefront. He has an easy gait, as if he's used to escorting girls who don't know him. He finds a bench overlooking the water and brushes off bits of twigs and leaves. We sit, his body angled towards mine. A soft breeze from the lake blows his hair off his forehead.

"My apologies. I'm handling this all wrong." He holds up his trembling hand. "Look. I'm giddy as a racehorse."

For the first time I notice his nervous smile. "It's okay," I reassure him, boldly taking his long, tan fingers and giving them a reassuring squeeze. His smile relaxes, but his eyes stay glued to mine. "But, please, tell me how we know each other. *When* exactly did we meet?" I hold my breath, waiting for his answer.

He hesitates, looking as if he's thinking back on fond memories. "I can't tell you that. All I can say is that for me it was awhile ago, but for you – well – it's still to come."

He's confusing me, but he seems to be confirming that I will continue to travel back in time. I release my breath. "You know about … my travelling?"

"I know *all* about it," he says with a serious tone.

"Did I tell you?" I ask tentatively.

"Yes. You told me many things about the future." He holds my gaze as if willing me to remember things that haven't yet happened, but I have nothing to offer him. He continues, "I'm not sure how I would have managed without you. Every time I skip, it's like being dropped in the cold lake. But you've helped me cope."

"Wait – you travel too? How long? Where have you been? When did we first meet?" I ask eagerly, desperate for answers. He smiles. His lips have a nice curve to them, and there's that adorable dimple.

"Whoa, Nellie, slow down," he says, touching my cheek.

He is completely comfortable with me, suggesting we really do have a shared past. But exactly *what* kind of past? "I'm sorry, but – wait a minute. Did you just call me Nellie?"

"I did." He laughs and his crystal blue eyes light up.

I see how I might enjoy spending time with him. "You know my name is Abbi."

"I do."

"So who's Nellie?"

"She was my horse."

It takes me a second to catch on, but then I say, "You were trying to rein me in like a horse?"

"You're getting a tad jumpy." His mouth twitches with humour.

I shake my head. Great, he's a comedian too. "I keep popping from one time to another with no rhyme or reason. You'd be jumpy too."

He runs his hand through the tall grass, picks a long,

slender blade and slips it into his mouth. With knowing eyes he says, "I understand."

"So, you know me from your past, and we're good friends?"

"Very good." A devilish sparkle lights his eyes, and I wonder just how good he's talking about.

"You know everything about me, and yet I don't even know your name?" I hate this feeling. It's as if I've woken up with amnesia.

His eyes dim as if he's wounded that I don't remember him, but then he says in the sweetest low voice, "My name is Will."

"Hello, Will." I let the sound of his name settle in. I have a friend in the past named Will, and he seems like a nice guy. A weight eases off my shoulders, and I breathe a little easier.

"I'm Abbi. You already know that, but I feel better officially introducing myself." I hold out my hand to shake his.

He glances at my hand and then back to me and says with a mischievous grin, "Oh, we're way past shaking."

I raise an eyebrow. Will dips his head sheepishly. "Abbi, I've missed you very much, and the thing is, we never had a chance to say goodbye."

It's my turn to smile. Do I let this adorable stranger kiss me again? He gazes at me with such devotion that I know we must have a history together. *Why not?* I think, and my stomach gives a flutter.

Will pulls the blade of grass from his mouth and leans forward. With our faces a few inches apart, his breath warms my cheek. He tilts his head and ever so gently kisses me. His fingers glide along my jaw as his lips coax mine to respond, and they do.

I can't believe I'm letting him kiss me, but by the familiarity of his touch, and how perfectly our lips move together, I know this is far from the first time.

Will reluctantly pulls away and lets the moment soak in. My eyes blink open as my pulse races.

"Is this goodbye or hello?" I murmur.

"Dear Lord, I hope it's hello," he says.

"You're not like the guys from my time." My voice comes out in a whisper.

"No. I suppose I'm not." He slides the blade of grass back into his mouth. Dappled sunlight seeps through the leaves overhead, sprinkling warm light on his hair and face.

I straighten my skirt and try to clear my head. "When exactly are you from?"

His eyes cloud. "Nineteen twenty-seven."

My jaw drops. "Seriously? Wait, how is it that you're travelling forward when I travel back?"

He looks out over the vast expanse of the lake, as if searching for an answer that isn't there. "If I had a nickel for every time I wondered that, I'd be a rich man. The God's truth, I don't know."

"Nineteen twenty-seven. That's so long ago. No wonder you had a horse. Were cars even invented yet?"

The corner of his mouth curls. "Yes, automobiles were common. My father owned a Model T, but we still used horsepower on the farm."

"Wow! You grew up on a farm … in the 1920s?" My

mind is reeling. As hard as it is to move back in time, going forward must be even more difficult. At least I have the benefit of knowing some history to guide me. Will is travelling blind with no idea what he'll encounter.

"Please, Will. Tell me everything you can. Maybe it'll help us figure this out. I've been totally lost ever since this started happening."

"Of course I will, but slow down. Allow me to take you to lunch. You must be getting hungry, and the food of this time is delicious."

Will isn't going to blow me off by running to some meeting or lecture like Professor Smith did. Will wants to spend time with me, and that's a huge relief. He gets what I've been going through, and that knowledge is a huge weight off my shoulders. Finally, I can take a breath and relax for a minute knowing I'm with a fellow time traveller, of all things. "Sure. I'd like that."

Will offers his hand to help me up, and I tentatively accept it. My hand fits perfectly in his gentle grip, yet I notice his hands are calloused. There's nothing I want more than to go home, and maybe this handsome farm boy has some idea of how to get me there. But at this moment, all I care about is that I'm no longer alone in this craziness.

We walk side by side, our shoes crunching on the gravel path. Will looks at me often, as if he's trying to make sure I'm real. I wish I shared the memories he has of us.

"Tell me how we meet," I say.

He smiles and his eyes go glassy as he remembers. "It was spring, the tulips were in bloom and I was fishing."

"That sounds nice. Where are you from?"

"A small town up north called Ephraim."

"So what was a small-town farm boy doing going to college?"

His jaw tightens for a moment, then relaxes. "It's complicated, but I couldn't imagine my future revolving solely around crops, livestock and the weather. All my life I've been curious, with a longing to learn about history, science and mathematics. My father disagreed, of course. He felt the only book a man needed to read was the Bible. I was desperate for more, so I left."

Will said it with such finality, as if it were a simple decision, but it must have been a pretty big deal. "Did he come after you?"

"He couldn't, not with the cows needing to be milked twice a day. My sister, Agnes, wrote and told me he was very angry. Can't say that I blame him. With me gone, Father had only Agnes and Mother to help with the livestock."

"I'm sorry. It must have been hard for you to leave."

"That it was," he says wistfully, bending to pluck a fresh blade of grass.

Will grows quiet and I wonder what he isn't telling me. What has he been through? What are the secrets that he keeps? But he doesn't offer more, so I change the subject.

"When did you first … travel?" I glance around to make sure no one overhears, but the students we pass are going about their normal 1961 lives, clueless that two time travellers are lurking in their midst.

"A few weeks after I arrived at school." He looks away.

I know the pain he feels, because it's mirrored in my own heart.

"So you travelled forward? I've only travelled back in time."

"That's right."

"Why do you think that is?"

"I don't know, but I believe the bells of the Carillon Tower have something to do with it," he says.

"Yes!" I say, excited that he's noticed this too. "The bells are the only thing that I know for sure happened each time. We should check it out. See if there's something there to give us a clue."

He shakes his head. "We've tried that." He gives me a wry smile and my stomach flips, but I brush the thought away. I don't need to fall for him and complicate my life more.

Will continues. "I even talked to the bell player. Of course, I didn't ask if he was sending me forward in time, but I did ask a lot of questions, and I learned that he never plays at night."

"But someone must be."

We stop at a crossing and wait for the light to change. Cars rumble past, emitting smelly exhaust fumes that would never pass carbon emission inspections in my time. The back of my dress sticks to my skin in the humidity.

"What about the professor? Maybe he can look into it if we can find him," Will suggests.

I stop short. "You know Professor Smith too?"

Will turns and comes back to me. When he registers my confusion, he pushes a hand through his hair. "I keep forgetting we don't share the same history yet. Most of my knowledge of him is from what you've told me. I met him briefly when he was a student, but he knew nothing of our time travels then."

"You're the other time traveller he mentioned!"

"I hope there aren't any others. This is complicated enough," he chuckles.

"Is this the first time we're all in the same place at the same time?" I blow the stray hair that's fallen in my face. I feel wilted, but the heat doesn't seem to affect Will.

"I guess so. You've seen him already?"

"Right before I saw you. And I'll see him again later today, I hope. He thinks my dorm room has something to do with my travel."

"That's good."

"But why hasn't my roommate travelled with me?"

He shrugs. "I've wondered the same thing about my roommates. I just landed in this time yesterday. I tried to find the professor but couldn't track him down. I went to his office this morning, but he didn't show. Apparently he was with you." He smiles at me. "So," he goes on, "it seems we have a few hours to dally away…"

I let a giggle slip out. It feels good to have an emotion other than sheer terror and confusion for a change.

"What?" he asks. "Grass in my teeth?"

"Dally. It's so old-fashioned."

His impish grin returns. "I guess I'm an old-fashioned fella. Trust me, you get used to it. Come along."

I sneak peeks at Will when he's not looking. He's lean and fit, with muscular arms. It must be from working on a farm. His skin is tan and his hair streaked blond from the sun. I notice a few stray hairs on the curve of his jaw where he missed shaving. Was he in a hurry today, anxious to meet me? He said he knew where I'd be.

We go to Rennebohms, a combination drug store and malt shop. The smell of hamburgers and grilled onions greets us as he opens the door for me. A long grey Formica counter with shiny red stools runs the length of one wall. Waitresses wearing crisp white aprons and little white caps hustle around in white trainers, waiting on the customers.

Will leads me across the black-and-white checkered floor, past the counter to a cosy booth. My eyes scan the menu: egg sandwich … Heinz soup? Liver sausage sandwich? Yuck. But I spot a Bucky burger that sounds safe.

"Twenty-five cents for a burger? The prices are amazing!" I say.

"Not to me," he laughs. "I'm used to a ten-cent sandwich and a five-cent cup of coffee."

A gum-snapping waitress arrives with water glasses. "What can I get ya?" She wears a lime-green nylon scarf tied around her neck and no makeup besides orangey-red lipstick.

Will gestures for me to go first. I order the Bucky burger, fries and a milkshake. He orders the same.

"This place is wild. Talk about a blast from the past," I say.

He laughs at the expression and watches me with such contentment on his face.

Sitting across the booth, we're forced to look at each other, which is both good and bad. He's certainly easy on the eyes, but he keeps staring at me as if I'm a figment of his imagination, as if he wants to somehow confirm that I'm real. Am I living up to his expectations? I nervously tear the edge of my napkin until it ends up with a border of fringe.

"So tell me, if you keep coming forwards, do you ever visit your family? They must have freaked when they first saw you looking the same."

Will bites his lip and shakes his head. "No. I never saw them again."

"Why not?" I can't imagine not being with Mom again if I had the chance.

"A few weeks after school started, I received a telegram that a smallpox outbreak hit my town. It was bad, and a lot of people died. Including my family." Will looks away.

"Your whole family? I'm so sorry." I stare at my shredded napkin, at a total loss of what to say. I lost my mom in time, but I believe that if I can get back home, she'll still be there. Will's family is gone forever.

He's quiet, and I don't want to invade his privacy. Finally he says softly, "It was a terrible thing. I planned to go home and give them a proper burial, take over the farm."

I look at him in surprise. He'd taken such a huge step to run away from that life, and yet he was willing to go back to it.

He seems to read my thoughts and shrugs. "There was no one else to do it." He takes a sip of water, seeming to gather himself. "But the next morning when I woke, a different fellow slept in my roommate's bed, and it turned out I had travelled forward an entire year."

"That's awful."

"It's in the past, and there's nothing to be done about it." We sit silently, his hands folded on the table in front of him. "I didn't mean to ruin our lunch."

I place my hand over his. "You haven't. Waking up with a stranger in the next bed was pretty much how it happened for me."

He gives my hand a squeeze. "I know." His blue eyes sparkle with kindness and a history I don't yet know. Apparently we've had this conversation before.

The waitress arrives with our lunch, and Will and I spend the next two hours at the diner, deep in conversation. He already seems to know everything about me, but I am desperate to know more about him. I discover that he loves being on the rowing team, that he had a favourite milking cow named Gertie and that he has a thirst for learning, which time travel has been interfering with.

"Did you ever make it back home then, since everything happened?" I ask gently, biting the straw of my long-gone milkshake.

"Yes, when I got my bearings after my first … trip, I wanted to see what had become of my father's farm and if anything remained. All the livestock had been sold, including my horse."

"Nellie," I sigh sadly, already feeling a sense of kinship. "How could that happen?"

He shrugged. "The bank repossessed everything. It had been well over a year. The animals needed immediate care, so others took care of them, and I'm grateful for that."

"Don't you have any other relatives – grandparents or aunts and uncles?"

"I do, back in Norway, but I've never met them. My parents came over before I was born."

"I'm so sorry."

It strikes me that Will is as alone in this world as I am.

CHAPTER 7

Later, in the Liz Waters "date parlour" (as Mom called it), Will drums his fingers on the arm of the wingback chair. I pace as we wait for Professor Smith. Girls come and go from the adjoining library, each straining her neck to get a good look at this cute guy I'm with. I notice a framed portrait of John F Kennedy on the wall.

Will taps his foot on the polished floor.

"Are you nervous?" I ask.

"Excited. This is the best thing to happen in a long while. That is, other than finding you." He gives me a lingering smile, and I wonder again about our supposed history.

A familiar-looking girl with short, curled brown hair and thick glasses approaches. It takes a moment before I realize it's my roommate, Janice. With her are some girls I don't recognize. "Abigail, who's your visitor?" she coos.

They all gaze at Will with his tanned skin and brilliant blue eyes as if he's fresh meat on the marriage market, and they're a pack of carnivores.

"Just a friend," I say, hoping they'll leave.

"Oh good." Janice grabs my arm with her clammy hand. "Introduce me."

I roll my eyes but play along. "Will, this is my roommate, Janice. Janice, this is Will. He's, he's–" I'm not exactly sure what to say.

"I'm Abbi's steady." Will stands to greet her, stretching his lean body to full height.

I do a double take at his word. So does Janice.

"Pleasure to meet you, Janice," he says, unleashing a charming smile.

Confused, she turns to me and hisses. "But you said – "

Will slips his arm around my waist and lets it linger on my hip. The warmth of his hand seeps through my dress like a red-hot brand. "Abigail is afraid her parents will find out about us, so she doesn't like to tell people. You see, I'm Catholic and they would never approve."

For a second I stare at him, dumbfounded. He gives me a quick squeeze, and I catch on. "Please, don't tell," I whisper to Janice.

Janice's jaw drops into an open-mouthed smile, apparently pleased to be in on our little scandal. "I promise."

"See you later then." I urge her and her posse to move on out.

"Bye, Will," she calls and heads upstairs, posse in tow.

"That is the lamest reason I've ever heard for a parent's disapproval." I turn towards Will and find myself conveniently in his arms.

He smiles down at me, enjoying the proximity. "It's a legitimate reason for us not to be together, and Janice believed it."

My hand rests on the soft fabric of his shirt. A small

patch of golden chest hair peeks out near his collar. "So, you're my steady?"

"Yes, I am," he says with a sureness that sends a zing through me.

"We'll see about that," I counter, but I have a feeling that, at least in his mind, he's telling the truth.

Professor Smith appears around the corner with a large black case in hand. I jump away from Will as if I've been caught in the act. Will gives me a smug nod, which I ignore.

"Professor! It's so good to see you." I step to join him. I know he promised to come, but after last time, when the bombing kept us apart, I don't count on anything to go as planned.

Will stays put, watching the professor closely.

"Hello, Abbi," Professor Smith says cheerfully, then glances at Will and startles. "Good gracious!"

Will smiles broadly. "You remember me?"

"Dear Lord, yes." The professor stares at him in disbelief, digesting this new tangle.

"It's Will," Will prompts and holds out his hand.

The professor comes forward and shakes it vigorously. "This is amazing – just incredible to have you both here. We've got a lot to catch up on."

Studious girls with curious eyes and conservative dresses peek their heads out of the library to see what all the commotion is about. It must not be everyday that a professor appears in the date parlour.

Professor Smith frowns at their interest and waves us out of the room. "I think we'd better find somewhere more private. How about the patio?"

I nod and lead the way. Clouds have rolled in, along with a brisk breeze that offers relief from the stifling hot day. Thankfully no one else is outside at the moment. Professor Smith sets down his bulky case, and we sit at a wrought iron patio set. He keeps glancing at Will and shaking his head.

"This is a monumental day. Will, a fella I met sophomore year, is here in 1961 with Abbi, my old–"

"Thorn in your side?" I offer.

"I was going to say old friend," he says with a tilt of his head.

"Oh, that too."

"It's great to see you again," Will says with a huge grin, as relieved as I am to have the professor in our presence.

"It's mind-boggling. Both of you look exactly as you did the last time I saw you. That is, except the clothes. No one would suspect you don't belong here."

I stare down at my boxy cotton dress and ugly shoes. I might blend in, but I sure don't fit in.

"You, mate, do *not* look nineteen," Will laughs, taking in the professor's scholarly tweed jacket, white button-down shirt and slacks. All he needs is a pair of brogues to complete his look.

"I suppose I don't. I'm married with three kids and another one on the way." There's a glint of pride in his voice.

"Holy cow!" Will shakes his head in disbelief.

"When love calls, anything can happen. Even to a boring chap like me." The professor grins. "Abbi, why didn't you tell me Will was here?"

Before I can speak, Will answers. "She didn't know, at

least not until a couple of hours ago."

The professor raises an eyebrow. I nod to confirm Will's story. "Apparently he and I have a history together," I say. I recall his delicious kiss from earlier and look down at the concrete patio blocks in hopes of hiding the blush that creeps up my neck. Will leans back with a cocky grin.

Professor Smith removes his glasses and rubs his eyes. "All right, Will. You'd better start from the beginning. Perhaps putting together both your experiences will be the key I need."

Will begins telling the professor what he'd told me. The professor writes frantically in a notebook, recording all the details.

But then Will stops and says casually, "Perhaps you and I can meet later and I can go into more specifics." I see Will catch the professor's eye.

He's holding something back. I'm sure of it, but I can't imagine why.

"Of course, of course," the professor says, picking up on Will's clandestine meaning.

The breeze gusts, whipping my hair around. "Hey, anything you tell the professor, you can tell me. I need to know this stuff too." But the professor ignores me, which is unlike him.

"Listen, I spoke with the director of housing, and he's called the head resident." He checks his watch. "She should be waiting now to escort me to your dorm room." He closes his notebook and returns it to his case.

I don't like the idea of them both keeping secrets from me but decide not to get into it right now. Instead I ask what he's hoping to find in my room.

"Perhaps there will be something that offers a clue as to why your room is serving as a portal for travel. But Will, I'm afraid you won't be able to join us."

"Why not? I've been to Abbi's room plenty of times."

My head jerks up in surprise. I turn to him for explanation.

A sheepish expression covers his face. "I told you we're close." He grins again.

The professor shakes his head and stands, not wanting to hear more. "I'm raising enough red flags by asking for an inspection of a coed's room. The housing department would frown heavily on a male student coming along as well."

"Ah, Smitty, you weren't a prude when I last saw you. If that's what happens with age, I don't want to grow up," Will jokes.

"Sorry, my friend. It's the rules."

Will rises. "Very well, then. I'll go and hang out at the boathouse for a while."

Suddenly I feel a pang of anxiety – Will can't leave! Now that I know I'm not alone in this, I need him. I grab his hand and try to keep the panic from my voice. "Do you have to?"

"Don't worry. I'll be waiting. In fact, why don't we meet outside my dorm, Tripp Hall, in an hour? There's something I want to show you." He gives my hand a quick squeeze. His eyes promise he won't let me down.

"Fine." But I'm still reluctant to see him go.

Will takes the steps down from the patio to the lake-side path and disappears. I reluctantly follow the professor back inside to the parlour, hoping Will keeps his word.

A stocky, red-haired woman wearing a thin set of pearls and a cloud of cheap perfume approaches. "Hello, Professor Smith, I'm Mrs. Chaplin. I understand you wish to do an inspection of room 4418."

The professor stands to his full height, shifting his expression from casual to professional. "Thank you, Mrs. Chaplin. I appreciate your accommodating my request with such expedience."

"Of course." She leads the way out of the parlour and down the corridor towards my room as I tag behind.

"Professor, may I inquire as to the nature of your inspection? It is quite unusual for a faculty member to request a tour of a ladies' dormitory room."

Girls step out of the way and stare at Professor Smith as we pass. He doesn't seem to notice.

"Yes, of course, Mrs. Chaplin. I'm doing a study on atmospheric pressures, their effect on sound waves and residual ambient effects. I believe I can gather valuable data from Miss Thorp's corner room. It is in precise adverse symmetry to the Carillon Tower, the lake and the hilltop."

I'm not sure what he just said, but it sounds like a load of bull to me.

Mrs. Chaplin pauses at the end of the hall. "That certainly sounds intriguing. We are honoured to assist you however we can here at Elizabeth Waters." Her pearls roll in and out of the folds of her neck as she speaks.

I pinch my lips to keep from laughing.

He notices my restrained laughter and winks. "Your cooperation is greatly appreciated."

At my dorm room, sappy pop music blasts from the

other side of the door. Mrs. Chaplin frowns and stands aside as I unlock the door and enter. I'd forgotten the room was a disaster of epic proportions. Janice is on her unmade bed, snapping gum and paging through a *LIFE* magazine as the radio blares "Teen Angel". She startles at our invasion, jumps up and stumbles over a discarded bath towel in her efforts to turn off the radio.

From the doorway Professor Smith's eyes travel to the array of ladies' undergarments dangling from the curtain rods and bookshelves. He struggles to keep a straight face.

Mrs. Chaplin, on the other hand, is horrified. "Ladies! The state of this room!"

"Sorry, we forgot to tidy up." I shove dirty clothes to the side with my foot and rush forwards, snatching down the oversize granny panties and atrocious-looking bras as quickly as possible. Janice's face turns beetroot red as she helps, stuffing the items under her pillow.

With most of the personal items now out of sight, we face Mrs. Chaplin, who is burning hot with irritation. She clears her throat. "Janice, Professor Smith needs to perform an inspection of your room."

"What for?" Janice asks, her eye bouncing to each of us in confusion.

"It's all extremely scientific, so if you would excuse us for a few minutes while he completes his research." She shoos Janice away like a bothersome gnat.

"All right." She collects her cardigan and heads to the door, glancing back at me as she goes. "Doesn't Abigail need to come too?"

"Abigail is a student in my advanced physics course

and will be assisting on this project." Professor Smith steps aside, allowing her to pass.

Janice looks at me quizzically, as if trying to figure out this new side of me. I shrug.

The head resident and the professor file in. The room is small and with all three of us, plus the professor's bulky case, it doesn't leave much room. Mrs. Chaplin's toxic perfume threatens to suffocate me.

Professor Smith ignores the mess and peers out of the window towards the bell tower. "You have a perfect view of the Carillon Tower."

"I do *now*," I say, hoping he gets my hint that there is a building blocking the view in the future.

"This is my bed, by the window. I can hear the bells perfectly." My unmade bed sits right up next to the window, giving me a perfect view of the treetops and nearby tower.

"May I set my case on it?" he asks.

"Sure. Excuse my clutter." I quickly pull up the covers and smooth the bed. "I like to keep things that are important to me nearby," I say, pointing meaningfully to the items on my bed, not the disaster of the room. "My quilt was given to me by my grandmother. She lived in Liz Waters too."

"The professor is here on official business. He doesn't need to hear about your grandmother's gift." Mrs. Chaplin's stale breath overpowers her perfume.

As Professor Smith unlatches the black case and pulls out instruments, I notice he's actually looking at the patchwork quilt and aged hatbox. "That's quite all right. It's nice to know you're following the family tradition by coming to the university. What was she like?"

He holds up a tuning fork and strikes it with a mallet, then slowly moves it through the room, but his eyes are studying everything on my side of the room, not his bogus instruments.

I stand at the head of the bed, running my hand over the wooden headboard. "Grandma was awesome." Mrs. Chaplin's brow furrows at my strange use of the word. I ignore her. "When I was younger, she would jump on our trampoline with me. And she loved to travel. She took me white-water rafting."

Behind me, Mrs. Chaplin snorts her disapproval, the old hag. Clearly not many women white-water raft or jump on trampolines in 1961. I don't know what the professor hopes to learn by hearing stories about Grandma. I look at him in question and tilt my head. He smiles and proceeds to perform imaginary tests while Mrs. Chaplin watches his every move.

"Miss Thorp, do you perhaps have an older sister who lived here at Liz Waters?" Mrs. Chaplin suddenly asks, studying me as closely as the professor is studying the room.

"No, I don't have any siblings. Why?"

"You remind me of another girl. That's all."

The professor removes a large black box and plugs it into the wall outlet.

"What's that?" I ask, looking at the odd machine.

"It's a tape recorder. Have you never seen one before?"

"Not like that," I say.

He presses some buttons and waves a microphone attached to a long coiled cord around the room. "Your grandmother sounds like a wonderful lady."

"She was." I run my hand over a swatch of blue floral fabric. It seems maybe it was an old dress once. "I wish I knew which room she lived in. I can almost picture her walking down these halls and going to the dining room with friends."

"Mrs. Chaplin!" A girl from down the hall suddenly appears in the doorway. "The tap in the bathroom broke, and water is spraying everywhere!"

"Oh my." Mrs. Chaplin looks towards the professor, then back to the panicked girl.

"I'm fine here. Only a few more minutes and I'll be ready to pack up. Feel free to investigate," he says with authority.

"Thank you, Professor. I'll return shortly." The flustered Mrs. Chaplin hustles after the girl, moving with surprising speed.

The professor tosses the microphone into his case, ending his fake pretense of testing the room. "I thought she'd never leave. Quickly, tell me anything you can think of in regard to this room and your time travelling."

I close the door and speak quickly. "Each time I travel, everything on my bed comes with me. The bed frame, the bedspread and whatever's lying on top of it. The hatbox was on the bed the day I first travelled." And then I add sheepishly, "I was kind of drunk when I fell into bed that night, and I forgot to move it."

The professor chuckles, then catches himself and nods. "What's the significance of the hatbox?" He snaps a picture of it with a boxy camera on a long, thick strap.

"It belonged to my grandmother. She put my name on it, so when my mother found it after Grandma died, she sent it to me. Do you think that's why I'm travelling through time? I first travelled the day I received it..."

"It's certainly an interesting piece of evidence that I've been wanting to look into."

I'm taken aback by this comment. I must have mentioned the hatbox to him some other place in time, which is so strange to think about.

He takes a picture of the view from the window to the tower and then my bed, the headboard and the furniture near it. "Does anything else in the room travel with you?"

I examine the room more closely, from the curtains, to the wardrobe, to the desk. "Other than the handbag I hook at the end of the bed at night, no. And each time I wake up, the room is different. Not everything. The furniture is always in the same place, but everything about it and around it is different, as if it all belongs to a different person. And see this calendar?" I step over to it. "There's always a Wisconsin Badgers calendar in this exact spot, like older versions of the one Grandma gave me the Christmas before she died."

"Let me get your picture next to it."

"Okay..." It seems like an odd request, and then it dawns on me why and I laugh. "You only want my picture because you want to be able to prove I'm real."

The professor laughs. "You've caught me." He holds up the camera, so I give him my best beaming grin and he snaps a shot, the bright, crackling flash momentarily blinding me. He continues poking around the room.

"I really hope you can figure this out." I run my hand over the quilt again. "And help me find a way back."

He smiles sadly. "I hope so too."

"But you're more likely to get to know Will in the future. I've only gone backwards and Will only goes forwards, so you have him to look forward to." Which is wonderful for Will and the professor, but it leaves me feeling more alone than ever.

"I suppose you're right," he says. "But I see you, as well, don't I?"

"Yes, of course. But for me, it already happened."

I sit on the edge of the bed, my safety zone, and stare out of the window into the distance. "Professor? What if it never stops? What if I keep going back until the beginning of time?" Panic inches along my skin like a heat rash.

"I don't think that's likely. Liz Waters was built in the twenties, maybe thirties. So if this room has something to do with it, I imagine it will stop there."

"Great! I'll live out the rest of my life in 1930?"

The professor pats my shoulder. "Try not to fret. I'll do everything in my power to help."

The door springs open and Mrs. Chaplin reappears. The front of her dress is soaked and her red hair is limp from her battle with the tap. She looks at the professor's hand on my shoulder and frowns. He immediately pulls his hand away.

"Just comforting Miss Thorp. All this reminiscing of her grandmother has made her melancholy."

Mrs. Chaplin glares at me. Geez. Does she seriously think I'd go for some old guy?

"Have you completed your examination of the room?" she asks with icy judgment.

"Yes, I've seen enough. Thank you." He returns his camera and the rest of the fake instruments to the case.

Within minutes we're back at the lobby. I walk him outside.

"Abbi, I'd like to go through the items in the hatbox. I don't know that it means anything, but it's worth checking. I find it intriguing that your grandmother keeps coming up. It's her quilt on your bed, her hatbox you were sent the day you travelled back in time and she even stayed in the same building."

"Do you think her ... ghost could be here?" I ask, kind of hoping it is.

He looks thoughtful. "I don't know about that, but perhaps the hatbox is a talisman or something."

"A talisman?"

"An object that holds some sort of power or energy."

"Like it's a horcrux, something enchanted like the effigy mounds?"

"Exactly," he says, though he looks a bit puzzled at my choice of words. "We shouldn't underestimate the existence and potential relevance of the effigy mounds. There's one at the top of Observatory Hill."

"Great, so now I'm travelling through time because this campus is cursed?"

"It's one of many theories. No reason to jump to conclusions."

"Easy for you to say. You're not speeding through time like pages in a flip-book."

"True," he says, sobering at my reality.

"Do you want me to show you the hatbox now?"

"No, let's meet at my office later, say seven o'clock? Don't tell me you've forgotten already?" He raises an eyebrow.

"What?"

"There's a smitten young man waiting for you."

I roll my eyes. "What am I supposed to do about him?"

Professor Smith considers me. "What do you want to do?"

"It's so weird. I mean, I hope we can help each other, but apparently we have a history, and I just don't know it yet."

"Why don't you ask him about it?"

"God, no!"

"Ah, young love. I remember it well," he says with a wistful smile.

"We are *not* in love, so don't encourage him." I'm not sure why I'm making such a big deal of insisting that I don't like Will, but the fact that he knows things I don't drives me crazy.

"Very well." Professor Smith shakes his head. "Now, I need to get back to my office and compile my notes. Seven o'clock."

* * *

Good to his word, Will waits patiently, leaning against a maple tree with brilliant gold leaves, a long blade of grass in his mouth. As soon as he spots me, a smile spreads across his face, and I'm struck again by how ridiculously handsome he is.

He pushes off the tree. "You sure are a sight for sore eyes."

I can't help but feel flattered. He adjusts his long stride to match mine.

Will guides me onto the lakefront path towards Picnic

Point. The light breeze off the water cools us. We walk in silence for a bit, our steps quiet on the packed earth. The blade of grass dangles from his lips.

"Why are you always chewing on grass?" I ask.

"I gave up smoking cigarettes, and it helps keep me from reaching for another."

"But why grass? Did you get that idea from watching the cows on your farm?" I tease.

He cocks his head and amusement glitters in his eyes. "A friend suggested I try it to help me quit."

"Smart friend."

As we follow the path along the lake, I almost feel as if time hasn't changed at all. The trees arch over us on both sides, creating a tunnel of privacy. The waves wash ashore with a calm steady swish against the bank, but then a car roars by on the road running parallel to us, reminding me of the behemoth vehicles of yesteryear.

"I can't get over the cars. My mom could have driven half the neighbourhood kids in that monstrosity."

"They're large compared to my time too. So cars go from being small, to big and then back to small again?"

"They aren't all small. There are still SUVs, trucks and even these giant things called Hummers, but most people drive smaller cars that are more fuel efficient."

Will just shakes his head at all of it. We pass a white wooden sign marking the entrance to Picnic Point. It's more secluded than the other times I've been here. Those times kids were on their way to a bonfire, or joggers and bikers were flying by on their daily workout. But in 1961, people don't seem all that interested in fitness.

He pulls the blade of grass from his mouth. "We

should do something special tonight. I could take you to dinner and maybe later we could watch the stars from Observatory Hill."

"Um, okay." I'm not sure about encouraging him with a romantic date, but I also want to learn as much as I can from him. "I'm meeting the professor at seven. You should come with me."

"I wouldn't miss it." Will smiles and returns to gnawing on his grass.

After following the main trail for a few minutes, Will turns onto a smaller trail to the left. A squirrel darts up a tree to spy on us as we pass.

"Where are we going?"

"There's something I want to show you," he says mysteriously, twirling his blade of grass in his fingers.

We follow a new path along the west shoreline to a narrower trail leading off deeper into the woods. The light dims under the canopy of oaks, maples and poplar trees, creating a mysterious mood.

"Rumour has it there's buried treasure out here," I say.

He smirks and looks sideways at me.

We follow the trail further, Will occasionally choosing a fork in the path. The trees grow denser and there's a fresh woody smell in the air. I can't imagine anyone finding their way back here in this maze, but Will knows exactly where he's going.

"Remember, after you take the first trail off the main one, you take two forks to the left and one to the right."

"Where are we going?"

He stops and turns around, his expression serious. "Abbi, this is important."

"Okay."

"What did I say?"

Geez, what is this a test? "Take the first trail, then fork to the left, then the right."

"No. Two forks to the left and one to the right. Repeat that." He watches me intensely with steely eyes and his jaw clenched.

"Two left, and one right."

He nods and relaxes. "Good. Don't forget."

Now I'm more confused than ever. But the path takes a bend and Will stops in front of a large fallen willow. It must have been there for years based on the moss and moist scent of decay.

Will steps off the path and through the thick blanket of fallen leaves. He climbs over the large fallen trunk and looks back. "Aren't you coming?"

"Oh, sorry." I follow clumsily, wishing I had worn trousers instead of a dress and impractical shoes.

Will takes my hand as I climb over the tree. His eyes meet mine and hold my gaze. I can't ignore his obvious attraction to me; he's certainly not trying to hide it. He seems like a good guy – I like him, and he sure knows how to kiss. But I *just* met him today.

Will drags large branches from the far side of the fallen log. I dodge out of the way to avoid scratches, or deer ticks, or worse. He pushes a pile of damp leaves away from the base of the tree.

"Would you tell me what you're looking for?" I slap at a mosquito.

"This." He pulls up a small trowel, rusted and worn from years in the elements.

"Yay," I say without a shred of enthusiasm.

He shakes his head, but I notice the corner of his mouth curl up. Further down the tree, he moves more forest debris.

I peer over his shoulder. "Now what are you looking for?"

"You'll see." He grunts as he lifts a rock the size of a toaster out of the way and begins to dig.

He piles the rich soil next to him, and suddenly, the spade makes a *thunk*.

"Oh my God, you found something." I squat next to him and peer into the hole.

He brushes a mosquito off his cheek with the back of his dirty hand, leaving a smudge. He looks at me with that playful glint in his eyes, and my heart rate takes off.

Will shovels away more dirt, then reaches into the hole and works the treasure free with his spade.

"What is it?" I ask as he uncovers something square wrapped in oilcloth.

"A tobacco tin."

"Why would it be here in the middle of nowhere?" I ask.

"Because I put it here."

CHAPTER 8

I stare at the unearthed treasure. "You did?"

Will nods, wiping the dirt away from the oilcloth. "There are a few items I wanted to have access to no matter what year I ended up in. I didn't want to risk trying to keep these items with me in my room. I have a safe deposit box at a bank, but I hear I might have trouble getting access to it once we hit something called the digital age, when social security numbers and passwords come into play."

"Oh, I never thought of that."

"Actually, you did. You're the one who warned me to take precautions."

I grin. "That was nice of me."

"Yes, it was." He laughs and unwraps the oilcloth, revealing a very old tobacco tin. The black letters on the olive-green container have been worn down over time, but other than a bit of rust, the tin is in pretty decent shape. "If I try to get access to the same safe deposit box in 1961, and I'm still eighteen instead of … fifty-one, that might be a problem."

I kneel next to him in the dirt and leaves, anxious to

see what treasures lie within. "So, open it. What's inside?"

Will grips the metal lid with his fingertips and carefully pries it off. The contents are wrapped in an old cloth. He's gone to a lot of trouble to protect his keepsakes. He gently pulls out the bundle and unfolds the linen to reveal a gold pocket watch, some bank notes folded in half and several silver dollars.

He wipes his dirty hands on his trousers and lifts out the watch. "This belonged to my father and his father before him. He gave it to me upon my high school graduation." Will cradles it in his hand and I can imagine the pain he's experiencing from the memories the old watch brings back.

Next he pulls out the coins. "Silver dollars become quite valuable in the future. Or so I'm told." He looks at me expectantly.

"Yes, they're kind of rare," I say.

He grins, as if he had been waiting for me to say just that, and I wonder if I've already shared that tidbit with him as well.

He points to a folded sheet of paper. "I recorded my bank account numbers here as a backup in case I lose them in the future. It's my only access to the money I managed to save. Someday, if I ever stay in one place, I'll need it."

"Will, how long have you been travelling?" I ask in awe. He's really thought through all of this. I need to get smarter and figure out how to make my life easier if I'm going to continue to travel.

"It feels like longer than it's actually been, I reckon," he says thoughtfully. I don't press for more.

"What's this?" I point to a small folded envelope.

Will dips his head in that adorable, shy way that I've come to like. "It's for you," he says, his voice sounding like a melody.

"Really?" I'm stunned. "What's it say?"

He shakes his head. "You can read it another time."

"But I want to read it now." I grab for the letter, but Will snatches the tin out of my reach.

"No. This letter is for you to read if you can't find me. I'll add to it every time I travel, at least every time that I can. That way when you travel, you can check the tin for messages, and I'll do the same."

"But I only travel back in time, and so far you've only travelled forward. I'll never get a new message!" My heart squeezes with frustration.

"It might change. You might travel forward. We don't know," he says in a reassuring voice. "And if you figure anything else out about why you think we're travelling, you can leave me notes and I'll get them."

It all seems pretty one-sided. He gets communication, and I get nothing? I move to sit on the old log, then cross my arms and glare at him. Doesn't he realize how scary this has been? If I travel again and he's not there, I'll be all alone again. And now he's keeping whatever helpful information he has in there from me.

"I hate this. All of it," I snap. "Do I ever write to you?" I ask.

"Yes," he says with a sheepish smile.

I leap off the log and reach for the tin. "I did? Is it in there? Let me see it!"

"No!"

I squat next to him and ask nicely, "What did I say?"

hoping my polite tone will convince him to share.

He avoids looking at me.

"What?"

He turns his head, his face a few inches from mine, and says, "You asked me not to tell."

I stand and throw my hands in the air. "That's the stupidest thing I've ever heard!"

"I think you were afraid it might change things for the worse." He seems miserable about not sharing this info. I wonder what else he knows that he's not telling me.

"How could this get any worse?" I whine and kick at the dried leaves on the ground. "So now I've changed my mind, and I want to know. Just tell me," I demand in my most authoritative voice. "It's my letter."

Will presses the lid back onto the tin, carefully wraps it in the heavy cloth and places it back into the ground.

"I'm serious, Will. You can't keep things from me. Do you have any idea how terrifying this has been?"

He cocks his head at me and raises an eyebrow. Of course he knows.

But that doesn't stop me. "See, you do understand, which is exactly why you need to talk. Apparently I told you how to protect your money. It goes both ways, pal."

I arch my eyebrows and wait for his response, but Will ignores me. His jaw is clenched again and the tension between us is thick as he pushes dirt back into the hole.

I want to club him over the head. "You are the most infuriating person I've ever met! You're full of secrets and innuendo. *'Trust me, we're quite close in the future',*" I mock.

"It's true," he says quietly, focusing on his task.

"Bullshit! When you meet me, whenever the hell that is, I won't bother giving you the time of day. We won't get close, and you'll have no reason to bother me. What do you think of that?"

His eyes flash in frustration, but his jaw is set. He says nothing.

"Nice knowing you. Later." I spin on my heel and take off.

"Abbi, wait!" Will calls, but I ignore him and run.

I don't like being kept in the dark, and that's exactly what he's doing. I glance back and see him dragging the branches over the hole while trying to keep track of where I'm going. I whip around the bend in the trail and dash through the woods before he has a chance to follow, taking every other fork in the path. All those years in track paid off.

Paying no attention to what direction I'm going, it doesn't take long before I know he isn't following. The dorky saddle shoes have rubbed my left heel raw, and now I have no idea where I am.

Great. Not only am I lost in time, I'm lost in the freaking woods too. Chirping birds mock me. But I'm on a university campus – I can't possibly be that far from either the lake or the lakeshore path. There aren't a lot of other options.

I limp my way down the path for a good twenty minutes until I hear voices. Another minute and I see small houses and a sign for Eagle Heights Graduate Student Housing. Once I get to a clearing on the edge of the settlement, I'm able to get my bearings and find my way back to the lakeshore path.

I keep a cautious eye out for Will, but I'm not even close to ready to talk to him again. He doesn't get to keep information from me like that. Thankfully he's either gone straight back to his dorm or is lost in the maze of trails trying to find me. It would serve him right.

It takes forever to get back to Liz Waters. By the time I reach my room, the back of my heel is bleeding through my white ankle sock. I whip off the shoe and fling it at my wardrobe.

"Whoa! What did that poor helpless shoe ever do to you?" Janice asks, coming through the door.

"It scraped every layer of skin off the back of my heel."

"If you wore your own shoes instead of mine, maybe that wouldn't happen."

"Oh. Sorry." I pick up the shoes and set them in the chaos of her side of the room.

"You're in a sour mood. Did you quarrel with your boyfriend?"

"He's not my boyfriend," I say sullenly, pulling off the bloody sock that's sticking to the open sore.

She pulls a bag out of her bottom drawer. "He seemed to believe otherwise."

"Well, he's not." I examine the broken blister on my heel and frown.

"Really? Well he sure frosted my cookies!"

I keep my eyes down to avoid rolling them at her.

"Here." She hands me a Band-Aid from her bag.

"Thanks." I try to be polite, but I can't take much more

of this. I want to go home. Somehow, someway, I must get back, away from all these strangers.

"Want to join me for dinner? No better way to get over a guy than food. I hear there's tapioca pudding for dessert."

I don't feel like going to dinner with Janice, and I hate tapioca anything, but I am starving. I sigh. "Sure. Give me a sec to find some shoes that won't torture my feet." Refusing to go out with Will tonight ought to teach him not to keep secrets from me.

After eating dinner with Janice and a couple of other girls from our floor, whose names I stubbornly refuse to learn, I gather Grandma's hatbox and walk the short distance to Professor Smith's office in Sterling Hall.

It's hard to believe that in a few short years, this build-ing will be bombed, but I can't let myself think about the possibility that he might die. Time wouldn't be so cruel. Would it?

I knock softly at his open door, wondering if Will is here too.

"Hello, Abbi. Please, come in," Professor Smith says eagerly.

I take in the small office. Will isn't here. I'm not sure how I feel about that.

The state of the professor's office makes my messy dorm room look immaculate by comparison. Two walls of shelves burst with books. Papers and boxes are crammed above them, with open folders and three-ring binders on top of that. Another wall is anchored by three tall filing cabinets, some of the drawers not quite closed, papers sticking out the top. A few crispy, water-deprived plants sit next to a dust-covered globe, and a pile of instruments that look like complicated rulers lie jumbled on a cluttered table. On the walls are several special achievement plaques and a bulletin board covered with papers listing complex equations, schedules and children's art projects.

"I brought the hatbox," I offer.

"Wonderful. Have a seat and let's take a look." He pushes a stack of papers in front of him off to the side.

"Are those your kids?" I point to a framed black and white picture of three children standing on a staircase in order of height. One has a huge cowlick, and another is in braids and missing her front teeth.

"Yes, they're all mine." He smiles affectionately and picks up the picture. "And the fourth one coming any day."

"That's really great." I always wanted siblings, but it wasn't meant to be.

"I'm a very lucky man." He puts the photo back and moves a dirty coffee cup out of the way.

"Interesting organizational system you have."

"Somehow my brain works better with chaos."

"Based on the condition of your office, you must be brilliant." I think of the library named after him in present day. I'm not sure what he's achieved to get his own library, but it must be big … unless the library is a memorial to his death? I shake the depressing thought away.

"Indeed!" Professor Smith chuckles. "So, what do we have here?"

I place the box on the corner of the grey metal desk

and remove the lid, releasing the familiar rosewater scent of Grandma's house.

"May I?" he asks, his hand poised to dive in.

"Go for it."

The professor removes the items, examining each one. "College memorabilia ... some photographs," he mumbles as he gently handles the items. He looks at a handkerchief embroidered with the name "Ruby" across the front, then glances at me.

I shrug. "I've never heard of anyone by that name before. Maybe it belonged to a college friend or something."

He pages through clippings of college dances, sporting events and photos of people I don't recognize, taking notes and photographs of each item as he goes.

"Oh, check this out," I say when I spot the picture of the somber-faced nun.

"Who is it?" He studies the photo.

"No idea."

The professor turns the picture over. "Me at the convent," he reads. He flips it back over. "Any chance this could be your grandmother?"

I shake my head. "It doesn't look like her, so I'd say no. Plus, Grandma wasn't even Catholic."

"Hmm. I suppose it could be a friend of hers. Maybe someone she met on a trip somewhere."

"Grandma travelled all over the world as an anthropologist." I picture the many souvenirs proudly displayed around her house: an ivory carving from India, bamboo baskets from Japan, the native masks from Kenya. She always brought home an authentic keepsake from each country she visited.

"Then perhaps she met this nun on one of her trips."

"It's possible."

I empty a velvet pouch, revealing two plain gold bands. One is large and thick, the other delicate and small. "Look at these rings." He opens his hand and I drop them into his palm.

"They look like wedding rings."

"They can't be my grandparents', because Grandma wore her wedding band until she died. My mom has it now."

"Perhaps they belonged to your grandmother's parents," he says, carefully studying each one. He pulls a magnifying glass from his top drawer and holds the rings under the desk light one at a time. "There's no inscription."

I lean forward to see but can't get close enough. "So there's a couple of old rings that may or may not have belonged to my what? Great-grandparents? I don't know if I've ever even heard their names."

"Do you know anything about your great-grandparents?"

"Not really. All I remember is my mom mentioning that an evil stepmother raised Grandma's mother, because her own mother died when she was a baby. Wait! There's a picture in here of Grandma as a teenager with her parents."

I riffle through football game programs, a crumbling pressed corsage and a yellowed list of house rules from Liz Waters. "Here it is." I hand over the photo.

The corner of the professor's mouth curls into a smile.

"What?" I try to see what he could possibly find in

the photo that makes him smile.

"Oh, nothing at all. They look like a nice family." He sets it down with the other items. "What else have you got?"

"Just old college stuff. No more pictures or anything interesting." I scan my memory for anything else I can tell him, but my brain is fried. Still, we spend an hour reviewing items in the hatbox in case there's some hidden meaning to any of them.

Professor Smith pauses as he's snapping photos. "Did you and Will have a good visit? Was he able to tell you anything helpful?"

I screw up my face with indignation but say nothing.

"Not getting along?"

I stare at the clay ashtray on his desk that holds paper-clips. It looks like something one of his kids made at school. "We sort of had a fight," I mumble.

"Already?" he laughs. "You barely know each other."

Professor Smith is way too entertained by this.

"Will is so stubborn. He refuses to tell me anything!"

"Did he say why he wouldn't?"

I clench my jaw and fight to keep my cool, but my voice comes out laced with sarcasm. "Apparently, I asked him not to."

A grin creeps over the professor's face.

"It's not funny!"

"I'm sorry. I'm sure that from where you're sitting, it's quite frustrating, but the fact is, I'm glad. It's a very responsible decision you've both made. We don't know how giving advanced information will affect the future. It could change things in a negative nature."

"Or do nothing at all. I don't see how telling me how far back I travel or who I meet can be such a big deal."

The professor cocks his head to the side. "You're the one who asked him not to tell your future self, so you must have had a good reason."

"Whatever," I huff.

As angry as I am at Will, though, I feel myself drawn to him. I'm both mad that he's not here, and worried about why he's not. What if he's right and we *are* something special, and I only have today before one of us travels? I realize that I want to see him again to get some things straight. Besides Professor Smith, Will is all I've got.

The black rotary phone on the professor's desk jangles loudly, startling me.

He frowns at it before answering, but soon he's beaming. "Tonight? How far apart are the pains? Uh-huh. Uh-huh. I'm on my way!"

He hangs up the phone and beams at me. "The baby is coming! I've got to go!"

"That's wonderful," I manage to say, though I can't help but feel abandoned. Together we return the memorabilia to the hatbox. I stand and secure the lid. "I'll get out of your way so you can go."

The professor stands, pats down his pockets and looks at his desk for anything he might need. "I'm sorry to cut our meeting short."

I collect the hatbox and head for the door. "Oh my God, are you kidding? You're having a baby!"

He pulls his keys from his pocket and locks his office door. Together we head towards the stairs.

"I'd like to meet you and Will again tomorrow, but if I can't make it, I'll call and leave a message for you at your dormitory."

"Sure … if I'm still here." A slow dread bubbles in the back of my mind.

He glances at me through narrowed eyes as we take the stairs. "Do you have reason to think you won't be here?"

"Well, I seem to zip through time like a humming-bird flitting from flower to flower," I say, lacking emotion, because I'm trying to mask my frustration.

The professor pauses at the landing. "Do you have pre-monitions about when you travel? Is it based on whether you're happy or sad?"

I think for a second. "No, I don't have a sixth sense or anything. But now that you mention it, I have been sad each time. It all began with my missing Grandma. I couldn't help it. Being on campus and so far from home made me miss her all over again. I don't know if that's relevant."

"I don't either, but one never knows." We continue down the last flight of steps and into the night air. He bounds towards the car park and calls back to me, "I'll see you tomorrow!"

"Congratulations on the new baby," I call back. And then I sigh.

* * *

As I walk the short distance back to Liz Waters, I'm happy for Professor Smith. The joy on his face was euphoric. He loves his family so much. And that just makes the loneliness of my situation even worse. I miss my mom more than ever. I have the professor, but only once in a while. I've met Will, who seems to know more about me than anyone, but refuses to tell me what he knows. I'm glad he showed me the buried tobacco tin, but why wouldn't he tell me more? I'd hike out to Picnic Point right now and dig it up, but it's dark and creepy, and I know I'd just get lost.

I hope that he'll be waiting for me at Liz Waters, but he isn't. I go to my room and wait but don't hold out hope he'll show up. Apparently he's snuck in plenty of times. Maybe he will tonight too?

But Will doesn't turn up. As the night grows late, I find myself listening for noises in the hall. Has something happened? Has he shot back in time and I've missed my only chance to learn more from him?

I press my forehead to the window and stare at the ground below. I scan the nearby woods, and my eyes are drawn to the warm golden stone of the Carillon Tower, peaking up over the treetops.

"What are you doing? Go to bed," Janice complains, rolling over and punching her pillow.

I think about sneaking out to look for Will, but I have no idea what room he's in at Tripp Hall. Besides, as a girl in 1961, I'm pretty sure I can't just march into a guys' dorm this late at night and ask for him. I'm nervous to go to bed, afraid that I'll travel again. If I slept somewhere other than my own bed, would it make a difference? Or would that somehow close my time travel window, stranding me here forever? I shudder at the thought and slip between the cool sheets, arching my head to see the bell tower and willing it not to chime. Maybe if I stay awake, it can't send me away? I hope.

The minutes turn to hours and I hear the bells chime, reverberating through the air. A thought niggles at the back of my mind that I'm falling asleep.

CHAPTER 9

I wake facing the wall. An alarm clock clangs loudly, like the bell at my old primary school, but I cling to my downy pillow and stare at the painted cinder block. I am afraid to roll over and see what torturous year time has dropped me into. Someone turns off the alarm, confirming I'm not alone.

"Abigail, rise and shine, sleepy head," a chipper voice calls. It's not Janice's voice, which confirms that I have indeed travelled again. I want to cry.

"It snowed last night. It's a perfect day!"

I stretch my head to peek out of the window. The air in the room is chilly. Sure enough, snow has collected on the bare branches of the trees outside. It's winter. This is new. I burrow back into my warm bedding, not ready to face this new time. Maybe I'll hide in bed all day.

Suddenly a pillow knocks me in the head. Great. I have a perky roommate. With a sigh, I roll over and push my hair out of my face to see who I'm dealing with. Will she be a bossy clean freak, or laid back and fun?

Sitting on the side of her bed, rubbing her hands together for warmth, is a girl who looks exactly like the girl in the picture from the hatbox. The picture I accidentally left back in present day on the bedside table. A girl who looks identical to my...

"Grandma?" I whisper in disbelief.

The girl looks up. "Did you just call me Grandma?"

Her delicate features are exactly like Grandma's, minus the joyful wrinkles and stylish grey hair. The bright amber eyes that never missed a trick are exactly the same, as are her high cheekbones and the curve of her lip.

"Uh, no. I was dreaming about my grandma," I say, staring at this svelte version of my grandmother as she plugs in a little kettle on her bedside table.

"What was your dream about?" She flits about the room wearing a blue bathrobe over a long flannel nightgown.

I can't think straight. My heart is pounding. My grandmother is standing right in front of me, clueless that her future granddaughter has travelled here from the future. Her waistline is tiny, her skin flawless. She can't be any older than I am.

"Was it a good dream or a bad dream?" She turns on a record player, filling the room with soft crooning music, and sings along to the melody, *"Gonna take a sentimental journey, gonna set my heart at ease. Gonna make a sentimental journey, to renew old memories."* She smiles and looks at me expectantly.

I try to talk, but can't get the words out. I clear my throat. "Good. It was really good." My eyes are glued to her. "I was lost and couldn't find my way home. Then my grandmother appeared."

"I like that dream. I never met my grandmother. She

died when my mom was only two."

I sit up in bed. Grandma never talked about her mother before. "What happened?"

"No one knows," she says, riffling through items on her bookcase with her back to me. "The story goes that she was fixing dinner one night, looked out of the window, had a scare and fell over dead. My mother was a few feet away in her highchair."

"Oh my God, that's terrible."

"Yes, it truly was," she says, setting mugs and spoons on her bedside table next to the kettle, which is now giving off a low whistle. "My mother grew up being shuffled from one relative's house to another until her father eventually remarried. Then she had to deal with an evil stepmother who shipped her off to boarding schools."

"I had no idea," I mumble. Except that I sort of did ... but now I have more of the story.

Grandma spins around with a grin, revealing a trace of her mischievous side that I rarely saw in her final year. "But I turned out perfectly, despite being deprived of a grandmother."

A knock sounds at the door. Grandma looks at me in a panic.

"What?" I ask. I can't imagine what is so horrible about a knock on the door.

She gestures to the kettle as steam shoots out of the top. "Answer the door, but don't let them in. I can't get written up again."

"For what?"

"Have you gone daft? The kettle!"

"Oh. Right." I jump out of bed wearing my baggy,

era-inappropriate T-shirt. My feet hit the cold tile floor, and I dance my way to the door, grabbing a bathrobe on the way.

The knock sounds again. I turn back to see Grandma unplugging the kettle and setting it on the floor out of sight, between her bed and the bedside table.

I tie the sash of my robe and open the door a few inches, blocking the view of the room. A girl with short red hair peers back.

"Yes?"

"Here's the invitation for you and Sharon to the Winter Carnival. I hope you both plan to come." She holds out a card with our names and room number printed neatly on the outside. "We'll be making decorations on Tuesday in the library if you want to help."

"Sure. Thanks." I accept the invitation and close the door. When I turn, I notice the wall calendar displays February 1951. I should be shocked, but I don't care. I'm with Grandma!

"That was close." Grandma retrieves the kettle and fills two mugs, then spoons in something from a box. She stirs them both and hands one to me. The sweet aroma of hot chocolate tickles my nose.

"Thank you." Even at eighteen, Grandma is already taking care of me.

* * *

During breakfast in the cafeteria, we look out at the freshly fallen snow on the patio. Grandma – or Sharon, as I should call her? – gobbles down her food.

"Hurry up," she urges.

I've barely eaten anything. I'm too busy staring at her perfectly unwrinkled skin and dancing eyes. "What's the rush?"

"Do you realize it's been three weeks since we've had more than a dusting of snow?" She waves her fork and knife in the air as she talks.

Suddenly she sets them both down with a clink. "Let's go sledging!"

"Um. Okay. When?" I take another bite of pancake.

"Now!" She removes the dishes from her food tray and stacks them neatly.

I wash down my food with a gulp of milk. "Don't you have a class?" Heck, I probably do too, not that I care.

She glances about the dining room, checking for anyone listening in, then whispers, "Today's a snow day."

"They cancelled class?" There may be six inches of snow, but that's nothing for Wisconsin.

"No, you silly goose. It's the official Sharon and Abigail Skip Class and Play in the Snow Day." She takes the plate of pancakes off my tray.

"Hey, I want those!"

"Too late, slowpoke. The early bird gets the worm." She clears both our trays, then stands up. With a quick covert look to see if anyone's watching, she slides her tray under her sweater.

"You're stealing the cafeteria tray?"

"Hurry up. Nobody's looking. Take yours."

I think she's a little bit nuts, but I'm willing to do anything she wants, now that I get to be with her again. Stretching my scratchy wool sweater over the metal tray, I slide it up so it looks as if I'm wearing flat body armour, or, more likely, a tray under my sweater.

Sharon makes a beeline for the exit and I follow. We scurry out of the dining room and scramble up the stairs and down the halls, until we're finally safe in our room. She pulls out her tray and falls giggling onto her bed.

"What was that about?" I join her in fits of laughter even though I'm not sure why I just stole a food tray.

"Now we have sledges!" She slaps her tray.

Fifteen minutes later, bundled up in wool coats and scarves and wearing bulky snow trousers, we stand atop Bascom Hill with the trays in our mittened hands as snowflakes float down from the grey sky, sticking to Sharon's hat and melting on her nose. She's radiant.

We're not the only ones taking a snow day. Students are scattered everywhere, sliding down the hill on everything from cafeteria trays to pieces of cardboard. One brave soul is using a shovel.

"Come on!" Sharon hollers, running to place her tray on the snow run where others have gone before us. The hill is pretty steep, but she's unconcerned. She sits down and pulls her wool coat up so it won't drag in the snow.

"Hey, Tom? Give me a push?" she calls, and a guy with an infectious grin and red nose ploughs through the snow to reach her.

"Big push or baby push?" he asks.

"Give it all you've got," she says, pulling her feet onto the tray.

Tom gives her a running push and off she slides. She goes a good thirty feet before her boot catches the snow. She spins into the fresh powder, letting out a hearty squeal.

I climb aboard my own makeshift sledge and tug

myself forwards with my hands until Tom gives me a push too. I scream as I fly down the hill, whizzing past Sharon before spinning out of control and biting the snow face-first.

When I get up, Sharon is bounding towards me laughing. "Are you all right?"

"Let's do it again!" I wipe the snow from my cheeks with the back of my snow-coated mitten. Sharon offers her hand and we climb the hill together and slide down again and again.

We build a snowman with other students and then a snowball fight breaks out. By the time we trek back to the dorm, we're exhausted, our woollen clothes are soaked, we're chilled to the bone and I'm utterly happy.

That afternoon, with our wet clothes draped over the radiator, we listen to old-time records by Perry Como and the Andrew Sisters, artists I've never heard of. Sharon pulls out her styling supplies and twists my hair into pin curls. "Are you sure you don't want me to cut your hair?" she asks. "It would be so much easier to style, and it would look lovely."

"You know how to cut hair?"

"No, but how difficult can it be?" she says optimistically, eyeing the scissors on her desk.

Touching a long lock, I say, "No thanks. I'll keep it as is." The tight, curly look suits Grandma well enough, but it's nothing I want to be stuck with when I finally get back to my time. Especially since she has no idea how to cut hair.

When she's finished pinning my hair, she pulls what looks like a shower cap with a hose coming out of it over my head. The hose plugs into a machine that she turns on. My shower cap fills with warm air and I smile to myself, feeling like an alien in an old cartoon.

We page through *National Geographic* magazines. Sharon scoots over and points out pictures of Machu Picchu. She yells to be heard over the noise of the hair dryer. "This is where I want to travel to this summer. It looks so exotic."

The ancient green mountains look familiar with the rocky-tiered ruins of a village below. I think I've actually seen old photos of Grandma at this place.

"But my mother keeps forgetting to send me my birth certificate, which I need to apply for a passport." She slumps back against her pillow.

Seems to me it would be unusual for a young woman to travel so far away in this day and age, but Grandma was never predictable.

"If I had a nickel for every time Mother promised to look for it, I could have gone five times by now. I think she's afraid of me leaving the country."

"What does your father think?" I yell over the sound of the humming dryer.

"That I should sow my oats while I'm young." She grins.

"He sounds like a good guy."

I think of the hatbox on my bed and the framed picture of Grandma and her parents. They both appear politely reserved in the stuffy formal portrait, nothing like the fun goofiness of their daughter. What would Sharon think if I opened it up and showed her? I hope she isn't a snoop and that she doesn't look into it when I'm not in the room. She'd be in for a shock.

"Oh, he is. Mother likes to tease about how she tamed him of his wild ways."

When my hair is dry, I'm amazed at how Sharon styles it to curl under and then swoops up the front and pins it in place. It resembles the look of her hair, despite it being so long, and I definitely look as if I fit in here now. I giggle to see what looks like a pin-up girl from one of those old calendars looking back at me in the mirror.

We stand in front of the mirror over my dresser. "See, you look beautiful with your hair done. Let me take your picture." She pulls a boxy camera from her drawer and aims it at me.

"Wait. I want you in it too."

"All right. Let me go and get someone to take it for us."

I laugh. "Silly girl. We don't need anyone's help." I pat the spot beside me and take the camera from her. "We'll take a selfie."

"A what?" She sits next to me, confused.

"We'll take it of ourselves." I examine the camera. "Where's the button on this thing?"

Sharon shows me a round button on top. I flip the camera around so the lens faces us and hold it up. Grandma and I lean our heads together and smile.

"Say cheese," she says.

"Cheese!"

As I snap the picture, a flash goes off, and for a moment I can't see. Then I blink and realize *this* is the picture that eventually ends up in the hatbox. The one that Jada and I looked at and thought we'd found my twin. I stare at the camera in my hand and think of all the years and places that picture will travel before it eventually comes back to me.

"Are you all right?" Sharon asks.

I look up at her wonderful face. "I've never been better." She leans over and we hug, and for an instant it's as if it's my dear old grandma hugging me.

When it's nearly dinner time, Sharon pulls out a pair of stockings. They look like tights that were cut off at the thigh. I watch, fascinated, as she slips a foot in and carefully pulls the sheer material up her leg, then slides a white band of elastic up her thigh to hold it in place.

Sharon glances up. "What's the matter?"

"Oh, nothing." I force down a giggle and turn to my dresser, finding I have several pairs too. Acting as cool as possible, I slide my foot in and gently tug the fabric up. Once I get them on and the elastic band tightly on my thigh, cutting off circulation, I go for shoes. Sharon snickers.

"What?"

"Your seams are crooked as lightening bolts."

I strain to look behind me and see two jagged seams zigzagging up my legs. Who knew there was an art to putting on panty hose?

"Here, I'll help you." She kneels behind me and, with little pinches that tickle, she tugs the nylon one way and the other until the back of my legs have two lines straight as railroad tracks.

After dinner in the cafeteria, I'm ready to snuggle in for the evening and see if I can figure out a way to stay here with Grandma instead of skipping backwards again. It occurs to me then that I haven't thought of Professor Smith or Will all day, but being with Grandma is far more important than either of them right now. I kick off my clunky shoes and search for a warm sweater in my dresser, wishing some modern-day pyjama bottoms and fuzzy socks had time travelled with me.

"What are you doing?" Sharon asks.

I slip into a navy blue cardigan and climb onto my bed. "Getting comfortable?"

"Oh no you don't. We're going out." She grabs my arm and pulls me to my feet.

"Where? It's snowing again."

"Yes! It's beautiful, it's Thursday night and we're going to the College Club, so dig out your makeup and let's get gussied up."

How can I say no? We primp and preen in front of the mirror, powder our noses and paint our lips red. By the time we're ready, several girls are waiting for us in the hall.

Bundled up in our thick coats and snow boots, we trudge our way up one side of Bascom Hill and down the other. I shiver as the cold February chill flows freely over my stockinged legs. When we cross Lake Street towards Library Mall, I see that the Memorial Library hasn't been built yet, creating another void in the landscape. In fact, Library Mall isn't built yet either. It's an extra block of State Street with houses and businesses, and vintage cars parked at the curb.

The College Club, or "Kollege Klub," as I see it's spelled, is located in a building I don't recognize. Inside it's a cross between a soda fountain and pub. The place is packed with students abuzz with the energy fresh snow and college hormones bring.

Sharon seems to know everyone. Tom, the guy from sledging, buys us our first beer. We spend the night dancing to the jukebox, drinking and cracking up over stories of how Tom befriended a baby skunk and made a pet out of it. Lots of guys talk to Sharon. She's a ball of fun, but it's Tom who monopolizes most of her time, flirting with her and making her laugh. When we finally return to our dorm room, I'm exhausted.

After changing into a soft flannel nightgown, I sit up in bed and lean against the cool outside wall. I pray I won't travel tonight. After everything I've been through, is this why I travelled? To see Grandma one last time?

I've been missing her so much, and now we're together again. Granted, she doesn't know me as her granddaughter, but this is the best gift I could have ever imagined, and I can't let it end.

"Tom sure seems to like you. Are you two an item?" I ask.

Sharon is fiddling with the lamp and alarm clock cords behind her bedside table. "Gosh no! He's just a good-time Charlie. I'm never getting married."

"Why not?"

"I don't see the point. Why would I sign up for a life of servitude and spend the rest of my days worrying about how to make the perfect pie crust or iron the wrinkles out of a shirt sleeve?"

I bite back a laugh. Grandma was far from a happy homemaker. She was incredibly independent. But then I worry whether history can be changed, like the professor warned. What if she never marries or has my mom? I'll never be born.

"If I marry, how will I see the world?" Sharon goes on. "I can't go to China or Greece or the Amazon." She shakes the electrical cords and almost knocks her lamp over.

"What are you doing?"

Her head pops up. "Making sure the cords don't cross and start a fire."

"Seriously?" I hide my grin.

"I'm quite serious. It would be tragic to wake up on fire."

"I can't argue with that. So tell me, how do you plan to pay for all your exotic travel if you don't have a wealthy husband to bankroll you?" I hope to steer her towards the marriage market.

"Well, I certainly won't be able to afford to travel if I'm a school teacher or a nurse." She pushes her bedside table back in place and climbs into bed. "I'll have torrid affairs with handsome men who are ridiculously rich."

"That's scandalous!" I say, and we giggle. I can almost see her going through with it. "But you won't marry any of your rich boyfriends?"

"Goodness no! I'd be bored silly with them after a trip or two." She pulls down her covers and slips her legs under.

Little does Sharon know that in a few years she will meet my grandfather while on a field dig in South America. She'll marry him, and they'll travel the globe together on research assignments.

But in case she can alter the future, I say, "I hope you change your mind, because if you don't have a family, then you'll never have grandchildren. Wouldn't it be fun to have little grandbabies to spoil when you get tired of travelling?"

She wrinkles her brow in thought. "That's true. I suppose grandchildren could be fun." She's quiet for a moment, considering the idea, and then blurts, "I think I'd like eleven of them."

I laugh. "That's random. Why eleven?"

"Because it's my favourite number, of course. I will teach them to ski and horseback ride, and when they turn eighteen, I'll take them to Las Vegas gambling!"

But she won't get eleven. She only gets me. She does teach me to ride horses and water ski, but by the time I turn eighteen, her cancer has limited her activities to quiet card games at home – although she did teach me poker. Towards the end we did a lot of jigsaw puzzles of the amazing places she visited throughout her life.

Sharon yawns. "I've changed my mind. Just for you I'll marry, but only at the last minute, after I've seen all there is to see."

Just for me, I think with a smile. How true that becomes. "Sounds like a solid decision." I relax just a little that she hasn't written off marriage entirely and that her line will continue on.

Sharon turns off her light. My bedside lamp glows. I look at her young form in the bed across from me and shake my head in amazement at the fabulous, impossible odds that brought us together. "Does my light bother you? I'm not tired and thought I'd sit up and read for a while."

"I don't know how you can be wide awake. I'm exhausted. As long as you aren't clacking away typing up a term paper, I can sleep through most anything," she says through a yawn.

But I can't afford to fall asleep and take a chance that those blasted bells might ring and suck me back in time again. If I'm awake, I can't travel, right? Finally, I'm in a place I want to stay, at least for a while before going back home. I'll sit up all night every night if that's what it takes.

"Good night, Abigail."

"Good night," I say, and then silently mouth, "Grandma."

* * *

It works. The next morning I'm awake, exhausted, but still here with Sharon. As soon as she leaves for class I collapse into bed and sleep for half the day. When I'm up and trying to decide what to do, I realize finding Professor Smith is my top priority, and after that, Will.

The year is 1951, so I don't think the professor could possibly be old enough to teach yet. I check his office in Sterling Hall anyway, and my suspicions prove correct. No Smiths on the faculty list. This campus is huge. How will I possibly find him? What is he doing in 1951?

I trek out to Tripp Hall, hoping to run into Will. I watch the entrance for a half hour, shivering in the cold, but no Will. Finally I ask a few guys if they know a Will, but no one does. I want to curse the stubborn guy for not telling me more about himself. I don't know his last name, what he likes to do or anything that might give me a hint at where he'd be, if he's here at all. I desperately want to dig up his treasure, but until the snow melts, I know I'd never find it.

Though I haven't been able to find Will or the professor, each day brings new excitement with Sharon. She goes from being my beloved grandmother to my best friend, and she's a whirlwind of energy.

Every night after another adventure, whether it's building snow forts overlooking the frozen lake or helping her spike the punch at the Winter Carnival, I make certain everything important to me is on my bed, especially the hatbox. I sit up until Sharon, and hopefully the rest of the dorm, is asleep. Then I wander the empty halls. It takes a good twenty minutes to make a full loop of each of the three stories and five wings. I also use the time to do my own version of research on time travel, lugging heavy books home from the library and pouring through them while everyone else sleeps. But most of what I've found is either fictional stories or too scientific for me to understand.

One night Grandma wakes up as I open my drawer for a warmer sweater to hold off the chill during my nightly patrol of the vacant halls. When I claim insomnia, she joins me, and we sneak into the cafeteria kitchen. She fries us up some grilled bologna and mayonnaise sandwiches.

A couple of times I accidentally fall asleep near dawn, but thank God, I wake up to Sharon singing. Usually it's Sinatra tunes, but sometimes it's Perry Como, whose smooth, "dreamy" voice I've come to love. Surviving on barely five hours of shut-eye a day isn't so great for my

GPA, but I know better than to assume I'll stay here with Grandma forever, so I don't worry too much about it. After a week, I receive a warning letter about my missed classes, but I ignore it. I know I'm only one bell gong away from being sucked back in time again.

On an unusually warm afternoon two weeks later, I venture out to enjoy the nice weather. The snow is melting, creating little streams that run along the edge of the pavements. Students mill about with their winter coats hanging open. I'm finally used to seeing all the girls wearing wool skirts that reach below their knees and hairstyles achieved by sleeping all night in painful-looking pin curls.

I find myself checking out every sandy-haired guy who passes. Could Will end up here too? He would have known the answer to this the last time I saw him, but, of course, he was too stubborn to say.

A student walks by and something about his gait catches my eye. His brown hair is buzzed short, so it definitely isn't Will. He turns a corner, giving me a glimpse of his profile complete with thick-framed glasses.

Professor Smith!

I race after him. "Professor!" But he doesn't slow. I push by a cluster of students and yell again, but still no reaction.

He puts his hand on the door to Bascom Hall. "Professor Smith!" I yell. This time he pauses and looks in my direction. "Wait up!" I call and run to catch him. He is so different, with the narrow face and skinny frame of a young man. The last time we met, he had the build of a man, but he hasn't filled out yet in 1951.

"I'm afraid you've got the wrong person. I'm not even close to being a professor," he says shyly, giving me a covert once-over.

Crud. Of course he isn't. He looks far more like a student than an instructor.

He peers at my face. "Oh my goodness, I know you."

"You do?"

"Yes. You're Abigail. It's me, Smitty. We met freshman year. On the Union Terrace," he adds, a broad smile of recognition covering his face.

"Right, now I remember." I'm totally freaking out inside. He and I have met before, but he doesn't appear to know about my time travel. And he goes by Smitty? My heart drops. This is not the professor I need to help me.

"That was what, three years ago? You haven't changed a bit," he says.

"So that must mean you're a senior," I say, hiding my dismay at learning I'll be travelling again, at least as far back as 1948.

"Actually, I'm in grad school. Once I decided on my major, everything kind of clicked." He pulls the door open. "It's nice to see you again. I wish I had time to catch up, but I'm running late for a lecture."

I can't let him slip away without knowing more. "Of course. But would you be free for coffee some time?"

He releases the door, adjusts his glasses and stares back at me as if I've said something shocking. "Certainly. How about tomorrow afternoon?"

"Great. Three o'clock, in the Rathskeller?" I offer.

"I look forward to it," he says with the hint of a smile and disappears inside the building.

Professor Smith's been a comforting authority figure to me, but now he's a regular guy running late for class. I'm devastated to discover that he doesn't seem to know anything about my time travels. Still, there's a sense of relief to see his familiar face ... albeit a much younger version. I didn't realize how much his existence means to me. I can't wait to tell Grandma. Of course, I won't tell her how I know him, just that I've met a guy and am meeting him for coffee. There are so few things I can tell her, but sharing my new friend, Smitty, seems safe enough.

I rush back to Liz Waters. Once inside, when my eyes adjust from the bright outdoors, I notice a barrel-chested man standing off to the side of the foyer, gripping his hat and wearing a somber expression. There aren't too many middle-aged men who venture into Liz Waters.

I dart past and weave my way through each wing, then barge into our room to tell Grandma about Smitty. She is hunched over an open suitcase with her back to me.

I stop short. "What are you doing?"

She turns, her face blotchy and tear-stained.

"What's wrong?" I ask.

"My mother died." She bursts into fresh tears.

I rush to her side and hug her. She weeps, her whole body trembling with grief. "I'm so sorry." I desperately wish I could make it better. My tough, gutsy grandmother has finally been faced with an insurmountable challenge.

When her tears subside and she's wiped them with a handkerchief, I lead her to my bed to sit. "What happened?"

"My mother's been ill on and off for a few months, but I had no idea it was serious. Father says that Mother didn't want me to worry and asked him not to tell me until near the end, but then the end came suddenly." She presses the handkerchief to her face. I lightly rub her back and lean my head on her shoulder.

She pulls herself together, dabbing at her tears. "My father's waiting for me now to go home for the funeral."

"Sharon, I'm so sorry."

I can't imagine losing my mom, and especially not getting a chance to say goodbye. Except that's sort of what happened to me. I lost her in time. Is Mom worried about me? Does she even know I'm not there any more? It's been easy to stay happy these past weeks with Grandma, but now the reality of being away from her comes rushing back.

Sharon sniffles, clutching the damp handkerchief. "Gosh, Abigail. I already miss my mother desperately. What am I supposed to do without her?"

I take a moment to consider what advice Grandma would give to me. "I guess you take it one day at a time." I brush her hair back from her face, thinking about how this wisdom applies to me as well.

"But I don't know how I'm going to get through the next hours." She twists the hanky.

"Then maybe you take it hour by hour, or minute by minute. If you can get through one, then you can get through the next." I squeeze her hand. "Tell me, what can I do to help?"

"I need to hurry and finish packing. I can't think straight enough to know what to take."

"Of course." I pick up a dress laid across Sharon's bed and carefully fold it. I realize I know so little about

Grandma's life. She settles in Ohio after college, but I've never even thought to ask her where she was born. "How far away do you live?"

"Sheboygan is a couple of hours east of here on Lake Michigan."

I carefully place the folded dress in the suitcase and then a slip and a nightgown, while Sharon gathers her hairbrush and other toiletries.

"I'm not sure how long I'll be gone, or if I'm even coming back." Her voice cracks with emotion.

My head snaps up. "Why wouldn't you come back to school?"

"If my father needs me, I'll stay at home. I don't think he even knows how to brew a pot of coffee, let alone how to operate the wringer washer."

My chest tightens. I can't be here without her. I've worked so hard to stay in one place, but if Sharon doesn't come back to school, I don't have anything to keep me here and I don't want to travel again unless I'm going home.

She places the last items in her suitcase, snaps the metal latches shut and looks around the room. "I suppose that's it."

I want to beg her not to go, but the sadness in her eyes reminds me this isn't about me. "I so wish that I could make this better."

Sharon slips on her long wool coat and picks up a smaller case that matches the larger one. "Having you for a best friend makes such a difference."

"Let me carry this." I lift the heavy suitcase off the bed and lug it down the hall. Suitcases from the fifties don't have the benefit of wheels or extending handles, so my arms are burning by the time we reach the foyer.

Sharon's father, the man I passed earlier, waits quietly in the corner, avoiding the curious glances as girls return from class.

"Abigail, this is my father, Walter," Sharon says stoically. "Father, this is my roommate, Abigail."

He turns and sets his weary eyes on me and nods. "Hello, Abigail."

"I'm so sorry for your loss." I know my words are inadequate. Then it dawns on me that he's my great-grandfather, and I can't look away from his face. Something about his eyes looks familiar, but I can't place it. Grandma doesn't really look like him, but maybe Mom does?

"Thank you. Ruby was a wonderful woman." He's fighting to keep emotion out of his voice. "Sharon, we should get started home." He lifts the suitcase with ease and heads outside.

I hug Grandma quick and hard, knowing I might never see her again. "I love you," I whisper and kiss her cheek.

"Back atcha, kiddo," she says with a sad smile and disappears through the main doors. I watch as she climbs into her father's car, a rolling beast stealing her away.

I wipe my tears, heartbroken to witness her losing her mother, and miserable to say goodbye. Back in my room, something niggles at my brain.

Ruby.

I open the hatbox, pull out the embroidered handkerchief and see "Ruby" in neat stitches. So this was Sharon's mother's hanky.

Night comes and it is the loneliest of my life. The anguish I experience at losing Grandma once again is more than my broken heart can handle. She is far more than my Grandma – she has become my best friend, a larger-than-life personality who has suffered a devastating blow.

My eyes grow heavy, but I don't dare chance falling asleep. I open the window to let in the cold air, and then later I wander the cavernous halls, making a slow torturous loop of every wing and floor.

As I trudge along, I realize that my pathetic "research" isn't getting me anywhere. My only hope to get back to my own time is the professor. It's time to refocus and work with him. But he is so young, and doesn't seem to know about my time travel.

It's time he did.

CHAPTER 10

A strong rapping pulls me from slumber. I blink awake, my eyes land on Grandma's empty bed, and my heart twists, but at least I didn't travel. The rapping sounds again.

"Coming," I call, trying to sound awake. I let myself go to bed as soon as the sun began rising early this morning. A quick glance at the alarm clock reveals it's now eleven-thirty a.m. I scrub my hands over my face to wake up. I slept like a rock.

"Miss Thorp, would you please open the door."

Crap. Is that the head resident? "One sec."

I whip off my old-fashioned nightgown, which I decided helped me fit in better than my old T-shirt, and yank on the dress I wore yesterday, twisting to reach the zipper in the back.

Impatient knocking sounds again. I pull open the door to the same irritated Mrs. Chaplin with the pearls and puff of perfume who disliked me in 1961. At least she doesn't know who I am. With her lips pursed, she glares down her bulbous nose at me.

"Hi," I say.

Her eyes trail from my uncombed hair down to my

bare toes on the cold tile. "Shouldn't you be in American Literature class right now?"

"Uh, yes. I was on my way."

She stares at my bare feet again and frowns. "It has come to my attention that you have failed to attend several of your classes for the past three weeks. Miss Thorp, your truancy is going to bring you only difficult results."

I resist blurting out that truancy is the least of my troubles. Instead I go for polite apology. "I overslept. I'm so sorry, and I promise you it'll never happen again." I shift from one foot to the other, wishing I'd taken the time to put on socks.

"Oversleeping doesn't explain why you've neglected to go to any of your classes for these past weeks."

"I've been sick. I think it's mono. I just haven't had any energy."

The head resident arches a drawn-on brow and I wonder if she even knows what mono is. "Under normal circumstances I'd be inclined to take your word, but considering I've witnessed you return from many a late-night party, your word carries little value with me. But it doesn't matter what I believe. You're to report to the dean of students and explain yourself."

While I don't relish the idea of facing the dean, at least Miss Sour Face will be off my back. I let out a sigh of relief.

"Miss Thorp, you seem unconcerned. I assure you this situation is quite serious. If the dean is not satisfied, you'll be expelled."

My head snaps to attention.

There's a snarl of satisfaction on her lips now. "If you wish to remain a student here at the University of

Wisconsin, you'll abide by the rules. This is your second warning." She holds out an envelope. "Here is the office and time for your meeting. I hope this will be the motivation you require to get back on track."

I glumly accept the envelope. "I will." Since when do college professors take attendance?

After she's gone, I hop back into bed to warm my feet. When I received the first warning note under the door, I blew it off. But a meeting with the dean, I guess I can't ignore that.

Later, after my grilling from the dean, I walk to the Union. The man was a stern old windbag with a talent for lecturing and citing university bylaws. Bottom line: go to class or get expelled.

I arrive early at the Rathskeller to meet Professor Smith. To my surprise, he's already there, sitting at a table alone. His coat lies over a chair with his cap resting on top.

"Hello, Abigail." He jumps to his feet as I approach.

"Hi – " My tongue twists as I change my greeting from "Professor" to "Smitty".

"It's nice to see you again. I must apologize for yesterday. You caught me off guard, and I'm afraid I was in a bit of a hurry. Please, join me." He eagerly holds out a chair.

"Thank you. I was surprised to see you too." I slip out of my coat and accept the chair. His hair is combed neatly and his shirt, which looks freshly ironed based on a scorch mark on the side, is buttoned to the top.

We look at each other and smile, but no words come to me. For some reason, I'm at a loss. I guess it's because there is so much riding on this moment. Where to even begin? Smitty shifts uncomfortably. Why is this so awkward? It's like we're on a first date or something, which is stupid because he and I go way back. Or, way forward, anyway.

And then we both speak at once. "What's your major?" I ask at the same time as he asks, "Would you like a Coca-Cola?"

We laugh, breaking the ice, and there's a glimmer of his older self that I see in his eyes.

"I'm sorry," he says. "I've wondered the last couple of years what became of you. And now that you're in front of me, I don't know what to say. How about that Coke?"

I smile at his nervousness. "Sure. I'd love one."

Smitty sighs with relief. "Thank you! I'll be right back." He jumps up to fetch my drink.

I've never seen him anything less than confident and composed. I chuckle to myself to think how much he grows up between now and when I know him in the future.

A minute later he's back with two bottles of cola and a basket of popcorn.

"Thank you. This is great." I clink my bottle to his.

"I never ran into you again after that time in freshman year. What have you been up to?" He asks.

I nearly choke and take a sip to stall and come up with a believable response. "I had to leave school. It was a family emergency," I eventually say.

He nods, holding the glass Coke bottle as if it were a lifeline. "I'm sorry to hear that, but I'm glad you're back and that we've met again."

This piques my interest about how we first met and how he's progressed so fast in school. He doesn't look much over twenty years old.

"How about you?" I ask. You said you're a grad student. How is that possible in only three years?"

He shifts in his seat as if this is a difficult question. "My life is school. I like to take heavy course loads, even in the summer."

"That's amazing. I wish I had your dedication." Instead I'm in trouble with the dean and have to figure out how to go to classes during the day and still stay up all night so I can be here if Sharon comes back.

I take another sip from my drink, wondering briefly what the caffeine content of 1951 Coke is and hoping it's a lot. "So, what did you decide to major in?"

"Mathematics," he says, matter-of-factly. "The world is a giant equation. Everything can be solved with maths."

And that's something I'm counting on. I need him to solve that giant equation of time travel, and if a maths equation will do it, that's fine with me. "I bet you'll be an awesome teacher someday."

"Stand up in front of a classroom of students? I could never do that! Look how nervous I am meeting you." He holds out his hand, and sure enough, it's trembling.

I laugh. He blushes and lowers his hand, then finds a scratch on the table to focus on.

"Oh, Smitty. I'm not laughing at you. I predict you'll be a brilliant teacher. So successful that someday a building will be named after you."

He looks up. "Thanks, but that's a peculiar thing to say."

"I suppose, but someday it'll make sense." A group of guys comes in and takes a table not far from ours.

They're loud and boisterous in contrast with our awkward silences.

Smitty takes a nibble of popcorn. "So, what's your major?"

I honestly have no idea what my major is, even after my uncomfortable lecture from the dean of students. "Oh, the usual classes," I deflect. "I guess the biggest thing going on in my life right now is my roommate, Sharon. She learned yesterday that her mother died."

"That's terrible."

"Yes. It's so sad. She's gone home for the funeral." I don't think I'll ever get that image of her crying out of my mind. In fact, it's the only time I've ever seen Grandma cry.

Smitty nods. "I never knew my parents."

I had forgotten this detail of his life but can't exactly say that. "You didn't? What happened?"

"I grew up in an orphanage."

"I'm sorry. Sounds like a difficult childhood." My talk of losing parents must have dredged up painful memories for him. I reach out and squeeze his hand.

"At times it was, but I got through. Enough about me, though." He squeezes my hand back, but doesn't release it. He peers at me through his glasses with hopeful anticipation. "With your roommate gone under such sad circumstances, I don't want you to be lonely. Would you allow me the honour of taking you to a movie tomorrow night?"

Holy crap. Is Professor Smith hitting on me? How am I supposed to let him down without crushing the poor guy's heart? I offer a weak smile, and his eager one falters.

"I don't think going out with you is a good idea."

He releases my hand and lets out a sigh of defeat.

"It's not that I don't like you – I do."

"You have a boyfriend?" he asks, dejected.

I shake my head, "God, no." But then I think of Will and add, "Actually, I'm not sure."

He leans away. I've hurt his feelings, which is the last thing I meant to do. How am I supposed to fix this? "Smitty, you don't understand. I'm not sure how much longer I'll be here. In fact, I might not be here this weekend, or even tomorrow for that matter."

"And you may or may not have a boyfriend. It's clear as mud," he says. The poor guy's face has gone from pink to red with embarrassment. I blow out my breath. Here goes nothing.

"Smitty, I'm going to tell you something. It's going to seem impossible and far-fetched. I just ask that you listen to me with an open mind."

"All right. I'm all ears," he says, but his body is angled away from me as if he's ready to bolt.

I look around the room, filled with a smattering of students eating or studying, to make sure no one is listening in. I rub my sweaty palms on my skirt and slide my cola bottle out of the way. "This is not the first time I've met you."

He nods. "I know that."

"No." I say as directly as possible, trying to catch his eye. "I've met you a few times before, and it wasn't freshman year."

He looks at me, confused. "I think I'd recall if I'd seen

you other times." And then he adds softly, "I had always hoped to."

I smile at his sweetness. "Here's the thing." I swallow the lump in my throat, look him straight in the eye and speak quietly. "I'm not from this time. I meet you in the future – your future – when you are a middle-aged man. But that's already happened for me."

Smitty goes still. I can't even see his chest moving to breathe. He studies me with his innocent brown eyes that are so familiar to me from his older years. Without a word he stands and gathers his coat and hat.

"Wait!" I hop up. "I know it sounds ridiculous, but you need to listen."

"I don't care to be made a fool." He moves to leave.

I reach for his arm. "That's not what I'm doing. I promise. Please, give me a chance to explain."

"Your little game has gone far enough. I liked you, Abigail." He heads out of the Rathskeller.

"Prof– Smitty, wait!" I grab my coat and run after him.

"You can't leave until you hear the rest of this. If you want to hate me after that, fine, but if I don't tell you now, you'll never know, and in the future, you won't be able to help me."

I don't know if it's the desperation in my voice or that he's curious as to what tale I've dreamed up, but he pauses at the door leading outside. I take advantage of his hesitation.

"Come on, let's find somewhere more private." I clutch his arm and drag him away and up a flight of stairs. There's a quiet room with couches and study tables, but students occupy them. I lead him up another level and another until, out of breath, we come across a huge event hall with marble pillars, opulent gilding and a mural on the ceiling.

"Wow! I didn't know this was here," I say in wonder.

"If you're from the future, you should know everything," he says with sarcasm.

"I've never been to the top floor of the Memorial Union until this very moment. I never got a chance … never mind."

He rolls his eyes.

There is a nook in the corner with a pair of wingback chairs. "This looks private enough." I head for the corner, toss my coat over the arm of an adjacent chair and sit. Smitty reluctantly does the same.

"Okay, future girl. Spin your tale." He sits rigidly with his arms crossed in defiance.

Here goes nothing. I curl my legs under my lap and begin. "When I started college here, it was the twenty-first century. My roommate was a girl named Jada."

He arches a brow but says nothing.

"I went to bed one night in my dorm room – in Liz Waters – but when I woke the next morning, everything was different. Everything on the walls was different, my roommate was a girl named Linda, the calendar on my wall read 1983."

"And we met," he says snidely, trying to predict my words.

"Actually, no. We didn't. I was scared. I didn't understand what was happening. The last thing I wanted to do was go to class. But now that I think of it, if I had, you might have been my professor – my physics professor."

Smitty grunts his disbelief.

"Now I really wish I had gone," I say realizing how differently things might have turned out if he were there and had seen me.

"Why is that?"

"Because the next time I went back, it was 1970, and we met. You said you were onto something. Something having to do with string theory. But by 1983, maybe you would have figured it out."

"I'm not a physicist. I'm a mathematician," he corrects.

"Then you need to change your programme, because in 1970, you teach quantum physics."

He shakes his head. "I already told you, I'm not going to be a teacher."

"Not just a teacher – a professor. That's why when I recognized you yesterday I called you professor. You've always been a professor to me, until now."

He frowns. "You're kind of a know-it-all."

I ignore his comment. "The point is that I keep jumping back in time, and I keep running into you. I think you're a crucial part of why this is happening, that you're supposed to solve time travel." I pause, leaning forward, and look him in the eye again. "I need you to help me."

His eyes soften. I can tell he's moved by my plea, but that he doesn't believe me. "And how could I possibly do that?"

"Because you're freakin' brilliant!" I blurt loudly and throw back my arms.

He cracks a smile. "But I don't *want* to teach. I want to work for a private corporation doing high-level mathematics. There is talk of creating a machine that can do math. Not just an adding machine, but complex equations like trigonometry and advanced calculus."

"Yes, that happens, but you don't invent it. You're here on campus, helping me."

"Abigail, this is a fascinating story, but you haven't given me any actual proof." He crosses his arms and pushes back his chair.

"What do you want to know? I'll tell you anything."

"All right." He thinks for a moment before continuing. "If you know me so well, why didn't you know that at this exact time I was here going to school? Wouldn't my future self have told you?" He cocks his head knowingly.

I can't help grinning. "Good point, but your future self happens to be extremely stubborn about telling me anything that has already happened. Professor Smith is a terrific guy, but he's dead set against sharing what he knows about where I'll be, or what happens."

He leans back in his chair again. "How convenient for your story."

"And … he refuses to let *me* tell *him* about the future," I say, still annoyed with the future Smith for that.

"Why does he, or should I say I, not want you to talk about the future?" he huffs.

"Professor Smith fears that if we know too much about our futures, we might do something different that will affect what happens. It could make it impossible for me to get back."

Smitty frowns. "Well, that seals the deal. You have nothing concrete to prove your point."

"Hold on. I'm not finished. That was the professor

who felt that way. You clearly have a lot of work to do before I'll consider you Professor Smith. You're not my teacher or mentor. Heck, at this point we're barely on the edge of friendship."

He grunts, which I'm not sure is agreement.

"You never told me anything personal, but I do know you have a bunch of kids."

He seems to perk up at that. "Where do I live?"

"You never mentioned, but I don't think it's far from campus."

He gives me a skeptical frown. "Easy guess."

"Fine. I don't know much about you, personally, but I know the future. What year is it? 1951? Is Elvis around yet? He'll be huge. And the Beatles. They're a singing group, just as huge as Elvis."

"I'm a numbers man, not a crooner. Try again." He scratches his fingernail against the upholstered chair. He's losing his patience.

"We put a man on the moon in 1969, I think. President Kennedy is assassinated around sixty-three."

"I've never heard of the man."

"You will."

"Telling me of supposed future events that I can't verify hardly convinces me of anything other than your vivid imagination. If all this is really true, why didn't you tell me about it when we met freshman year?"

I consider his question, hating this bizarre predicament I'm in. "Honestly, I don't know – because I haven't experienced it yet. But there must be some reason."

Confusion clouds Smitty's eyes.

"You see, I only seem to go backwards in time, not

forwards. So you met me three years ago, but for me it hasn't happened yet. It will be the fourth time I've met you, but it will be the first time you meet me."

He looks at me in wonder. "You have no memory of our time together three years ago?"

"Nope. I haven't been there yet," I repeat, trying to tamp down my frustration. "If you tell me now, I'll know what to expect. How do we meet?"

Smitty shifts in his seat. "If you don't remember, I'd rather not say."

"Why?"

"It was embarrassing." His eyes dart away.

I throw my hands up. "See? You're as bad as your future self, all filled with secrets."

He rubs his forehead. "This is quite a tangled story you're telling me. How could this possibly be?"

"I don't know. Time travel is the only explanation I have. We could have this conversation again when I get there to meet you for the first time, but since you clearly don't know anything about it, we must not have."

Smitty stands up and paces. He is, at least, considering my story, which is a good sign.

"Isn't there some sort of proof?" he asks.

I think of the hatbox and all the items in it, but from what I've seen, most of it is from this time, when Grandma was in college. Nothing from the future. There's the macramé handbag back in my room. It still holds the bandana from 1970 inside, but I'm not sure that's enough to convince him. Then I get an idea.

"I know. See the holes in my ears? Everyone pierces their ears in my time. I've had mine pierced since sixth grade." I move my hair and pull the collar of my dress back to reveal the tattoo of a star on my shoulder that represents Grandma, up in the heavens. Smitty leans in for a closer look, lingering a little longer than I think necessary.

"Why would you have yourself tattooed?" he asks.

"In my time we call it a tat."

"*Why* is my question. You're not a sailor. You weren't in the military."

I let my collar slide back into place. "No. I got it when I turned eighteen, shortly after my grandma died. My mom wouldn't let me get one any sooner."

"Your mother sounds like a smart woman."

"She is," I say with a sigh, missing her. All this talk is getting me nowhere.

"What does she think has happened to you back in your time?" Smitty asks with a spark of interest. Maybe I am making progress.

I picture mom's face as we said goodbye and then her car pulling away. "I have no idea. I don't know if I disappeared off the face of the Earth, or if time is standing still back there. God, I hope she doesn't think I was murdered or something." I hadn't thought of that before, and now that I do, it depresses me more.

"You don't have any proof that stands the test of time. Get it?" Smitty laughs not realizing how helpless I am. If he did, he wouldn't be making jokes.

"I don't," I answer, dejected.

"Are you sure you aren't a creative writing major?" he teases.

"Positive. Listen, you clearly haven't become the professor yet, so I'm going to tell you something important, something that you didn't want to hear. Do not work late at your office in Sterling Hall on the night of August twenty-third in 1970."

"Why?" he asks, bewildered.

"That, I won't tell you."

"See, you're no help. This only works if you tell me something important."

"This *is* important," I stress.

He crosses his arms again and glares at me. "Sure it is."

"Smitty, I will only say this one last time." He has to listen to me, and he has to remember. I stare him straight in the eye and repeat the words, this time in a serious voice, like the doctor who told us my grandmother was dying of cancer. "Do *not* work late at Sterling Hall on August twenty-third, 1970."

I hold his gaze and refuse to look away.

Smitty shifts uncomfortably. "Why, do I die or something?"

For a moment I say nothing. I'm not sure if I'm messing with the future but hope I can ensure his safety. I whisper, "I don't know."

He swallows.

"I slipped back in time again before I could find out."

He considers my words. "I won't say that I believe in time travel, because I don't. But I think *you* believe what you're saying."

"I'm not lying," I say in dead seriousness.

"Perhaps, perhaps not."

"You don't have to believe me, but in time, you'll see that everything I've said is true. Even you commented that

I look the same. For all I know when I leave this time, I go straight to your freshman year."

"So, you'll see me again soon," he says dryly.

I shake my head. "I hope not. I'm not ready to leave this time. I want to be here when Sharon comes back. If she comes back."

"Why do you care so much about Sharon?"

I level him with a steady gaze. "Because she's my grandmother."

CHAPTER 11

I spend the night staring at the stars hanging in the frozen sky outside my window like sparkling crystals, willing myself not to fall asleep. As the tedious minutes drag by in slow torture, I replay my conversation with Smitty over and over.

I suppose it doesn't matter if he believes my story. One way or another he'll figure it out, and hopefully I haven't ruined the future by telling him. After my comment about Sharon being my grandmother, he turned a bit pale. I'm sure he thinks I'm nuts, but I also saw a sliver of curiosity in his narrowed eyes. As a future physicist, he should be keeping an open mind to all possibilities, but at the moment he far more resembles an awkward bookworm.

The next morning, instead of crawling into bed and catching up on sleep as I usually do, I head to class like the rest of the students. I can't afford to get kicked out, not if I want to be here in case Grandma returns. Not to mention losing my place here at Liz Waters and possibly never getting back home. Anyway, the professor is here, and more than anything, I need to convince him to start thinking about time travel.

But my immediate issue is finding the Home Economics Building for a food science class that starts in five minutes. I'm standing on the corner of Charter and Linden, at a loss for which direction to go, when the young professor appears, weighed down with thick books.

"You're still here," Smitty says with a touch of sarcasm.

I smile, glad to see his gawky form ambling towards me. "Were you hoping I'd be gone?"

He ducks his head and grins. "No, just making an observation. You said you might jump back in time at any given moment."

"I told you I have no control over when or where I go when I sleep."

He snorts his disbelief.

"Hey, I spent the whole night trudging through the cold halls of my dorm trying to stay awake to keep myself here." It's curious how long I've been able to stay in this time, and then I remember something I thought of last night. "Smitty, I did think of one thing you told me. It might not mean anything to you yet, but you made a comment once about how you almost took a job out of state. I think it was with some big company in New York."

His eyes go wide and his jaw drops open.

"Oh my God, that means something!" I squeal and clap my hands.

"How did you know?" Smitty is totally bewildered.

"You told me. You said it off the cuff. Something about

how it was a good thing you didn't take the job in New York. It's happening now, isn't it?"

He nods. "How could you know that? No one knows. I received the letter offering me the job yesterday. Did you sneak into my room?"

"Of course not. I don't even know which dorm you're in."

"I'm not in a dorm. I live in a boarding house on Monroe Street."

I give him a satisfied smirk. He's starting to believe.

Smitty suggests we find a warmer, quieter spot than a street corner to talk. We duck into a nearby building and find an empty study room with a scratched-up wood table and four hard chairs around it. A single small window with a view of the next building adds the only natural light.

Smitty spends the next two hours asking questions, most of which I have no answers for, like why I travel and how I travel. I explain what we had figured out with the Carillon Tower and the bells, that it only seems to happen at night, and maybe only around a full moon. There are so many variables and yet nothing I know for sure.

"Does anyone else travel through time like you?" He looks up from the loose-leaf paper he's been scribbling notes on.

I hesitate, not sure if I should say.

"There is someone else!" He points at me with his pen.

"Yes. And you've met him."

He leans back in his chair, surprised. "Who?"

"Apparently you met him in your sophomore year. His name is Will."

Smitty's brow furrows as he thinks back. "Did he have blond, kind of sandy-coloured hair?"

"That's right!"

"I remember him because he was always chewing on a blade of grass."

"That's him," I say wistfully, suddenly feeling nostalgic and missing someone I met only for a day. I think of the humour in Will's eyes, his steady confidence that offered me hope and his ability to annoy me with his secrets.

Smitty watches me as if he's analyzing a lab rat. Then, as if coming to a brilliant conclusion, he blurts, "You're sweet on him!"

"No!"

"Yesterday you said that you maybe had a boyfriend. He's got to be the one, but why did you say maybe?"

I laugh at the strangeness of the situation. "Because I've only seen him once and it didn't end well. Will more or less said that the two of us were an item, but since I'd just met him, it was pretty one-sided." Except for that kiss – he'd caught me off guard with that. And yet it was so ... familiar.

Smitty is back to recording notes so thankfully doesn't see my expression. "When do you meet him?" he asks without looking up.

"He never told me." I frown. "So, you never saw us together?"

"No, I only talked to him once or twice. He was in one of my classes."

"Physics?" I ask.

"That's right. But then he didn't show up one day and

I never saw him again," he says thoughtfully.

"You'll see him again. Trust me." And the hope that they'll have each other to talk to going forward is a relief, even though I'll be who knows where and likely by myself.

"How do you know?"

I grin. "Because I reintroduce you two in the future."

Smitty holds his head with his hands. "This is so confusing."

"Tell me about it."

"So in the future, you said there's a building named after me."

I nod. "A physics library."

"That's impossible. I'm nobody. I don't have two nickels to rub together," he says in disbelief, but there's also a glint of excitement in his eyes at the prospect of becoming someone important.

I shrug, not sure what to say.

"What year do you come from? What year is the library built?"

"I don't know if I should say."

"Are you kidding me? You ask me to believe your ridiculous story about time travel, and then you refuse to tell me what year you come from because you think, or maybe you know, that I'm dead?"

I hated it when he and Will kept information from me, so I give in and tell him.

He drops his pen and falls back in his seat. "By then, I'll be dead."

"We don't know that," I say with a gulp. "Not for sure."

He studies my face. His earlier excitement is replaced

with resignation. "I think it's pretty obvious we do."

"Well, then live a healthy life and make sure you stay alive. And don't smoke. Do you smoke?"

"Everyone does."

"Lung cancer is one of the biggest killers out there. Quit. Today."

He smiles at my bossiness. "Are you certain you're dating Will? I mean, it hasn't actually happened yet, and I think you and I would get along mighty fine."

"I can't go out with you," I say gently.

Smitty picks up his pen and rolls it between his fingers. "You see, I've been on my own my whole life. I'd really like to find someone special I could settle down with. I have trouble talking to girls, but with you it's easy."

"I'm sorry, but I'm not the one for you. I never stay in one place for long. Go and find yourself a nice, pretty, smart girl, and not some needy chick trying to trap you for her MRS degree. I promise, you're going to get married, have a bunch of kids and be deliriously happy."

A hopeful smile spreads across his face.

* * *

Two days later the ding of my dorm room bell wakes me from a dead sleep. The bell means I've either got a message or a visitor. What am I in trouble for this time? A knot develops in my gut as I realize I've overslept and missed my morning classes. Again. After barely staying awake last night, I was so tired, and I wanted a quick hour of sleep. But in my fog I must not have set my alarm.

I dress and trudge to the lobby to see what new disaster

awaits, and then it hits me that maybe Will is here. Yesterday I made the trek out to Picnic Point to see if the snow had melted enough to find his treasure, but it was still deep and undisturbed other than some rabbit tracks.

Still, I race the rest of the way, hoping to find Will's reassuring face. Instead, Smitty is shifting uncomfortably with a large book tucked under his arm. His eyes dart away shyly when girls peek at him as they pass.

I walk up behind him. "They won't bite. I promise."

Smitty jumps. "Oh, hello, Abigail," he says with obvious relief.

"It's Abbi. At least that's what my friends call me."

"Abbi it is." He beams as if I've let him into a special club.

"Are you really that uncomfortable around girls?"

"Of course not! It's just that I've never been inside a ladies' dormitory before." He adjusts his glasses as if they're a pseudo security blanket.

I hold back my laughter. "So, what's up?"

"I've been doing a lot of thinking about everything you said, and I'm trying to find a way to prove your story."

I sigh. I thought he believed me.

"Yesterday I did some research in the university archives and discovered something I think you'll find interesting." He pulls a large yearbook out from under his arm.

Just then the front door opens, letting in a blast of cold air and snow. I pull my sweater tight and see Sharon struggling through the doorway with her luggage.

"Let me help you." Smitty rushes forward to take her large suitcase and carries it to the middle of the foyer.

"Thank you," Sharon says, brushing snowflakes off

her coat, her cheeks rosy from the cold air.

Smitty gives me a smug lift of his chin that says, "See, I can talk to a girl."

"You're back!" I run past him to hug her.

Sharon smiles weakly. "Father insists he can take care of himself and that my mother wanted me to finish school and get my teaching degree. I didn't have the heart to tell him I changed majors to archeology."

Smitty watches us with interest.

"Sharon, I'd like you to meet my friend Smitty. Smitty, this is my roommate, Sharon."

He raises a knowing eyebrow in my direction. "It's my pleasure to meet you." He zeroes in on her, and I immediately know what he's thinking.

"How do you do?" Sharon replies politely.

I yank him aside and whisper through clenched teeth. "You are *not* dating my grandmother!"

"Why not? You told me to find a pretty girl. She definitely qualifies." His gaze travels from her bright eyes, over her stylish figure, down her slender legs and back up.

I turn my back to block Grandma from hearing us. "Because I know who my grandfather is, and it's not you! You might screw everything up. Including my existence!" I hiss. "And you can't ever tell her what I told you. Ever! At this rate I'll probably disappear right in front of you."

Smitty cocks his head. "From what you've told me, you won't be here. So, you'll never know."

That cannot happen. I'm starting to understand why the professor was so stubborn about not talking about the past – or the future. I give him my most lethal glare.

Finally Smitty whispers, "Fine! But I hope you're not

screwing up *my* fate while fixing your own!"

I peek to the side and find Sharon watching us with interest, so I leave it alone. "Thanks for stopping by Smitty, but I need to help Sharon get her things back to our room." I push him, not so gently, to the door.

"Oh, but the yearbook." He holds it out.

"Great. Thanks." I take the heavy volume and tilt my head towards the exit. The less time he spends near Sharon, the better. "See you later. Bye-bye!"

I grab Sharon's large suitcase and lug it towards our wing.

"All right, bye then. Nice meeting you, Sharon," Smitty calls after us.

She catches up with me. "Your friend is kind of cute. What's the story?"

"It's recent. He asked me out, but I said no."

"He's adorable, in an academic kind of way. Why would you say no?"

I don't like the way she's looking back at Smitty. "You know, you're right. I think I'll talk to him tomorrow and tell him I changed my mind."

***

Once we're back in our room with the door securely shut, I put the book Smitty gave me face-down on my bed and turn to Sharon. "So, how are you?"

She frowns, hangs up her coat and sits on the edge of her bed. "It was horrible. I'm exhausted from crying, and when my mother's casket was lowered into the ground, I thought my father was going to crumble. He's destroyed by her death. I still can't believe he brought me back to school so soon."

I sit down next to her. "Maybe he needs some time alone to process losing her."

"Maybe. It's all so strange. The house is eerily quiet without her. She used to play the radio and bake bread every day. The smell always warmed the whole house. I don't think she had baked bread since I was home over Christmas. Dad says she went downhill so fast."

"I'm sorry."

"I don't know how I'm supposed to go to class when all I can think about is my mother." Her eyes well up and she wipes away a stray tear.

"There's no reason you have to go back to class right away. Take as long as you need." Heck, I hadn't gone to a single class until three days ago, and I've missed more since then.

I go to my dresser drawer and dig for candy bars. "Let's eat chocolate, and if you feel up to it, you can tell me more about your mom. I'd like to know about the woman who produced the most amazing girl ever."

"Abigail, you're the best." She hugs me.

Sharon puts on a Sinatra album, placing a penny on the needle to keep it from skipping. I pile all our pillows onto her bed, and we climb on top. I open a chocolate, eager to hear stories about my great-grandmother.

Sharon takes a bite, chews thoughtfully and starts talking. "My mother was wonderful. You see, I'm pretty certain my father wanted a son, but he only got me. He taught me to do all sorts of boy things like shoot a gun, play basketball and ski. Mother never seemed to mind. We'd come home trailing in mud from our boots. She'd ask if we saw any bears or elephants." Sharon giggles a bit, remembering. Then she adds quietly, "I don't think my mother received much love as a child, and that's why she was so good with me."

"Why do you say that?" I gnaw off another bite of the chocolate bar.

"Like I told you before, her mother died when she was a baby. Later, when her father remarried, she got stuck with a nasty stepmother. I met the woman a couple of times when I was young. I remember my mother standing between me and this shrill, prune-faced lady as if she was protecting me."

"She sounds terrible."

"My mother was shipped off to boarding school when she was young. I guess I'm lucky. At least I got to have a mom for more than eighteen years. That's better than she got. What's your mother like?"

I choke on my chocolate. She's asking about her future daughter. Tears spring to my eyes, but I quickly shake them off. "Um, she's great. She isn't much of a housekeeper, but she's super smart. She works at a job she loves, and she's always been there for me."

"She sounds very progressive. I think I'd like her."

"I know you would." But I can't help the ache in my heart, missing both my mom and Grandma. I know I'm lucky to be with Sharon now, but I miss the older version of her too.

She climbs off the bed and comes back clutching her handbag. "Abigail, I've discovered a dark secret that

I have to share with you, but you must swear not to tell a soul."

I set the rest of the chocolate bar on her bedside table. "Of course."

She opens the bag and pulls out a small folded piece of paper.

Suddenly, there's a loud knock on the door. Sharon jumps and stuffs the paper back into her handbag before opening the door. "Oh, hello, Betty," she says.

"Hi, Sharon. I have an official letter for Abigail. Mrs. Chaplin told me to put it directly in her hands." Betty wears a somber expression.

I join them at the door. Betty holds out a white sealed envelope. I stare at it, afraid I know what it is, but I don't want to worry Sharon. "Thanks for dropping it by," I say in a cheery voice, accepting the envelope.

Betty disappears without another word. Sharon closes the door. "What's that about?"

"I'll look at it later. Tonight is about you." I toss the envelope onto my bed.

But Sharon picks it up and reads the return address. Her brow creases with concern. "Abigail, this is from the dean of students. Maybe you should open it."

"I already know what it says. I made the Dean's List for Academic Achievement," I lie.

"That's wonderful!" she says with relief and sets the letter down.

"I know, right? Now what were you about to tell me? The suspense is killing me."

"Oh my gosh, yes." She again removes the slip of paper from her bag and hands it to me.

An ominous feeling comes over me as I recognize this piece of paper with its torn corner.

"Read it." She urges. "It's my birth certificate."

But it's not just any birth certificate. It's the exact same copy as the one I saw in the hatbox that first night. I glance at my bed where the hatbox rests in the lower corner against the footboard. Somewhere in time, my version of this very birth certificate has been left behind.

My mind races as I scan the paper. The print is tiny with names of a hospital, doctors and officials.

Sharon peers over my shoulder.

"What am I looking for?" I ask, not sure what she wants me to see.

"Look at the part where it lists the mother." She points to the line.

"Yeah?" It reads "Ruby M Phelps."

"Next to that. It says number of live births." She slides her finger to the spot.

I squint. Sure enough, in fine print there's a small box next to the words "Number of Live Births". "It says two," I say and glance up at her for explanation.

"Don't you get it? I'm an only child. But, according to this, my mother gave birth to another child before me."

"Maybe you had an older sibling who died while you were still a baby?"

"Abigail, I couldn't have had another sibling. I was born a year after my parents married. This baby had to have been born *before* they were married." I can tell from her expression that this is a terrible scandal.

"Maybe your mother was married before your father and had a child with her first husband," I offer, trying to ease her away from thinking badly of her mom.

"No, that couldn't be." She paces our small room. "Mother was eighteen when she met my father, nineteen when they married and twenty when I was born. She was never married before. I'm sure of it."

"You should ask your dad. I bet he could tell you."

"Heavens, no! I could never speak of such a thing." She sits beside me. "And even if I did, what if he didn't know about the baby? What if it was some secret my mother kept? Father would be devastated. He loved my mother so much."

"He's probably seen your birth certificate before. He must know," I say gently, handing it back to her.

"I suppose, but I could never ask about a baby born outside of wedlock. It's too shameful."

"So, basically, your mother had a baby as a teenager. So what?" I assume there wasn't much in terms of birth control back then. Heck, I have no idea what women use for birth control in this era either. Do they even have any?

Sharon shakes her head in denial. "It doesn't fit Mother's character. She was always so proper and well mannered. It would have been a terrible scandal. I just lost my mother, but now I know that I have more family. Somewhere out there I have a brother or sister. I have to find them. But why didn't Mother ever tell me?" Sharon grabs a pillow and hugs it. "There was a girl from my high school who suddenly moved to Kansas to take care of her sick aunt. But later I heard that she didn't have an aunt in Kansas. Her parents sent her away because she had *disgraced* herself. What if the same thing happened to my mother?"

"Maybe it's a clerical mistake, and it was supposed to say one."

"No. I don't think so." She shakes her head slowly. "When I was eight years old, I begged my parents for a baby brother or sister. Looking back, they acted strangely. When I wrote to Santa Claus that year, I said the only gift I wanted was a baby for our family. When I read my letter aloud, my mother started to cry. My father took the letter away and asked me to write another one asking for a toy instead."

"Wow."

"So you see, maybe Mother was crying because she had to give her first baby away."

I have to agree, it sounds likely. "But how could we ever figure it out?" I ask gently. I can't imagine tracking a lost baby down, especially without the Internet.

"I don't know, but there must be a way."

I love her determination. "All right. We'll do this together. We'll search everywhere we can think until we find that baby."

She turns to me with hope in her eyes. "Promise?"

"Cross my heart." I make the motions across my chest. "We'll start first thing in the morning."

Sharon hugs me tight. "Abigail, you're the best friend a girl could ever have."

Later, after she's finally fallen asleep and I'm sitting up awake, I open the letter from the dean. My heart pounds as I unfold the single sheet.

NOTICE OF EXPULSION.

My breath goes out of me. It's official. I've been kicked out of college and must vacate the dormitory in twenty-four hours. I glance over at Grandma, sleeping through the turmoil of losing her mom and now the mystery of a secret baby.

Time isn't playing fair. If I fall asleep, I might be sent to another time. But if I don't, I'll be kicked out of here with nowhere to go. What will become of me? Will I be stuck in this time forever without my bed in room 4418 to transport me home?

Not sure what to do, I lie in bed. Frustrated and miserable, I run my fingers over the different patches of fabric that make up my quilt. I wish Smitty was already a professor. He'd be able to help us. I'll have to track him down tomorrow and break the news that I'm getting kicked out. My arm brushes against the yearbook he brought. Trying to figure out what he wanted me to see requires more energy than I'm up for tonight. I can't even think straight. I crumple up my expulsion letter and toss it at my wastebasket, but miss.

My thoughts wander to Grandma's lost sibling, the missing baby. I gasp. Could *this* be what she was mumbling to me about before she died? She said I'd promised to help find the baby and to keep trying. At the time I thought she was delirious or losing her mind to the brain tumours. But she wasn't. Is that the whole reason I'm travelling? To help Grandma solve this mystery?

But how can I keep my promise? When I can't come up with any obvious ways to track down a missing baby in 1951, my mind wanders to Will. I wonder where he is and if he's having a better time of it. My eyes slip closed as I picture him walking along the lakeshore path with that blade of grass in his mouth.

CHAPTER 12

I wake up slowly with my face pressed against something hard. I open my eyes and realize it's the yearbook Smitty gave me. I fell asleep. Shit! I jerk upright.

Everything on Grandma's side of the room is wrong. Her bed is covered with a navy blue bedspread and embroidered throw pillows. She's gone.

No!

How could I have let this happen? Grandma just returned from her mother's funeral, and now I've abandoned her when she needs me most. "Arrgh!" I punch my pillow.

I don't know where I am in time yet, and I don't care, because it probably doesn't include Grandma. I finally thought maybe I had an idea of why I've been tumbling through time. But I've been yanked back again. How can I help Grandma if I've left her behind?

I sit on my bed, my only oasis from this storm, surrounded by foreign objects that belong to a stranger. A pit of dread grows in my gut. Of course there's a new wall calendar. I groan. It can't be good. Other than landing in Grandma's time, it's never been good.

My new plan is to stay in bed and hide from time, but curiosity eventually gets the best of me. I climb out and glare at the cursed calendar. September 1948. Too early for Grandma to be on campus. I hate this place or time or whatever it is. Without Grandma, I want to go home more than ever.

I glance out of the window. Leaves cover the branches of the trees outside. A few are turning a golden hue. At least it isn't winter any more. I pull on a scratchy cotton shirt, plain wool skirt and shoes that I make sure are from my own wardrobe.

Out in the hall on the door, I see my name printed neatly on a paper acorn alongside the name Dorothy. I haven't seen her yet, and that's fine with me. With any luck I can avoid her all day. I've conveniently wasted so much time this morning that the halls are empty.

After having a wash, I return to my room. It looks so unfamiliar now after weeks spent sharing it with Grandma. She made the room a haven filled with fun, laughter and safety from the elements of time travel. What do I do now? I'm not up for discovering this new year.

And then I think of Will and his buried treasure. It's September – the ground won't be frozen yet. I can go and find it! With renewed energy, I pull on a grey sweater and pull my hair back into a ponytail. Probably not the style in 1948, but I'm beyond caring. I grab a pen and fold up a piece of loose-leaf paper from the desk to write my note. I push them both into my macramé bag, which is bound to look out of place here, and dash down the back stairway instead of the main entrance. I might be stuck in the forties, but I have no intention of mingling with the other students unless I absolutely have to.

The rich fall air smells like paradise after the snowy winter of 1951. My feet crunch on the cinder path along the shoreline as I rush past Adams and Tripp Halls.

Is the young professor here? Probably, but he'll have no idea who I am, so I'm not even interested in looking him up at the moment. I'll worry about that later. But this must be the time I meet Will.

As I make it down the peninsula of Picnic Point in search of Will's tobacco tin and the message he promised he's left for me, I'm surrounded by a colourful rainfall of gold, orange and rust leaves.

I find the first trail off the main trail and take it. What did Will say the directions were? Right, left and left? Shoot. I make it to the first split and take a right, scooting along the thin trail. I take the next two lefts, but nothing looks familiar. Then again, Will brought me here nearly fifteen years in the future, so things will have changed. I search for the fallen tree but find none. So much for my sense of direction.

I retrace my steps all the way back to the main trail and decide to try the opposite route. I've sweated through my clothes. This time I go left at the first fork and pass a clump of red sumac. At the next fork, I'm tempted to veer right but stick to my plan and take another left. Branches brush against my shoulders, and I hear the sounds of small creatures skittering out of my path. At the next fork, I go right. The path winds around a bend, revealing a giant tree trunk lying on the forest floor in all its glory. I climb through the brush, snagging my sweater as I go.

My pulse races at the thought of finding Will's treasure. I walk around the fallen tree to the other side. As before, a pile of dried branches crowds the decaying trunk. I can picture Will dragging them here to hide his precious few belongings. I pull a large branch away, and another, until I find a mound of leaves. This is where Will pulled out the spade to dig with. I kneel on the ground and push the damp leaves aside.

Something small darts over my hand and I scream. A tiny mouse scurries away. After that I use a stick to clear the remaining debris. Sure enough, I find Will's spade, crammed under the log.

Thank you, Will.

With spade in hand, I locate the big rock. I try to nudge it with my foot, but it's too heavy. I clank the spade against the rock in case any more creatures are lurking.

Leaning over, I try to lift the rock, but I still can't move it. Using both hands and leveraging my weight with a heave ho, it finally gives way, throwing me off balance. I land on my butt in the damp leaves.

I scramble over to the newly revealed spot. The dirt doesn't look as if it's been disturbed in a long time. Does that mean Will is not here after all? Kneeling before my target, I dig into the rich soil, piling it in a mound beside me. Earthworms wiggle their frustration at being relocated.

Will the tin be here? It has to be. With each spadeful of dirt, I feel closer to Will. I'd given him such a hard time that day we met, and now I wish I could apologize. No matter how frustrating he was, I feel desperate to connect with him, the only person in time who understands what I'm going through.

The spade hits something hard. *Yes!* I frantically dig around it, unearthing my prize. I pull back the oilcloth, revealing the tobacco tin, and sigh with relief.

Doing as Will did, I pry the lid off with the tip of the spade, carefully brushing away the dirt so it won't fall inside. I wipe my hands on my dress and lift out the contents.

There are the coins and bills Will placed for safe-keeping, along with the pocket watch and a sturdy key I hadn't seen before. I ignore the papers and go for the envelope he wouldn't let me see.

The folded paper springs open once released from the tin. I slip it out and read.

Dearest Abbi,

My heart is shattered without you here by my side. We knew this day would come, but it doesn't soften the desperate ache in my soul. You assured me our paths will cross in the future, but until I set my eyes on you again, I will be a useless excuse of a human being, rowing away my sorrows.

If you ever read this, which I pray you do, please

don't think me mad with my declarations of love. I fear you may expect me to be a man of courage and strength. What you will find is a lost boy, looking for meaning and direction in this crazy world you and I share.

Abbi, you brought me solace and made my life worth living again. Each night I say a prayer that the bells will chime and take me to a time when I will gaze upon your sweet face again.

All my love,

Will

Oh my. I lean against the fallen tree, ignoring the rough bark that pokes into my back.

My heart races from his unexpected love letter – a bit corny and over the top for my day, but undeniably sweet in any era. If only I could reach out to him just for a second.

I turn to the next page and find another note.

My dearest Abbi,

The saying "absence makes the heart grow fonder" is boloney. Desperate would best describe my general sense of being. It's torture to know you're out there somewhere, hidden in time.

I long to know that you are safe, but my wishes have been ignored by fate. You have not left me a message, so perhaps you were unable to find the location of my treasure.

I've wondered if perhaps you are like many women who lack a sense of direction, and that you've never found this spot again. And now I smile as I picture your annoyance at being compared to a helpless woman of the past.

Should you ever locate this spot, be assured that I am well enough. I have become more adept at fitting in and making a life for myself. We don't have much choice about that, do we?

Each evening I look into the night sky and gaze at the stars, knowing that somewhere in time, you are doing the same.

Until we meet again,

Will

I hug the letter, breathless from his words. I regret not doing more to open up to him the day we met.

I pull out the pen and paper I brought and try to think of what to write. He probably knows almost everything that happens because I will have already told him. But still I smile as words form in my mind and I put them to paper.

Dear Will,

Clearly I've found your treasure, so you'll have to take back your words about me being helpless! I've landed here in 1948, but you probably know that because I plan to tell you when we next meet. By the way, you never told me when that happens, which, as you know, annoys the heck out of me.

Last night I left my grandmother. I assume I've told you about her. I'm devastated all over again, but today I've found your letters and am so relieved and happy, you can't imagine. I only spent a few hours with you in 1961, but now, having read your words, I can't wait to see you again and discover this magic connection you say we share.

I saw Smitty in 1951. He asked me out! My last night

there, I had the chance to introduce him to my grand-mother. He got all excited about her too, so I had to ward him off. How the poor guy ever finds love, I can't imagine.

My great-grandmother Ruby died. My grandmother is heartbroken. I'm now on a new quest, which you probably already know about, so I won't mention it again.

By the way, couldn't you have found a better spot for your treasure? A mouse ran over my hand and I almost had a heart attack.

Okay, now I'm babbling, but it makes me feel less alone. I'll go now, but know that my latest roommate will probably throw me out when she sees my dress and shoes covered in dirt, and all because of you!

Hope to see you soon.

Your partner in time,

Abbi

I smile as I sign my name, imagining Will's reaction when he reads this someday. I fold my letter and slide everything back into the tin. I notice a few black and white pictures tucked behind some papers.

I remove them gently. The first is a photo of a family

dressed in old-time clothes standing on a pier. There is a man, woman, girl and little boy. I peer closer and discover that the cute little boy in the shorts is Will.

The next picture shows the same family at a beach in hilarious full-body swimsuits. My heart breaks for the little boy holding a toy bucket. How did he survive after losing everyone in his family?

I flip to the next picture and gasp.

Will and I grin at the camera, our arms draped casually around each other. We look so happy, as if we were laughing the moment before the picture was snapped. The clothes we're wearing don't help me figure out the year. I turn the picture over, but there are no dates written on it. Knowing Will, he left it undated on purpose.

Holding the picture by the edges so as not to ruin it with my dirty fingers, I study it for a long time. Will has an easy confidence about him. His smile is inviting and reaches his eyes, which sparkle even in this old photo. His nose is narrow and straight, framed by full eyebrows and strong cheekbones. His head is pressed to mine as if we both need to feel connected.

I really want to take the picture with me, but then it won't be here for Will, and he might need it more than I do. Hopefully I'll find him here in 1948 and won't need a picture to remember him by.

Reluctantly, I return everything to the tin, wishing I'd brought some sort of small token to leave for him. Burying the tin makes me even dirtier, and by the time I cover the rock and log with the branches, I'm a disaster.

On the long walk back to Liz Waters, I can't get Will out of my mind, not that I want to. Why is time bringing us together and then ripping us apart? And why did I end up with Grandma and the professor, only to leave them again? There must be some sort of meaning to this madness, some order to the chaos, but what?

Professor Smith had better get his butt in gear and start learning physics so he can figure this out.

* * *

Famished from skipping breakfast and spending the morning digging up Will's tin, I shower, change into clean clothes and head to the Union for an early lunch. It would be quicker to eat in the cafeteria at Liz Waters, but I don't want to pretend to know people or make small talk. It's easier to remain anonymous at the Union.

From the outside, the Union looks exactly the same as I knew it, and inside isn't much different. The smell of burgers grilling makes my mouth water. I grab a tray and slide it along the order counter. Students wearing white paper hats and aprons work behind the counter, taking orders and preparing food.

"May I help you?" a guy asks as I browse the menu neatly written on a chalkboard. Something about his voice sounds oddly familiar and gives me goose bumps.

"Yes. I'll take a hamburger and a chocolate milkshake, please," I say, turning to look at him. A tall pimply-faced student is jotting down my order.

"Here you go, miss." He looks up to hand me my ticket, and I see familiar brown eyes peering at me from behind wire-rimmed spectacles.

Smitty?

"Thank you," I mumble, accepting the slip of paper and soaking up this wet-behind-the-ears version of Professor Smith.

Noticing my curious stare, he lowers his eyes and wipes his hands on his apron. "It'll be out in a few minutes."

"Thank you," I repeat. Even from when I last saw him, he looks markedly different. He is stick skinny with a long neck and gangly arms, and acne mars his face. In later years he becomes rather handsome.

I pay for my food and find a seat at a small table in the Rathskeller where I can watch him. He works behind the counter, hesitating at each decision. He pours milk into a glass, then drops a large scoop of ice cream in, and milk splashes out, sopping his apron.

His awkwardness is bizarre. A coworker gives him instructions, and Smitty adds more ingredients and then pours the whole thing into a blender. As soon as he turns it on, mixture shoots out like shrapnel.

I cover my giggle. A few minutes later he delivers my lunch. Ice cream dribbles down the side of the tall milkshake glass.

"This looks delicious," I say, trying to put him at ease.

He sneaks a quick glance at me. "Enjoy your lunch."

As I devour my juicy burger and suck down the milkshake, I watch Smitty clear dishes and wipe tables. As he lifts a tub of dirty dishes, he turns directly into the path of another employee delivering a tray of hot food. I almost shout for him to look out, but it's too late. Smitty careens into the other guy and sends food flying.

Horror registers on his face as he realizes what he's done. He should be working on complex equations, not in food service.

"Smitty!" an older worker calls.

"Yes, sir?" he says in a defeated voice.

"Why don't you take your break and collect yourself?"

"Yes sir," he answers, more dejected than ever. He removes his white paper hat and unties his apron. He steps out onto the terrace and sits in an orange sunburst chair overlooking the glistening lake.

I can't bear to see the poor guy this miserable. I wipe my mouth and go out to join him.

"Having a bad day?" I take the chair across from him.

Startled, he sits up straight. "You saw that?"

"Hard not to." I smile. "Don't sweat it. We all have bad days."

He shakes his head and stares at the ground. "But does anyone else have *all* bad days? I can't seem to get anything right. Maybe I'm not cut out for college."

"Why would you say that?" Is he out of his mind? He's the perfect student.

"I'm so behind. Everyone else seems to know what they're supposed to do and how to fit in." He adjusts his glasses as if seeing more clearly will help.

"And you don't?"

"Not really." A leaf lands on our table. He flicks it away with his fingernail, glances up at me and then refocuses his gaze out over the lake, as if looking me in the eye is too difficult. "Where I grew up, life was much simpler. Now everything is new and such a struggle. I've never worked at a restaurant before, and the harder I try, the worse I am." His sigh is filled with regret and self-loathing.

"Maybe you shouldn't try so hard," I suggest.

He looks at me as if I'm an idiot. "How would trying *less* help?"

"Well, you'd be less nervous. Right now, you're strung so tight that you're setting yourself up for failure. Give yourself a break. Relax and slow down."

He shakes his head, rejecting my advice. "I can't slow down, there's too much to be done." His toe taps rapidly on the ground, and he pushes back his glasses nervously.

"Maybe you need to find a different job. What else are you good at?" I speak more slowly and quietly in an effort to calm his racing nerves.

"My other job is in the campus library. That's better than here. The worst I can do there is misshelve books."

"Or knock over a bookcase. That would be bad," I tease.

His expression turns to fear. "Don't say that!"

The breeze blows strands of hair in my face. I tuck them behind my ear. "You have two jobs? That's a lot."

"It's not enough. I need to find a job I can work on Sundays. Living expenses are higher than I thought, and my money is going fast."

"When do you find time for homework if you're working so much?"

"When I'm not working, I'm studying, which I enjoy. The rest of my time I sleep, which I can't seem to ever get enough of."

"Lack of sleep I can relate to," I say. "Well, it sounds like you're doing great. Just remember, no matter how bad things seem, they'll work out. So never lose hope.

Hold your head high and don't let anyone get you down. Believe in yourself."

Despite my pep talk, he sags in his chair with his shoulders hunched miserably. "Why are you being so nice to me?"

"Why shouldn't I? You're a great guy. But if I could make a suggestion, you might consider looking for a job working for a maths or physics professor. I think you'd be a lot happier."

"That's not a bad suggestion. I do have an interest in maths."

"One more thing. Is there any chance you know a guy named Will?" I don't think he does yet, but it's worth asking.

"No, not that I recall. Why do you ask?"

"Oh, just hoping to find an old friend."

"Sorry I can't help you." He stands, stretching to his full height. "I'd best be getting back to work. Thank you again for your kindness."

"No problem. It's been nice talking with you."

He slips his paper hat back on. "I hope to see you around sometime."

"Trust me. You will."

***

After leaving Smitty and hoping I cheered him up, I go to my physics class. Maybe there's a clue that I've missed by skipping class. But the professor is old and monotone, and the lecture is way over my head. There's certainly no way I'll solve time travel based on his lectures.

On the way back to the dorm I stop at the Carillon

Tower, so tall and mysterious with only a couple of small windows partway up. What secrets are hiding inside its walls, and why have I never heard the bells play during the day?

I place my hands on its rough stone surface. *Send me home. Send me back to where I'm safe and have family I love.* I close my eyes and lean my forehead against the cool stones, but nothing happens. No bells chime, no lightning strikes out of the blue sky and I'm still here wearing saddle shoes and a scratchy wool skirt.

I walk down to the Liz Waters pier. It wasn't here during any of my other time jumps. One more thing that's different and out of place. I watch the boats out on Lake Mendota. Is Will out there rowing? Does it even matter? And what about my promise to Grandma that I'd help her find her long-lost sibling? How am I to do that now when I don't know when or where the child was born, or where or who the father is?

That night I lie in bed pondering everything that has happened. I look through the 1930 yearbook that Smitty gave me in 1951. It's a heavy monster that must weigh at least five pounds. I turn to the Badger athletics section and find two pages featuring the rowing team.

And then I see him. There's Will posing with the 1930 team. He's wearing one of those stoic expressions that guys give in sports pictures. His hair is the same as the day I met him, shaggy and a couple of weeks past needing a haircut. I stare at his grainy black and white image for the longest time.

"Who are you, Will? And why did you come into my life?" I whisper, but no response magically appears.

I page through the rest of the yearbook. It must have been Will's picture Smitty wanted me to see, or was there something else? I get to the section on Liz Waters. There are five group photos of the residents, one for each wing. I run my finger along the row of faces and see one that seems familiar, but I'm not sure why. I crosscheck to the list of students until I match up the girl with the name. Ruby Phelps. My handkerchief. Grandma's mother who just died. She lived in Liz Waters too?

"Who are you, Ruby? What happened to your baby?" I stare at her fine features, willing her to telepathically send me the answers to my question. She smiles serenely back. I close the book and lie down. What must it have been like to have a baby so young back then? Had she already become a mother when this photo was taken?

My body is exhausted. I don't know if it's from my emotional upheaval or too many all-nighters. There doesn't seem to be anything else I need in this time. I've met the young professor, I found Will's letters and he hasn't magically appeared, so I decide to leave my destiny to the hands of fate by snuggling in and closing my eyes. It's decadent to relax into my pillow for a change instead of dragging myself through the halls of Liz Waters like a zombie. Later, from somewhere deep in REM land, a chorus of bells rings through my dreams.

CHAPTER 13

Big band music crackles through the room. I'm in a new time and not even surprised. Peering around the room, I'm relieved to see that I'm alone, and I lie back and stare at the ceiling. Last night I thought I didn't care whether I travelled or not. Turns out I was wrong. I'm sick and tired of being whipped through time like a feather in a wind tunnel.

Time travel is sucking the life right out of me. Always trying to find my way has my nerves in a constant state of high alert. It's exhausting. My eyes well up with emotion. Maybe I'll stay in bed from now on and see how that works out. If I don't leave the room, I won't have to face this new world.

The door opens. I wipe away my tears of frustration. A girl wearing a skirt that reaches well below her knees, a button-up blouse and her hair in a short wavy bob enters. I immediately dislike her, because she isn't Grandma.

She takes one look at me and shakes her head. "Well, at least you're awake. If you hurry, you can still make breakfast."

"I'm not hungry," I mutter, hoping she isn't a talker.

"Suit yourself, but don't dilly dally too long." New Girl hums as she collects her books, turns off the radio and, with a final, disappointed shake of her head in my direction, leaves me alone again.

Thank God. I roll over and stare at the items on her tidy side of the room. Her books are stacked according to height. I spot an embroidery hoop with a floral pattern she's working on. There's a small frame with a picture of a young man on her bedside table. Boyfriend, maybe?

My bedside table holds a wind-up alarm clock, a room key and a Union membership card. I reach for it. *Abigail Thorp* is typed neatly on the card. And then the wind goes out of me as I spot the year. 1930.

That's an eighteen-year leap. It's too far. How can I possibly fit in here? The only answer that comes to me is that I can't. I'm about to cry again when I realize that the yearbook on my bed is from 1930. Will has to be here! I push my worries to the back of my mind and leap out of bed to check the wall calendar. Yes! It's April 1930. This has to be when we meet.

I rush to my wardrobe. The dresses are longer than any of the others I've had to endure. Bell-shaped hats are stacked neatly on the shelf above, and all the shoes have chunky heels and a round toe. There isn't a single pair of flats or trainers. How on earth do these girls get around campus? I pick out a yellow dress with cap sleeves and a flowing skirt, along with a cream-coloured sweater. The dress has long lines and is fitted in all the right places, a nice improvement from earlier decades. Who knew that the styles this far back in time could be so flattering?

I'm not sure what to do with my hair, though. The girls in the yearbook had mostly short hair with some weird wave on the side. That's not going to work for me. A ponytail and leaving it down both seem wrong, so I put it in a low braid and hope that's good enough.

In the cafeteria, I pick a table in the far corner to discourage anyone from joining me. I push thick porridge around my bowl and wonder what the best way to find Will is. I could stalk the boathouse. He'll have to show up there eventually if he's here, but what if he isn't? My heart sinks to think that just because Will was here at some point in 1930 doesn't mean he's here now.

***

After breakfast I step outside to brave my new world. I'm not going to class. I've got a fresh attendance slate in 1930, so skipping one day shouldn't matter. I may be gone from here tomorrow anyway. There's a cool breeze, but the sun shines brightly, warming the day. Nearby flowering crab trees perfume the spring air.

So where should I go? I know the professor isn't here. He likely isn't even born yet. Grandma isn't either. But according to that yearbook, Will might be here. He's my only hope at finding a friendly face. I walk down the creaking boards on the pier in front of Liz Waters and look for rowing boats on the lake but see none.

After a few minutes of watching birds swoop gracefully over the water, I head towards Picnic Point. The paved path of my day is now a gravel road shared with extremely old-fashioned cars rumbling past. The cars are all black and look as if they're made out of tin cans. The skinny black tyres seem more suited for a bicycle than an automobile.

At the entrance to Picnic Point, I follow the main path with the intention of checking for Will's treasure. Even if there's nothing new in there, its presence gives me a sense of security. A connection to him.

When I reach the fork in the path, I'm stopped in my tracks. There's Will, leaning against a tree with a fishing line cast out into the water. I can't believe my eyes.

His head is down, deep in thought, or maybe he's nodded off. Dusty blond hair blocks much of his face, but I'd recognize the clean lines of that profile anywhere. His knee is bent and a cigarette hangs carelessly between his fingers.

Blood pumps through my heart at full speed. I look around, unsure what to do. Does Will know me yet? If this is our first meeting, the ball is finally in my court. I know things he doesn't, and he'll need me.

I approach, stopping at a birch tree ten feet away. Deep in thought, he doesn't notice my presence. His expression is somber. This is not the carefree Will I met before.

"Hey, stranger," I say tentatively, testing the waters to see whether he knows me.

He looks up, distracted. I've pulled him away from some far-off place.

"Hello," Will says politely but turns back to his fishing, confirming that he's totally unaware of who I am. I'm torn between a tinge of disappointment and a feeling of protectiveness. I can relate to how he must feel.

"How long have you been here?" I stand a few feet away. Will looks at me as if I'm being pushy, which I suppose I am.

There's a silent void between us, and no recognition sparks in his eyes. Not only doesn't he know me, but he doesn't appear to want to.

"A couple of hours," he says, his eyes focusing out over the water.

I experience a sense of relief at just being near him. I don't know him well, but at this point I'm pretty sure I will. If there's one thing I've learned, it's that time doesn't lie.

"Nice day we're having," I say, trying again.

He frowns at my interruption. I bite back a grin and sit on the grassy bank, adjusting my skirt so I'm not showing too much leg for 1930. "Am I bothering you?"

He's quiet for a minute, then takes a long drag off his cigarette, the tip glowing bright. Then he exhales the smoke in a slow grey stream. "You're scaring the fish away is all."

In my day guys usually perk up when a girl pays attention to them. But apparently Will is immune to me. I nod towards his empty bucket. "Doesn't look as if you've been having much luck."

He speaks with thinly veiled annoyance. "Miss, is there something you need?"

I smile to myself. Do I give him a hard time or lay it on the line now? Do I try to shock him? It would serve him right. "No. But I've travelled a long *time*."

His jaw clenches and he looks at me, incredulous. Then he shakes his head and looks away as if he's bored.

"Thirty years," I say, referring to when we first met.

His expression changes to tightly reigned surprise. He sets the fishing pole down and faces me, his blue eyes flat. It hurts that he sees me as a stranger. Now I understand how bad he felt when I didn't recognize him the day we met. "I wasn't born thirty years ago," he says. "Neither were you."

I arch an eyebrow. "In the future."

His breath catches. I have his attention now. Will releases his breath and his shoulders sag. I'm reminded of my hopelessness when all of this first began, and I feel bad for him. If he's from the 1920s, then he probably hasn't travelled much yet. But again he says nothing, just takes another long drag of his cigarette and blows it out the side of his mouth.

"It's safe to talk to me. In fact, you were quite chatty in 1961." His back stiffens. I'm irritating him, but I can't just give up and walk away. He stares at a distant boat on the lake. I try again. "You showed me where you buried your tobacco tin. Want me to take you there? I know where it is."

His face shows astonishment, but he says nothing for a full minute before turning to me and saying blankly, "Miss, what is it that you want?"

"Listen, if you'd give me a chance, we can help each other. We've met before."

"That's unlikely," he says.

"Unlikely, but true." Suddenly saying the words that I am from the future sounds too much like a cheesy sci-fi flick.

Will takes another drag of his cigarette, stares at his

fishing bobber and exhales the smoke, clearly wishing I would leave. I thought he'd be interested in seeing me, but he wants nothing to do with me.

I examine this 1930s Will. He's wearing a faded green button-down shirt that's showing its wear. The fabric looks buttery soft against his skin. His sturdy brown trousers are casual with braces, and his scuffed boots look as if they've walked some miles. He wears a cap that shades his eyes from the sun, but not from me. A cool breeze off the water ruffles his hair. He's lost deep in his thoughts, thoughts I'm not yet a part of. And then I remember and want to kick myself for being so insensitive.

"I'm sorry about your family," I say gently.

Pain colours his eyes.

"And I know how hard it is to be all alone."

He clears his throat and speaks softly. "How do you know about that?"

"You told me," I say, watching his reaction carefully.

Will shakes his head. "I'd remember telling you, and I'm certain I've never met you before."

"Will."

He looks at me with raised eyebrows, surprised I know his name.

"I'm like you. You told me, in the future."

I want to reach out and comfort him, but that would only push him even further away. He's got everything on lockdown. He tosses his cigarette into the lake, pulls in his line and gathers up his fishing gear.

I stand and step closer. "It's true. You told me in 1961. We met at the Union."

He stands and puts his hand up. "Stop. Please. Stop."

"But–"

"I'm sure you're a nice gal, and clearly you know a few things about me, but I can't take anything more today. I'm at my limit." There's a rawness in his tone. He picks up the bucket and walks away.

I start to follow. "Will, wait! I have so much to tell you."

He pauses for a moment. "Please. Leave me be. I'd rather not know." His voice comes out in a soft plea that convinces me not to follow.

His lanky figure disappears down the path with his head hanging low. He's having a rough time of it, but why wouldn't he want to connect with me – the only person who really knows him? It makes no sense.

I sit and lean against the tree in the spot Will just vacated. I feel as if I'm here for some purpose. I'm sure of it. Because why else would fate spin me through time with no rhyme or reason? I'm here with Will again. That has to mean something.

I flick a stone into the shallow water and watch the rings it makes. If there is some pattern to this chaos, why can't I see it?

* * *

It's been a full day since I saw Will fishing on Picnic Point. I decide to wait and see if fate brings us together again, so I spend the morning in a literature class listening to a mind-numbing talk on circular journeys. On my way back to the dorm I wonder if there's any way I can find out what happened to Ruby's baby. Obviously the Internet is not an option. There must be court records, or hospital records of a birth. If I can find either of those places, would they just hand over the information? I doubt people are as paranoid about identity theft in this era as they are in mine, so maybe there's a chance? I remember seeing a hospital on University Avenue, so I decide to start there.

I find the massive building easily and am affronted by the sterile smell of alcohol and cleaning supplies. A woman at the information desk directs me to the medical records on the basement level at the end of a long dim hall that looks like a great setting for a horror movie. My steps echo on the tile floor as I approach a short man with thinning hair behind the desk. He looks up and raises an eyebrow, irritated to be pulled away from his newspaper, it seems.

"Hi. Um…" I stall and then stand straighter. "I was hoping you could help me find a record for a patient."

"Name?"

"Ruby Phelps."

"Date of admission?"

"I don't exactly know."

That eyebrow of his shoots up again. "Was it a recent stay?"

I feel my face going pink. "Is there any way you can just check by the name?"

"And what relationship are you to the patient?" he asks, finally getting suspicious of my motives.

I can't exactly say she's my great-grandmother. "A friend."

"And why is it you can't ask your friend for this information directly?"

"I know it's an odd request, but you see, she had a baby, and I'm trying to find out what happened to the baby. If it's ... okay or not."

"Miss, this is a highly unusual request."

"I know, but, please, could you check?"

He huffs. "This institution is not in the habit of handing out medical records willy-nilly. Do you in fact know that she was admitted to this hospital?"

"No."

"I see. It appears you are on a wild goose chase. And since we are only one of four hospitals in town, may I suggest you ask your friend these questions instead of taking up my valuable time." He picks his newspaper back up. Valuable time my ass.

But he's right. Finding out if Ruby was ever here was a long shot. And maybe she hasn't even given birth yet. "Sorry to have bothered you," I say, dejected, and turn to go.

As if it's an afterthought, he says, "You might also check the *Wisconsin State Journal*. It lists names of patients admitted to area hospitals as well as birth records."

"Thank you. I will."

And so I spend my afternoon at the campus library paging through old newspapers until my eyes cross, but still no mention of a Ruby Phelps.

Frustrated with hitting a dead end, I trudge back to Liz Waters and my thoughts shift back to Will. Where the heck is he? I decide fate is for the birds. If I want to find him, I'd better go and look.

Hanging out by Tripp Hall gains me a lot of curious

looks from the male students on their way to and from class, but there's no sign of Will. I see some guys running sprints over on the track and get an idea of where he might be.

I follow the lakefront back towards the old boathouse located between Red Gym and the lake, scanning the water again for signs of rowing boats.

I spot the dock from a distance. A bunch of guys are hauling a long, narrow boat out of the water, and afterwards they gather around the coach. I retrace my steps towards the dorms so I can try to catch Will on his walk back, if he's here. I find a spot on the hill near Liz Waters and wait, wrapping my sweater closer as the air is cooling fast.

It's a good fifteen minutes before some guys appear wearing white rowing T-shirts and shorts. They glance at me as they pass. Then I spot Will walking alone, his head down, another cigarette between his fingers.

I wait until he's close and then step onto the path in front of him. One glance at me and Will tenses.

His reaction is like a cold slap. "Hi." I face him squarely, an unavoidable blockade.

"Hello," he says, then steps past me and keeps walking.

What? I rush to keep up with his long strides. "You're not even going to talk to me?"

He takes a drag of his cigarette and exhales, leaving the scent of fresh tobacco in the air. "Miss, I'm tired and hungry and want to go and eat supper."

"Seriously?" I snap, running out of patience. "I'm here.

I don't especially want to be, but I am, and so are you." The breeze picks up and blows my hair loose. I shove the strands behind my ear.

He keeps walking.

I stop and call after him. "Will, I need you."

He turns and faces me, that tortured look on his face again. "Trust me. I'm no one you can count on. I have nothing to offer. You'd be best off staying far from me."

"Please. Don't go. We can help each other."

He hesitates and seems to consider my words, but just when I think I've got him, he shakes his head. "No one can help me."

And with that he walks on.

"Dammit, Will! You were a pain in the butt in 1961 and you're an even bigger pain in 1930. I didn't ask for this either."

But he doesn't pause; he just disappears around the bend. I want to scream, but other students are on the path, and they're looking at me as if I'm crazy. I storm out onto the pier in front of Liz Waters. The water laps against the pilings.

I'm so sick of all of this. I have no control over my life, and now the only person I can possibly count on won't even talk to me.

A couple strolls out onto the pier with a blanket and a basket of snacks. It must be nice to belong to this time and not have a worry in the world. I don't want to watch them flirt, but I don't want to go back to my dorm and my nosy roommate either. Picnic Point and the Union will just be filled with cruel reminders that I'm in the wrong century. There's literally no place on this campus I can go to be by myself and escape. But there are two boats and a canoe tied to the dock. No one can bother me out on the lake. Maybe I can row away from this 1930 nightmare. What the hell.

I climb into the cleaner looking of the two boats and untie one of the lines holding it to the pier. "Could you toss me that other line?" I ask the guy on the date, pulling his attention away from his girlfriend for a moment.

"Are you sure you want to go out? Looks as if it might rain."

I glance at the cloudy sky. It doesn't look too bad, and if I don't get out of here right now, I'll have a major meltdown. "I won't be long." I manage a tight smile as he tosses the line and I situate myself on the wooden seat. The boat drifts away from the pier. While I've canoed and kayaked plenty at summer camp, I've never actually manned a boat before. But it can't be that hard.

I dip the oars into the water, but I've reached too deep and nearly lift myself off the seat trying to pull them back. Okay, this is harder than it looks. Luckily I get in a few good strokes and have soon moved away from the pier and the curious eyes. I dip my oars again, but this time I dip too shallow. They skitter over the top of the water with a splash, and I fall onto the gritty floor of the boat from my overzealous pull.

I scramble back into my seat, hoping the couple on the pier didn't notice, and row more carefully after that. The breeze carries me away from shore and the site of my frustrations. The further I row, the better the view. Liz Waters, the almighty rock, looms grandly on the hillside.

The Carillon Tower pokes above the trees, majestically overlooking campus and, sadly, ruling my destiny.

From further out on the lake, the students at the Union Terrace look like tiny figures. I'm free from all of it and finally alone. Not a sign of 1930 in sight.

I raise the oars, slip them inside the boat and let myself drift. The lake is vast and the water dark, and I'm just a tiny meaningless blip like a water bug on the surface.

A breeze gently pushes the boat, and the water laps against its side, soothing me. Geese fly overhead, back from their southern retreat. I let myself relax and think back to easier times, like when my biggest problem was getting rid of that sloppy drunk at the bonfire and Colton saving the day. It seems like forever ago.

And then I wonder if Will's tobacco tin was still buried there when I was at the bonfire that night. What will happen to Will in the future? The terrifying possibility strikes me that I may never know if I can't get home.

The wind picks up, blowing cool air off the water. I wrap my sweater tighter and hug myself. I look to shore and realize it's a small speck in the distance. I've let myself drift too far. Crap.

I slip the oars back into the water and aim the boat for shore as a light rain begins and punishes me with cold drops. Within a minute it's a steady downpour and my sweater acts like a sponge. I grimace and pull harder on the oars stroke after stroke, until my arms ache. After five minutes of heavy rowing, I'm still a long way from shore and there's a growing puddle of water in the boat. My hands begin to blister and keep slipping off the wet oars. When my hand slips again, one oar pops out of the holder and over the side. Scrambling, I reach for it, but the choppy water has already carried it out of my grasp.

"Dammit!" I scream.

I try rowing with the one remaining oar, but it only sends me in a circle. With no other choice, I lift the unwieldy oar from its holder and stand carefully, wobbling to keep my balance as the rain pours down on me. I attempt to paddle after the oar that's floating away, but it's no use.

"Why can nothing go right?" I yell. "I hate you, world! You hear that? I hate you!"

But the pelting sound of the rain on the water muffles my complaints. I plop down onto the seat, careful to place my remaining oar inside the boat, and cover my face in defeat.

My shoes are soaked, my fingers are more wrinkled than the time I spent two hours in my friend's hot tub, and one of my blisters has broken open. I want to feel sorry for myself, but it's my own stupid fault for taking out a boat.

I hear something and search for the source. Through the rain, I see a boat heading in my direction.

Thank God. I don't know how I would have made it back on my own.

As the boat comes closer, I see a lone figure rowing. There's no jerking or oars popping up out of the holders. The strokes are long, smooth and strong. The figure comes into view and my suspicions prove true.

It's Will.

CHAPTER 14

"Have you gone daft?" Will yells over the downpour of rain and pulls his boat up next to mine.

I can't help myself. I grin.

"Clearly, you have." His jaw is clenched in anger as he reaches into my boat and grabs the tie line that's floating in the rainwater. He secures the rope to the back of his boat and then turns to me. "You think you can step over?"

"Of course. I'm not helpless."

He gives me the eye. "I believe you've just proven otherwise."

Rainwater runs down his face, and he blows it out of his mouth. Like me, he's soaked.

Will grabs the sides of the two boats with one hand. He braces his legs to keep balanced and reaches his other hand out to me. "I'll hold the boats as steady as I can."

My heart pounds, and I don't know if it's because he came for me, the fact that I'm in the middle of the lake during a rainstorm or because even with his hair soaked and pushed back to reveal his irritated expression, he is more handsome than I realized.

Freezing to my core, I reach for his outstretched hand.

He grasps mine firmly, holding me steady as I clamber awkwardly in my dress and heels out of my boat, over the paddle and into his. The boats wobble and I scrape my leg on the side, but Will holds them together long enough for me to land safely. He keeps hold of my hand until I'm seated, making sure I don't flip us both into the choppy lake.

As the torrential rain continues to pour, he releases the boats and lets them drift apart, my boat still tied to the back of his.

"Are you all right?" he asks with true concern.

"Never better." My teeth are chattering.

Will frowns, then expertly handles the oars, turning the boat towards shore. I didn't realize how far I'd drifted until I see how hard Will has to work to get us back. His sleek muscles strain under his T-shirt with each steady pull. The rain runs down the top of his nose, dripping off the tip. I smile despite the miserable conditions.

"What are you so happy about?" he asks between pulls, not amused.

"I knew you'd have to talk to me eventually, but I never imagined this is how it happens."

"We'll deal with that later. Right now let's get to shore before you freeze to death." Wearing only his wet T-shirt and shorts, his arms and legs are a mass of lean muscle and goose bumps, and his cheeks are chafed red.

Will rows us to the pier of the boathouse. He nimbly jumps out and ties off the boats, then offers his hand to me. My muscles are stiff with cold and I can barely stand, but I put my icy hand in his and he pulls me up easily.

"Why didn't you take us back to my dorm?" I follow

him down the pier, the rain still pouring down. My shoes squish with each step.

"I wasn't keen on rowing another half mile in the rain. I'll take the boats back to the pier after it lets up."

The boathouse is filled with rowing boats and canoes. Up close, the rowing teams' boats are impossibly long, spanning the length of the building. There are more boats suspended above us and dozens of racks holding paddles, ropes and other nautical gear.

Despite being out of the rain, I can't stop shivering. Will leads me past two guys working on a trailer.

"Hi fellas, we got caught in the rain. Mind if we use the club room to dry off?"

The other guys eye me. Water drips off my clothes like a leaky tap. I don't think they see too many women inside the boathouse, let alone one looking like a drowned rat.

"We're almost finished here. Lock up when you leave," one says with a knowing smirk.

Will ignores him and directs me to a stairway leading past the rows of suspended boats and up to a second-floor room. He flicks on a light and heads straight for a fireplace against the back wall.

"Take off that sweater before you catch your death. I'll have a fire going in a jiffy."

The room is filled with old sofas and chairs that look like cast-offs from a car boot sale. Framed photos of rowing teams as well as plaques and trophies from various regattas line the walls and shelves. A large braided rug covers the floor in front of the fireplace.

Will lights old newspapers in the hearth. The flames

catch and soon a small blaze appears. I can't stop shivering. I slip off my sweater, heavy with rain, then crouch near the fire, hugging my knees and waiting for the warmth to hit me.

While the fire flickers to life, Will disappears and returns with a stack of small towels. "Sorry these aren't any nicer. They're used to wipe down the boats. And here is a change of clothes – they're the smallest I could find. There's a bathroom at the end of the hall."

I stare gratefully at the grey UW rowing sweatshirt and cosy sweatpants he's holding out.

"Don't worry, they're clean," he says, as if I'd turn my nose up at dry clothes.

"Thank you." I say, accepting the bundle. "And thank you for coming out in the rain to rescue me. I don't know what I would have done if you hadn't."

He nods. Still holding on to his anger. At a loss for what else to say, I go in search of the bathroom.

I wring out my hair with a towel and slip on the over-sized clothes. The soft fleece caresses my cold skin. When I return, barefoot and carrying my damp dress, stockings and ruined shoes, I see Will has placed two wooden chairs before the now crackling fire.

He turns to me with his brow creased, his irritated expression back. "You want to explain why you were out in the middle of the lake during a rainstorm?"

"I didn't plan to get stranded. Those boats are terrible – someone should invent a better system for keeping the oar in its hooky thing." I hold my cold wrinkled fingers up to the fire. "Oh yeah, they do. In the future."

He cracks a rare smile and tries to hide it by rubbing

his hair with a towel. "You didn't answer my question," he says, his hair now sticking straight up. The light of the fire colours his face. "Well?"

I sigh and stare at the fire for a minute, reliving that trapped feeling that convinced me to take the boat out. "I'm so tired of it all. I don't fit anywhere. There's no place I can go to escape" – frustrated, I wave my hands in the air – "*time!*" My throat tightens with emotion. But I refuse to shed one tear in front of him.

Will is standing in his wet clothes and trainers, a towel slung around his neck, his hair jutting out at wacky angles. "So you took a boat out in a rainstorm." He stares at me as if he thinks I'm an idiot.

"It wasn't raining at the time."

He shakes his head.

"Hey, if you would've just taken a minute to talk to me, I wouldn't have done it, okay? I'm not a total moron. I think I'm allowed a little meltdown after falling back through time again and again." I move to the hearth to get closer to the heat. "You were a nice guy the last time I saw you. Now you're kind of being a jerk."

Will flinches. "You certainly do speak your mind."

"The world changes a lot, trust me," I say with resignation, the wind gone out of me.

He takes his seat. We're silent, neither of us knowing where to go with this. The fire pops. At least I'm finally beginning to warm up.

When Will speaks again, it's with a kinder tone. "How many times have you travelled?"

I think about it, ticking off years on my fingers. "This time makes six … I think."

"Six!" He jumps out of his chair as if I've jabbed him with a fireplace poker.

The number depresses me more now that I've said it out loud. "How many for you?"

"Twice, but that's two more than I can bear." There's panic in his eyes at the prospect of more time travel.

I nod in perfect understanding. "I don't know how long I'll be in this time, but, in the future, you told me we're good friends." I look at him earnestly. "I could really use a friend right now."

Will leans against the fireplace mantle, his expression softening. "When you approached me yesterday, I'd just received some terrible news." He rakes a hand through his damp hair, leaving it in slightly better condition. "I don't know how to survive this thing that's happening to me. I thought it would be best to avoid making any friends or connections, because I have no idea what tomorrow will bring ... But you're making me see things differently."

"So, friends?" I ask.

A smile curls his lips and, for the first time since I left Grandma, I feel that maybe I'll be okay for a while.

Will changes into a rowing team tracksuit identical to mine. We look like a bad version of Thing 1 and Thing 2. He tosses his pack of wet, ruined cigarettes on the hearth and frowns. After putting a kettle of water on the fire, he joins me.

At first it's awkward. We seem to have come to terms that we're destined to help each other, but how do we begin?

Will squats down and adds another log. Sparks fly into the air like fireflies at dusk. "You know who I am, but who are you? I don't even know your name."

"I'm Abbi. Everyone else since I started travelling seems to know me as Abigail, but to my friends, I'm Abbi."

He catches my eye, and we both smile.

"You realize this is a peculiar paradox. The fact that you know me from your past, which is in my future?"

"Believe me, I'm well aware of how bizarre this is," I say, staring into the fire. I hold my hands up to warm them, my fingers still like prunes.

"You've got blisters." Will takes my hand in his.

"It's okay. I deserve them."

He runs his finger lightly over my sore palms. Shivers run up my arms. He lets go of my hand, stands and begins to pace. "So when are you really from?" he asks.

Will's eyes nearly pop out of his head when I tell him. "That's a very long time in the future."

"I know. Every relative I've ever known hasn't even been born yet."

"And every person from my time will be dead by your time," he adds sadly.

And that's how we begin. Will makes us bitter coffee, full of grounds, and for the next hour, I catch him up on my travels and he tells me about his. I explain how I met the professor and how I think he's the key to helping us.

"But I can't talk to Professor Smith any more, at least not as long as I keep going backwards in time. It's going to be up to you. Once you meet him, you must do everything you can to help him. He becomes a brilliant physicist in the future, and I hope that he can find a way to send us both back to our real times." And then I share with him the Sterling Hall bombing, the Smith Physics Library and the uncertainty of the professor's survival. It ups the stakes, as if we're working on a ticking time bomb.

Will considers my words. "While we're here, we'll look into every possible clue, and I'll share our findings with this professor ... when I find him."

"And we should research the Carillon Tower. I've never been up in it, but maybe we can find a way."

"Wait – you think those bells that ring in the middle of the night have something to do with it?" Will looks at me in surprise. The light of the fire flickers over his face, casting warm shadows in the hollows of his cheeks.

I nod. "Yes, I hear them too. There's got to be some connection."

"And the effigy mounds..." he suggests.

"Are you going all woo woo on me?" I tease.

His brow wrinkles. "I don't understand. What is woo woo?"

I laugh. "It's believing in spirits and special powers."

"All I know is that the Indians were quite serious about their customs and beliefs. They've been around longer than anyone else, so perhaps there's something to it." Will glances at the clock and frowns. "We need to get you back before curfew." He hops up and scatters the embers in the fireplace.

We gather our damp clothes and head outside. The rain has stopped. The air smells fresh and full of promise. "What about the boats?"

"I'll return them after I escort you back to your dorm."

The walk back is cool, and I'm glad I'm not in my wet clothes, although my shoes still squish when I walk.

"When I saw you yesterday, you seemed upset. Or

maybe sad is a better word," I say.

Will presses his lips together, and I realize he doesn't want to talk about it, but then he opens up and says, "I just found out that my father's farm and everything he worked his lifetime to build are gone. After my family died, I should have…" He shakes his head in frustration.

"You told me. I'm so sorry."

He nods stoically. "As my father's only living heir, the farm was put in my name, but then I shot forward in time and the stock market crashed. The banks were in trouble, no one was making payment on the property, so it was repossessed by the bank."

"Can they do that?"

"They did. Everything my father worked so hard for is gone. Other than a small bit of money I have stashed away, I'm destitute."

"Will, that's terrible."

"I thought that I'd always be able to return to the farm if I had to, but it's no longer mine. I'm alone with no means of support. I don't know what I'll do now."

"We'll figure something out. You're not alone any more." I reach out and give his hand a quick squeeze.

A cold breeze blows the trees and a sprinkle of rain falls on us from the leaves above. By the time we reach Liz Waters, the shoulders of our sweatshirts are damp.

"Well, this is me."

Will says nothing, just stares up at the Carillon Tower on the hill, his eyes dark with concern.

"What's the matter?" I ask.

"What if one of us travels tonight?"

I understand his nervousness. I feel it every day. "When

I was with my grandmother in the fifties, I forced myself to stay awake nearly every night. Then I'd nap a few hours after the sun came up. It worked, and I never travelled, but I was exhausted most of the time. I missed all my classes and ended up getting expelled."

"I can do that. I can't let you go, after you worked so hard to get my attention." His mouth curls up at one corner and he playfully nips my chin with his thumb.

I'm relieved to see his softer side again. "I got your attention, huh? Is that how you knew I was out in the middle of the lake during the rainstorm?"

"I may have been watching you from afar," he admits. "Your rowing skills were comical."

"All right, so, we have a plan. Don't go to sleep until dawn. Do you want to meet someplace around noon?"

"How about the bell tower?" He points to our nemesis.

"Perfect. I'll see you then." I notice a woman inside getting ready to lock the doors. "I've got to run."

Will calls after me. "Abbi, please stay awake tonight. I don't want to be alone any more."

I stop at the doors. "I promise."

Will waves and turns towards the boathouse.

* * *

Back in my room I pull off my wet shoes. I'm exhausted, and all I want to do is sleep, but I promised I wouldn't. This is going to be a long night.

A high-pitched clink sounds. I look around, but my roommate is snoozing peacefully with an eye mask covering half her face. Her hair is tied in rags all around her head. I've learned that her name is Mildred, which seems about right.

I hear the sound again. Something is hitting my window.

Scrambling over my bed, I peer down to the ground below and see a girl waving frantically. I point to myself. "Me?"

She nods and points to the seldom-used rear exit at my end of the wing.

I nod, slide into some slippers and sneak down the back stairs. As I crack open the door on the ground floor, a girl with porcelain skin and delicate features smiles at me.

"You're a doll." She slips inside. Before the door closes, she turns and waves to someone hiding in the shadows. "We lost track of time and that wicked Miss Peabody has locked up this place like a virgin's vault."

I laugh at the expression. "Happy to help."

The girl grins and I have this strange sensation that I've seen her before, but where? We head up the stairs side by side.

"Are you on fourth floor too?" I ask, racking my brain for clues as to who this girl could be.

"No. I'm on third." She's wearing a boxy coat with a wide fur lapel. Her light brown hair is in a short wavy bob. "What room are you in?"

"Forty-four eighteen."

"This is my stop," she says when we reach the third-floor landing. "Thanks again!"

"Of course. I'm usually up late and my roommate Mildred sleeps like the dead, so feel free to throw rocks at my window any time. I'm kind of a night owl."

"Me too, obviously. But you have to room with Mildred Broadbent? I'm so sorry."

"Why do you say that?"

"She's such a tattletale. If your skirt isn't the exact proper length or you're a minute late, she's sure to report you. But you probably know that better than I."

"All I know about Mildred is that she spends more time on her hair than anyone I've ever met and she wears a sleep mask, so she looks like a creepy raccoon in the dark."

The girl giggles and pushes open the door to her floor.

"By the way, I'm Abbi," I whisper, hopeful I've found another friend in this new time.

"Swell to meet you. I'm Ruby." And she disappears down the hall.

CHAPTER 15

Just before noon I wait for Will at the Carillon Tower. There is a concrete landing in front, a dirt path around it and thick woods around three sides creating a cocoon of mystery. I still can't believe I met Ruby last night. Instead of searching all day for records about her, I could have just gone down a flight of stairs and introduced myself. My world keeps getting more freakishly crazy. When I woke up this morning, I looked for her, but she was already gone. With Ruby only a floor away, it shouldn't be too hard to connect with her again, but how will I ask about a baby? "Can I borrow some bobby pins? Oh, and by the way, ever given birth? And where have you hidden the kid?"

Will appears, cresting the hill, tall and lean with a casual gait. A cigarette is pinched between his lips, and his wispy hair blows in the breeze.

He removes the cigarette and says with a bashful smile, "We made it."

"Nice to see you too." He's the epitome of thirties college fashion in a knitted tank top and collared shirt.

"So you think this might be the key to our ... problems?"

He gestures to the bell tower, thick and formidable.

"Hard to say, but it seems to be one of the constants."

He cranes his neck and looks up the steep stone walls that rise several stories above us. "I don't understand how ringing bells can cause us to travel through time."

"Maybe it creates a rift in time. I tried to do some research at the library, but I couldn't find anything. I don't know how anything like that would work, but it seems we should at least check it out."

"Perhaps there's a secret chamber in there with a time machine waiting to be discovered," he suggests, wiggling his eyebrows.

"With my luck I'd drive it the wrong direction and end up surrounded by cavemen," I joke, thinking of movies I've seen, my only working knowledge of how time travel might work.

Will tries the door without luck and then leans his shoulder against it. "Locked up tight as a drum."

"That's a bummer."

"Yes, indeed, a bummer." Will tries out the expression, and I bite back a grin.

"Maybe we could pick the lock," I suggest.

"Do you have a hairpin on you? That might do the trick."

I shake my head. I was in too big of a hurry to worry about trying to pin my hair into an appropriate 1930s fashion. I settled for a low ponytail at the back of my neck. It's ironic that *my* hairstyle looks plain and old-fashioned next to all these girls with their short sassy bobs. "But I can get you as many hairpins as you need. Want them now?"

"We probably shouldn't pick the lock during the day."

He studies the door and takes another drag of his cigarette. "I believe it will take a little stealth on our part."

"Then tonight?"

"Yes."

We stand in silence. I kick at pebbles on the pavement and wonder if I should say goodbye until later and go back to my room. I'm relieved when Will asks, "How about a walk?"

We head towards Bascom Hill. The day is sunny and cool, but warming up fast, and I undo the buttons of my cardigan. We walk silently for a while, both in our own heads. There's so much more to tell him, but for just a moment, I'm enjoying this feeling – letting myself pretend we're two ordinary college kids on a beautiful spring day.

Finally I say, "I was thinking about the problem of your money last night."

"You mean lack of it." He gives me a sideways glance.

"Yes. But you said you still have some. I can help."

"Oh, did you time travel with a satchel full of money?"

"No, but I know some things about the future that should help you make a few surefire investments."

Will looks skeptical.

"For example, my best friend from high school, her grandfather worked for Polaroid. They were a big camera company, and later Apple computers are huge. I'll write down the products that I know become super successful, like Nabisco and Oscar Mayer, and if you keep going forwards, you can check to see if they exist yet and buy stock."

"I know nothing about how to buy stocks, and since the market crash last year, I don't figure it's a smart idea."

"The market will recover, eventually. You're going to have to learn a ton of new things. The world changes. A lot."

"Sounds tricky." He tosses down his cigarette butt and steps on it. I wrinkle my nose and step sideways to avoid it. Right away, Will reaches into his pocket and pulls out another.

I roll my eyes and go on. "I'll help as much as I can, but you have to do this. If you get stuck in God knows what year and have nothing, how will you get by? Money makes life a lot easier, and trust me, the future is expensive."

My problem is the reverse. How do I take money to the past? Each time I've travelled there's been some cash on my bedside table or in my top dresser drawer, but how do I make sure I have enough in case of emergency? I can't exactly use 1960 dollar bills in 1930.

Will strikes a match to light his new cigarette and draws on it like a seasoned chain smoker.

I wave my hand in front of my face. "And stop smoking. You'll end up with lung cancer. Plus your breath smells like an ashtray."

He frowns. "You sure are bossy. Are all women in the future as headstrong as you?"

I have to laugh. "I'm just trying to help. And in the future women *are* strong, they aren't all 'helpless, poor me,' like so many women in this time."

A smirk appears on his face. "You mean like last night when you were stranded out on the lake?"

"I did not cry 'help me, save me!' I would have figured something out eventually." Except that I did have a major pity party. "But okay, yeah, that wasn't my best move," I admit. Will smiles down at me and seems to strike a silent deal – he snubs out his cigarette with the toe of his shoe.

"Swell. I'll invest and pray to God I'm able to collect on it." He sinks his hands deep into his pockets.

I rack my brain for more details that might help him. "The US will enter World War II in the early 1940s."

"Another world war?" He looks incredulous.

"Yeah. It's a bad one, so do whatever you can to avoid getting drafted."

Will lets out a worried sigh. He shouldn't have to think about these things. Maybe I'm making things worse instead of better.

"You're going to be okay. Hey, I remember learning that when the war happened, car companies did really well because they started building tanks and planes."

"I hope your plan succeeds. I don't have much, but I did squirrel away some money after my parents' death." His voice drops to a whisper when he says "death".

"Oh, Will. It's awful that you've had to deal with all of this." I touch his arm.

He puts his hand over mine and simply says, "Thank you."

When we reach State Street and walk towards the capitol building, I see that everything looks different. There are old-fashioned shopfronts, green postboxes on the corners and elaborately styled streetlights with glass globes on top. "I can't believe how everything is changed."

"You and me both. Just a few years ago, there was still

the occasional horse-drawn buggy. Now look at us dodging street cars and delivery trucks."

We pass a travel agency with a poster in the window advertising honeymoon trips to Niagara Falls. I stop for a closer look.

"What is it?" Will asks, following my gaze.

"Reminds me of my grandma, Sharon. She loved to travel." I look back at him. "She was my roommate when I landed in 1951."

"Egads! Are you certain?"

I nod. "In my time she'd recently passed away, so it was amazing being with her. But when I left her, she was so upset. Her mother had just died, and she had discovered some upsetting news. We were on a mission, but then I travelled and abandoned her."

"What was the mission?"

"She'd learned that she had a sibling she never knew about – a baby her mother had before Sharon was born. I was going to help her find out what happened."

"So now she has to solve the mystery without you."

"That's just it. I know for a fact she *doesn't* solve it. Remember," I point at myself, "I'm from the future. And you want to hear something even more bizarre?"

He nods.

"Last night I think I met Sharon's mother, Ruby."

Will stops short and stares at me. "You met the woman who just died?"

I nod. The whole thing is crazy.

"Your grandmother's mother. That's unbelievable. That makes her your what, great-grandmother? What did you say to her?"

"Not much. I helped her sneak in after curfew. She'd been off with some guy. I didn't realize who she was until the very last second."

Will shakes his head, still digesting the situation. "What are you going to do? Ask her what she's done with the baby?"

"Maybe she hasn't had it yet. I don't know."

"You think she's ... with child now?" He practically blushes saying the words. Apparently *pregnant* is a dirty word in this time.

I shrug. "She didn't look it, but I only saw her for a minute, and I wasn't exactly checking her out. Maybe she hasn't met the father yet."

Will shakes his head. "If she's sneaking in from some late-night tryst, I assure you, she has."

"You don't know that." I want to give Ruby the benefit of the doubt.

"This whole situation is unbelievably strange."

A couple turns the corner in front of Rennebohms, their hands linked, looking all gooey-eyed at each other.

I lean over and whisper in Will's ear, "I think it just got stranger."

"Why is that?" he asks, his face close to mine.

The girl spots me. Her face lights up, and she rushes over. "Oh my goodness, it's Abbi, isn't it?"

"Yes! It's great to see you, Ruby!" I can't believe she's here. "This is my friend, Will." I turn to him, hinting with my eyebrows. But I am shocked to see that Will already seems to know them.

"Holy smokes! Hey old pal, how've you been?" Will asks, heartily shaking the hand of Ruby's date

"You know each other?" I ask, dumbfounded.

"Sure do. I met Ruby and Walter … a while back."

Walter? As in my great-grandfather? My jaw drops. He's right in front of me, looking young and handsome with the same bushy eyebrows and with Ruby at his side. Will was right – she *has* met the father.

They're all staring, waiting for me to say something. "It's nice to meet you, Walter," I finally manage.

"Likewise," he says. "Will is responsible for introducing Ruby and me. He and I sat together in a physics class, and during a crowded lecture, this gentleman here gave up his seat for this little lady, and she's been sitting next to me ever since." Walter beams at Ruby.

I turn to Will, who nods. "It's true. I couldn't let the poor gal just stand there, and I thought Walter might need a little nudge in the right direction."

Walter claps Will on the back, and Ruby laughs and says, "He sure did!"

My mind is reeling … *Will* introduced my great-grandparents to each other.

"And Walter, Abbi is the sweet gal who let me in last night," Ruby says. "He and I lost track of time and I missed curfew," she adds with a blush. "Abbi is a true lifesaver."

Will chokes, and the sound turns into a hacking smoker's cough. I give him another hearty whack on the back.

"In that case, you must let me treat you to a drink." Walter motions to a nearby diner.

"You don't need to do that. I was glad to help," I say.

"I insist. Allow me to treat you and Will. You've both done us a kindness."

"He won't stop until you let him have his way," Ruby

says, clutching his arm. "It's much easier to go along."

"All right, I'd love one." What the heck? I'm going to hang out with my great-grandparents. Surreal. I glance at Will.

He grins back. "I can't think of anything I'd rather do."

Walter holds the door to the diner and we enter. Out of his earshot, I tug on Will's shirtsleeve and whisper, "He's my great-grandfather!"

Will laughs softly and shakes his head.

The smell of fresh coffee and grilled food fills the air. We slide into a booth, Ruby and Walter on one side, so close their arms are touching. Will keeps a respectable distance between us on our side. We each order a different cold drink. This experience is like the precursor to the coffee shops of my time when I'd go to Starbucks with friends and drink flavoured coffees. Our drinks show up in tall glasses with long straws. Mine is a sour cherry drink. Will's is a root beer float. I can't stop staring at Ruby and Walter, so young and full of life. They glance at me, a little uncomfortable with my steady gaze. "I'm sorry, you both just seem so in love."

They smile at each other and my rudeness is forgotten. I take a mental snapshot of this scene with my great-grandparents and hope to remember this moment always.

"Will, I haven't seen you around campus since that day you played matchmaker for us. Where the devil have you been?" Walter asks.

"Well," Will pauses, probably searching for a plausible reason. "I needed to help out on the farm, and I wasn't able to get back to school until this semester."

"That's unfortunate, but I'm glad to see you again."

We're sipping our drinks when out of nowhere, Will says, "Walter, have you ever been inside the Carillon Tower?"

I can't believe his bluntness. I kick him under the table, but he doesn't flinch.

"Inside, you say?" Walter scratches his head. "Can't say that I have, but yesterday I was in one of the tunnels that run beneath campus."

"I didn't know there were tunnels," I say.

"Oh yes, miles of them, but you need a good light with you. Some are quite dark and dangerous."

Ruby turns to him in surprise. "What were you up to in the tunnels?"

"I needed someplace to hide after campus police caught me riding the fire escape in Science Hall."

"What is so special about a fire escape?" Will asks.

"It's loads of fun to ride," Ruby says, swirling her straw around her glass. "But you have to sneak up to the top floor of Science Hall. The graduate students working up there don't care for undergrads interrupting their research." She puts on a hoity-toity face and says "research" in a playful, mocking voice.

I smile and say, "I've never heard of such a thing." It cracks me up to discover that my great-grandparents are much more fun than the stoic family portrait in my hatbox would indicate.

Ruby continues, "Walter took me to the fire escape on our first date."

He shakes his head. "Aw, shucks, Ruby. Now you're making me look like a cheapskate. She left out that I took her to the movies first."

"That is an imaginative date. I'll have to figure out

how to top it." Will peeks at me, his blue eyes dancing.

Whoa. Is he planning to ask me out?

"What has you wanting to get inside the Carillon Tower?" Walter asks.

I raise an eyebrow at Will and think, *Because he hopes to find the secret of time travel within its stone walls.*

"Why else? Because it's there." Will laughs, showing off that contagious smile of his.

Walter slaps the table and our glasses jump. "In that case, I'm your man for the job."

CHAPTER 16

Ruby and I, dressed in dark coats and stockings, sneak out the back exit of Liz Waters just before eleven. She puts a rock in the door, propping it open a tiny bit, and winks at me. She's done this before.

We follow the pavement close to the woods, then turn the corner and climb the short hill to the Carillon Tower. It shoots upwards, with the twinkling stars in the inky black sky as a backdrop. The dim light from the corner street lamp doesn't reach the tower, casting the area around the hulking black giant in ominous shadows fit for a horror movie.

"Is it always this quiet at night, or is it because we plan to break the law?" Ruby clutches my arm as we approach cautiously. "Where are the fellas? This is not a night I want to be out alone."

I scan the woods for the guys, but they aren't here yet. A car approaches, and we scramble around the back of the tower to hide. As the car rumbles past, someone jumps out of the shadows.

Ruby and I scream.

"Gotcha!" Walter says and pulls Ruby into his arms.

"You nearly scared me to death! Shame on you!" She swats him playfully.

Will appears at Walter's side with a flashlight and an easy smile. "Nice evening for a stroll, ladies." He tips his cap as if it's every day he sneaks around in the dark, breaking and entering.

"I can't believe we're going to do this." Ruby pulls her coat tighter. "I feel like a cat burglar!"

My heart pounds with anticipation as we gather around the door. My arm brushes Will's, and his friendly gaze lands on me.

"Have you had a change of heart, Ruby? Maybe you girls should go back and let the men handle this," Walter teases.

"Not on your life. I want to see what's up there too! But we'd better not get caught," Ruby says to Walter. "I can't afford to have Miss Peabody call my father."

"I won't let that happen." He puts his arm around her and kisses her temple.

Will turns to me. "Abbi, are you still with me on this?" He winks and rests his hand at the small of my back. I step closer. "Atta girl," he says.

If there's something in that tower that can help us determine what keeps hurtling us through time, we need to know.

"If there's any sign of trouble, Ruby, run into the woods," Walter tells her.

"I will," she answers.

"So we're all set?" Will asks, looking to each of us.

Everyone nods. Ruby presents a long hatpin, and

Walter, a screwdriver. I hold out the bobby pin and say, "I solemnly swear we're up to no good."

With a chorus of snickers, we circle around the front door as Will shines the light on the lock.

"Good thinking to bring a flashlight." I huddle next to him for warmth.

"Thank Walter for that. He borrowed it from a pal who works for university maintenance."

"It's all in who you know." Walter takes the hatpin. He straightens it and slides it into the lock, jiggling it about, but nothing happens.

"Try using it with the bobby pin at the same time," I say. "That's how they do it on TV."

They all turn to look at me oddly. "TV?" Ruby asks.

For a second I think she's kidding, and then my brain clicks on. "Oh, I meant radio. It's how they do it on the radio shows."

Will gives me a meaningful look. He doesn't know what TV is either, but clearly he knows it's from the future and that I shouldn't have mentioned it. Oops.

Walter jiggles both pins. "This isn't working. The lock is strong and sure." He hands Ruby the pins and brings out his screwdriver. But there is no place to use it. The screwdriver is useless.

Ruby peers over my shoulder and whispers in a panic, "Someone's coming! Quick, scram!" She and Walter run behind a nearby oak at the edge of the woods.

Will clicks off the flashlight, grabs my hand and pulls me behind the tower. We wait, my back against the cool stone wall, and Will gently grasps my shoulders. My heart pounds so hard in my chest, I'm afraid it'll give us away.

He gazes down at me and smiles, seeming unconcerned that we could be busted at any moment. His face
is so close I feel his breath on my forehead. He smells of
mint and woods and … home, I realize with surprise.
Will's eyes, dark and mysterious in the shadows, lock onto
mine, and I forget to breathe.

"All clear," Walter calls, interrupting the moment.

Will gives my shoulder a warm squeeze and then
releases me.

"It was only a student walking home," Ruby says,
appearing with Walter.

"I don't think a screwdriver is going to get us in," I say,
refocusing on our task and trying to get the feel of Will's
touch off my mind.

"That's all right, because I found another way." Walter
points to a small window partway up.

"This is why I asked for your help. I knew you'd be
good in a jam." Will pats him on the shoulder.

The two guys start feeling the large stones for places
to grip. I doubt either of them has ever taken a rock climbing class. Still, they both attempt to scale the wall, trying
to wedge the toes of their shoes into the crevices between
the stones. Walter is wearing thick shoes and immediately
falls off. Will makes it up about three feet in his leather
loafers before losing his grip and sliding down.

They begin to try again, but I have an idea. "I think
I can reach the window if I stand on your shoulders."
Two years of high school cheerleading taught me a thing
or two.

The guys stare at me.

"What?" I say.

Walter links his hands and holds them out. "Here, Will. I'll boost you up."

They totally ignore me and look like a couple of monkeys wrestling as Will attempts to climb on Walter.

"You guys, I know how to do this."

Ruby giggles when they fail for the third time, scratching their heads in defeat.

"Seriously? Would you let me try?" I bark.

Walter and Will stare at me again but this time at my legs.

"Abbi, you're wearing a dress," Ruby says under her breath.

"Oh, please. I'm sure they will be total gentlemen and not peek up my skirt." I think of the uncomfortable garter belt and stockings I wrestled myself into.

Will fights back a smile, covers his mouth with his hand and looks away.

"*I* might," Walter admits with a sly grin.

Ruby yanks him away. "Walter, you're terrible! No, you won't."

Shaking my head, I bite back a laugh, then take off my coat so I can move more easily in just my cotton dress and sweater. I shiver and kick off my heeled leather shoes and step next to Will. The dress certainly doesn't help any, but I'm pretty sure I can do this. I hike it up above my knees and wonder for a minute what these two guys would make of miniskirts.

Will raises an eyebrow, but slips off his coat too. "Abbi, I fear this will end badly. You saw how difficult it is. Leave it to us."

It's clear he doesn't believe I can do this. "Seriously? You need to give women more credit. There's a lot you don't know about me."

"I suppose I'll have to work on that," he says with a wink.

"Will, plant your feet further apart and squat down a little. I'm going to step on your thigh, here, with one foot, and then up to your opposite shoulder with the other."

He looks at me as if I'm crazy, but reluctantly does as I say, squatting awkwardly next to the tower.

"Now hold your arms like this for me to grab." I raise my arms up and towards him. "Keep them steady as I go up."

"Yes, ma'am." Will takes his position.

Ruby watches, her jaw open in wonder as if we're a circus team doing a death-defying trick. Walter stands by, ready to catch me if I fall.

I place my stocking foot on Will's thigh near his hip. This would be a lot easier in trainers, but that's not an option. I grab his outstretched hands and place my other foot on his shoulder, straining the seams of my skirt. He wobbles, but holds tight.

"Hang on." I step up, pushing hard against his arms, and carefully stand using the wall for balance. The whole manoeuvre takes a couple of seconds.

A low whistle sounds behind us. "Well, I'll be," Walter says.

Will holds me easily. He's even stronger than he looks.

"Grab on to the back of my calves," I instruct.

There's a long silence before Will asks, "Did I hear you correctly? You'd like me to place my hands on your legs?"

I realize this must be pretty racy for 1930. "Uh, yeah. Unless you want me to fall, I suggest you do it." From my ankles, his hands slowly grope their way up to my calves. Heck, it *feels* a little racy.

"Can you reach?" Ruby asks, bringing me back to reality.

I inch my hands up the rough stone and can almost touch the window ledge. "Not quite. Can you get me any higher?"

"Hang on. Walter, give me a hand and let's try to boost her up further."

Strong hands grasp one foot and then the other. I wobble.

"On the count of three," Will says.

I cling to the wall, and on three I'm lifted an arm's length higher. I reach for the window ledge and check for a way to open the window. But the window has a metal frame and cross bars. There's no screen and it doesn't look as if it was built to be opened.

"What in tarnation are you doing?" a stern voice demands.

Walter falters at the sound of the voice, releasing his hold. I topple down, skinning my hands against the wall.

Will fumbles to catch me as I land helter-skelter, elbowing him in the head. He accidentally grabs my breast with one hand and my thigh with the other. He wavers, but doesn't drop me. After an awkward second of realizing where his hands are, he sets me down quickly.

We spin around, me smoothing my dress into place, and find a man in a university maintenance uniform, hands on his hips. "Are you trying to break in?"

"More or less," Walter confesses.

We glare at Walter.

"Why didn't you ask to borrow my key instead of my flashlight?" the guy says.

Walter shows a rascally smile. "Gee, Frank. It never occurred to me you'd have one."

"I swear. I'm smarter than all you knuckleheads put together." He looks us over. "What tomfoolery are you saps planning to do up there?"

Will steps forward. "Actually, I'm the one who needs to get up in the tower. I assure you, sir, it's for purely self-serving reasons."

"And those would be?" Frank crosses his arms in front of himself, but it's clear he's curious, not angry.

Will whispers something in his ear. The man grins broadly, showing off crooked teeth. He pulls a key ring from his pocket, selects a key and slaps it into Will's hand.

"There you be. I think I'll take one last cigarette break and stroll to the observatory and back. If you can't accomplish what you need to by then, you're a damn fool."

"You're a good man," Will says, holding the treasured key.

Frank heads down the hill away from us. "Don't I know it."

We huddle around Will. "What did you say to him?" Walter asks.

"A gentleman never tells," he answers with a knowing glance at me.

Walter chuckles.

"Let's get on with this." Will helps me on with my coat and then slips into his as I put my shoes back on. At the front door, he slides the key into the lock and turns it. The massive door clicks and swings inwards silently, revealing a pitch-dark room. The flashlight lands on a set of metal stairs leading up.

"Walter, would you and Ruby keep watch while we go in?"

Some sort of telepathic male communication passes between the two, because Walter nods. "Of course."

"But I want to see the view from the top," Ruby complains, tugging on Walter's sleeve.

Walter whispers something to her. She looks from me to Will then back to Walter and giggles.

"Besides, that place is filled with cobwebs and mice. Stay down here where I can keep you safe."

Ruby shudders. "Oh, that's fine then. I'll stay."

I grab Will's arm in a grip that says, *Are we seriously going into that?* but he's unfazed and steps through the doorway.

"Stay close," he says over his shoulder.

"Not a problem." I hustle to follow his beacon of light. Will takes a step up. I put my hand on the metal handrail. It's gritty and rough, and then my hand brushes against a cobweb. I jerk my hand away and follow Will, taking the middle of the stairs and praying my legs don't brush against any more cobwebs.

There's a dank, musty smell from the cold tower. I hear a skittering movement. "What was that?"

"I didn't hear anything," Will says softly.

"Slow down, will you?" I grab his coat-tail and inch closer.

Step by step we continue up flight after flight until

we finally reach a landing and a small room. A sliver of moonlight shines through the window, creating shadows where the flashlight doesn't hit. I stand close behind Will, not ready to let go of him.

He shines the light on the bulky covered form against the wall. "Must be the organ under that tarp."

"Now what do we do? What are we even looking for?"

Will switches the flashlight into his other hand and pulls me next to him so I'm not hiding behind him like a terrified child. "I don't know. Maybe there's a sign that says, 'Press here for time travel'."

He scans the walls and moves the beam upwards, looking for any possible clues that could help us. The light brushes over the figure of someone standing in the room. I scream and shrink against Will, clutching his arm in a death grip.

"What?" He turns his light back to the spot, but I bury my head in his chest.

"It's only a bell." He laughs.

I raise my head for a peek. Sure enough. I see a dark bell about the size of a person's head. "I thought it was a man." I release his arm and smooth his jacket.

"You are a big scaredy-cat. No one else is up here. You don't believe in ghosts, do you?" he teases.

"I didn't believe in time travel either until very recently, so I'm not counting anything out." I shift my feet in case any spiders try to crawl up my legs.

"So, who's up here playing the bells on the nights we travel?"

Will continues to shine the flashlight around. "Maybe it's the wind."

"It doesn't feel drafty in here." But just then a whoosh of air rushes by my face, and then another.

I screech and dive back into Will's chest. His arm falls protectively around me.

"Bats," he says, ducking his head.

"Are you kidding me?" I squeal. "They're flying rodents!" I tighten my hold, noticing his solid chest and lean waist. My face is near his neck, which happens to smell amazing.

He laughs, yet still holds me close. "I won't let them get you, I promise."

"Is everything okay up there?" Walter calls, his voice echoing off the walls.

"Just a little folly with bats."

Will chuckles, his chest rumbling beneath my hands. "You are enjoying this way more than you should," I say near his ear.

"What's that? Having a beautiful gal cling to me?"

I loosen my grip, even though I'm flattered. "All right Sherlock, now what?"

Will keeps his arm around me. "I don't know. I was hoping once we were up here, the answers would reveal themselves." He glances at me and smiles. Here we are in a bat-infested bell tower in the middle of the night, and he's as calm as if we were searching for four-leaf clovers in a park.

"What did you say to Frank earlier to get the keys?"

Will shrugs. "I told him I planned to get you up here and kiss you."

"Oh?"

This would be a perfect time for him to do just that,

and when he doesn't, I'm a little disappointed.

Will releases me and tugs the canvas cover off the organ. He runs his hand across one of the wooden handles. "I thought it would be a keyboard, not a bunch of wooden knobs."

I stare at this device that somehow has played a role in our time travels. "What if it started playing right now?"

Will runs the flashlight over each knob. "Do you think we'd travel?"

"And if we did, where would we end up?"

"All I know is, if it starts playing, I'm holding on to you," Will says.

His words send a warm rush all over my body.

"Where you go, I go," he adds softly.

He may not want to kiss me, but he wants to stay with me.

"Do you think other people hear the bells like we do on those nights?" he asks.

"I've wanted to ask someone, but because I end up in a different time, that's been impossible."

I hum the haunting melody that plays on the nights I travel. Will joins me in the tune, the low timbre of his voice blending with mine.

Our eyes lock in that tiny room at the top of the tower, the moonlight casting a silver glow on us. We're mesmerized as we hum the exact same melody. But when we reach the part where the melody goes off key, Will's version is different. Where my song goes flat, his goes sharp.

"Oh my God. They're different!" I say.

"What does that mean?" He seems as stunned by this revelation as I am.

"My version goes down, and yours up. Is that why … I go back and you go forward?"

"It's a valid theory."

"We may not have found a time machine in here, but at least we have one more clue. Let's cover this back up."

Together we lay the tarp over the wooden organ knobs. The sudden weight hits the keys, and bells gong so loud I scream again. It sends vibrations deep into my bones.

"Skedaddle!" Will grabs my hand and we scramble down the steps, the flashlight beam bouncing off the walls along with the reverberating gong.

The second we spill out the door, Walter and Ruby are there.

"You trying to wake the dead?" Walter exclaims.

"Sorry about that. Quick, lock the door before campus police show up."

"Give me the flashlight. You take the gals back, and I'll get the key and flashlight to Frank."

Will hands over the flashlight. "Let's go." He leads Ruby and me alongside the woods so we can duck in if someone shows up. Back at Liz Waters, Ruby slips in the back door with a wink, leaving me alone with Will.

"That was the most fun I've had in a long time. Abbi, you are a fascinating girl." He looks at me as if really seeing me for the first time.

CHAPTER 17

"Abigail, you can't miss class again. You'll be written up," Mildred's nagging voice insists in my ear.

"What time is it?" I mutter without opening my eyes.

"Eight-thirty. You're going to miss breakfast."

I groan. Staying awake all night is killing me. "I'm not hungry."

Mildred harrumphs, slamming her desk drawer. "This isn't right."

It's times like these that I long for modern conveniences like sound-blocking headphones. "Stop worrying about me. I couldn't sleep last night."

"I know you're playing truant," she snaps as if it's some great revelation.

"Please, just let me sleep." I pull my pillow over my head, determined to be left alone.

Mildred mumbles something and closes the door. Thank God. I drift back to sleep.

It can't be five minutes later when I'm startled back awake by someone pulling the pillow off my head.

"See, Miss Peabody. She refuses to get out of bed," Mildred whines.

Oh no! She's brought in the head resident. I bolt upright, pushing my messy hair out of my face.

Mildred glares at me with her arms crossed and hip hitched. "This is the second day in a row, and I know she's not sick."

"Why do you even care?" I snarl at Mildred.

"Abigail, what is this about?" Miss Peabody asks, tapping her foot.

I rub the sleep from my eyes. Miss Peabody towers over my bed. She's exceptionally tall and skinny, resembling a stork. Her beaked nose doesn't help the look either. "Lately I can't sleep at night. I don't know what it is. If I can sleep in, I'll be fine the rest of the day."

"This is not how the respectable young ladies of Elizabeth Waters present themselves. You are to get yourself up and dressed immediately and go to class. What is your first class of the day?" she asks with the efficiency of a drill sergeant.

"She has Eighteenth Century Literature," Mildred pipes in.

I stare at Mildred, dumbstruck. "How do you even know that?" I sure don't.

"Up with you," Miss Peabody says. "You may consider today a warning. One more unexcused lateness, and you'll receive a demerit. Oh, and do something proper with your hair. It's an embarrassment." She turns on her heel and leaves.

"Oh my God, you people are killing me."

Mildred glares at me. "Then obey the rules."

"I pity the man who marries you."

Her face pales. "What a horrible thing to say!"

Someone laughs. Ruby is at the door, already in her coat, ready for the day.

"And what do you want?" Mildred snaps.

"I'm certainly not here to see you," Ruby says and saunters in.

"Fine. I'm going to class like a responsible person." Mildred gathers her books and stomps off.

Ruby closes the door. "She's a nasty one. Watch your step around her. If you don't do things her way—"

"It's the highway?" I offer.

"That's a good one. What was Miss Peabody doing here?"

"Just making sure I never get a decent amount of sleep." I yawn. "Do you think there's any chance I could switch my morning classes to afternoon ones?"

"It never hurts to try." Ruby sits on Mildred's neatly made bed and grins. "Last night was terrific fun."

Memories flash of me clinging to Will in the bell tower while he held me tight. "It sure was," I agree.

"I can't believe you went up in that dark tower with Will. Dish! Did he kiss you?"

"No. He's kind of shy," I say, which is totally not true.

"Horsefeathers. We need to give him a little push. I'll have Walter tell him to invite you to the spring dance." She lights up with excitement.

"Please, don't do that. We're just friends." Friends who need to support each other in this time-travel nightmare. I get up and my feet hit the cold floor. Why doesn't anyone put a rug in here?

"But you make such a handsome couple," Ruby says in a dreamy sort of way.

"Look at you, playing matchmaker. What about you and Walter? You seem pretty serious." I seize my opportunity to ask some nosy questions. Unless she's already had the mystery baby, Walter must be the father. I search through my dresser drawer for a pair of warm socks.

"He's wonderful. We're going to get married."

I startle and look at her, beaming with happiness. "Ruby, that's great. Congratulations!" So maybe Grandma's birth certificate was wrong after all?

"But we're going to elope. You see, my father would never give his blessing."

Standing on one foot, I pull on a sock, then switch and hop while I put on the other. "Why not? Walter seems great."

"It's my stepmother. Father listens to whatever she says." Ruby picks up a throw pillow from Mildred's bed and punches it. "She's the meanest woman on this Earth!"

I climb back on my bed. "Why should she care who you marry?"

"Because Father loved my mother first, so my stepmother disapproves of everything that has to do with her … which includes me."

"She sounds awful."

"She's been pushing a bookkeeper from town on me for two years. He's a weasely little man who works for his father's firm. He's extremely boring, and I wouldn't marry him in a million years."

"You definitely belong with Walter."

Ruby beams at me. "I think so too." She tosses the pillow and heads for the door. "I must get on to class, but I'll see you later tonight?"

"Absolutely."

* * *

After struggling to give my hair a slight bit of thirties wave, I toss the archaic iron on the floor and pull my hair into a low bun. It may not be the exact style of the day, but it's the best I can do. I can't imagine how these girls get the wave in their hair every day. Who's got that kind of time? I'll have to ask Ruby for tips.

Rather than go to class, I march straight to the registrar's office to change my schedule. Who knows how long I'll be here, but if I'm going to make it, I might as well try to stay out of trouble.

A stuffy-looking man wearing a droopy bow tie sits behind a massive desk. He doesn't want to make the change. But when I mention my monthly curse and tear up over my inability to get a full night's sleep due to *hormonal* changes, he turns red and scribbles his signature on the change slip as fast as he can before dismissing me. I'm officially transferred out of all classes beginning before noon, but now my afternoons are packed.

Elated, I race to find Will at the meeting place we picked last night – the Abe Lincoln statue at the top of Bascom Hill.

He pulls a cigarette from his lips. "You look quite satisfied with yourself."

"My class schedule now begins at noon," I announce

proudly. "I can officially sleep in and get Mildred the snitch off my back."

"Brilliant idea. I'll have to look into that myself." He takes a puff from the cigarette.

"Will, you really need to quit those nasty things." I frown.

"I'm not hurting anyone." He grins at me and flicks grey ash into the grass.

"Trust me. You don't want lung cancer. Please try again to give them up." This time I say it nicely and flutter my lashes.

He shakes his head but tosses the cigarette and snuffs it out with his shoe. "How's that? Just for you." He gives me that devilishly sweet smile that lights up his eyes and shows off his dimples.

"Thank you," I say, getting that warm feeling again. A thought pops into my head. "And the next time you get the urge for a cigarette, try chewing gum or..." I look around and pull a long blade of grass growing next to the statue. "Try this!"

Will stares at the blade of grass. "You want me to chew on grass?"

I laugh. If only he knew. "It's worth a try."

He accepts the blade and slips it between his teeth. "Oh yes, this is much more enjoyable than a smoke. If I start to moo and give milk, please say you'll let me smoke again."

"Deal. Now that I've switched my schedule, I have a class in a few minutes. It seems such a waste of time when I know I'm only here for a while, but I don't want to get expelled again."

"I'll walk with you." He takes my books and curls them under his arm. I'm beginning to understand why in the old days women used to swoon over men.

Will adjusts his stride to my pace. "Abbi, I've been doing a lot of thinking, and I really hope you don't … leave."

There's a definite comfort hearing him say those words, but there's only so much I can do to try to stay.

"Before you arrived, the only good thing left in my life was rowing."

"You like it that much?"

"I do. It reminds me of home. I lived on the water, and sometimes the only escape from my father was to row."

"Your father was … difficult?"

Will takes the blade of grass from his mouth, looks at the chewed end and frowns. "I could never please him. He was terribly strict, and he insisted I farm the land with him, but I wanted so much more out of life. I guess I don't really have anything tying me to my time any more." He slips the grass back into the corner of his mouth.

"Well, I'm glad you have rowing now. Did I tell you that the professor, when he was a freshman, gave me an old yearbook from 1930 that has your picture in it? It's how I knew for sure you were here. I didn't know if the days overlapped, but I really hoped they did."

"I look forward to meeting the good professor. When did you say that happens?"

"He said you meet during his sophomore year, so that would be around 1949, but don't judge him too harshly that first time." I picture the nervous, pimply-faced student and smile. "He's not the all-wise and brilliant man you're going to expect. He's still finding his way."

"I'll keep that in mind."

We walk for a bit and I wonder what he's thinking, and then he speaks again. "I must say, Abbi, last night was great fun. Your great-grandparents are swell."

"They are. A couple weeks ago I didn't even know their names, and now I'm hanging out with them. It's wild."

We stop in front of the Social Sciences Building. "Here's my class."

He leans against the light pole, still holding my books. "So, when will I see you again?" he asks, peeking from behind his long eyelashes.

"When would you like to?" We aren't dating or anything, but it sort of feels that way.

"Would you like to meet at the library later to study?" He smirks.

I wrinkle my nose. "Sure. Maybe some of your brains will rub off on me."

* * *

After sitting through two lectures, I head back to the dorm. As I approach Liz Waters, Walter runs up to me, panic flashing in his eyes.

"Abbi, you've got to help me find Ruby. It's an emergency." He's out of breath and flushed.

"Of course. What's wrong?"

"My father's had a terrible accident. I have to go home, but I can't find Ruby to tell her." He wrings his cap in his hands. "They've buzzed her room, but she's not there. I don't know if she's at class or where she could be, but I must speak to her."

He paces before me. "What am I to do? I can't miss the bus to Sheboygan. There isn't another one for three days, but I can't leave Ruby like this. We had plans. Important plans."

My heart goes out to him. "Ruby told me of your plans to get married."

He looks at me in surprise and nods.

"What do you want to tell her? I'll give her your message."

"That I'll be back as quick as I can. Hopefully no more than a few days. My father has an ice delivery company. If someone isn't there to deliver the blocks of ice, he'll lose everything. My brothers are only ten and twelve, so they're too young to drive the truck."

"I'm so sorry, Walter."

His face is etched with pain. "Tell her I'll write as soon as I arrive and explain everything."

"I will. Good luck, Walter!"

He rushes to a taxi waiting by the curb.

* * *

Two hours later, Ruby is crying on my bed. When she finally arrived back to the dorm, I broke the news about Walter.

"Oh, Abbi, I can't wait for much longer." Her head is in her hands and she's mopping up tears with an embroidered hanky.

"What will a couple of weeks matter?" I say, trying to cheer her up. But she looks at me sadly and opens her coat.

CHAPTER 18

"Oh, Ruby…"

"Please swear you won't tell a soul," Ruby begs, hugging her pregnant belly, her eyes wide with fear.

"Of course I won't. I promise." I sit next to her and hold her hand. My mind is racing. I have found the mystery baby! And yet, all that matters right now is that Ruby is terrified and needs my help. "Does anyone know?"

She keeps her hand protectively on her baby bump. "Only Walter."

"How have you kept it a secret from your roommate? You look pretty far along…"

"My nightgown and robe keep it covered fairly well. I've had some close calls, and it's getting more difficult now that the weather is warmer. It looks suspicious if I wear my coat so much."

I can't take my eyes off her round belly. "What are you going to do?"

Her expression changes to determination. "I will wait for Walter. We've been wanting to marry sooner, but there's so many problems we have to work around."

"It can't be that hard." I immediately regret my words.

I have to remember that things like this are much more complicated in 1930 than in my day. The last thing she needs from me is judgment.

"Neither of us has any money. Our school expenses are paid by our fathers, but if we marry, we're on our own. Walter wanted to graduate before the wedding so he could get a job to provide for us. I need to hide my pregnancy for a little longer. Except now he's gone. Oh my gosh, Abbi, what am I to do?"

"Ruby, I'll help you. Together we'll find a way to hide it as long as it takes. I wish you and Walter would have snuck off to a justice of the peace before now."

"If his father learned he married before graduation, Walter wouldn't get the plot of land promised to him. We're counting on it to live on."

I admire her steadfast trust in Walter. But I don't see how Ruby can hide her pregnancy much longer.

"How far along are you?"

She rubs her belly. "I'm not sure."

I try to guess, but I have no experience in this department. "What does the doctor say?"

She gasps. "I couldn't possibly go to the doctor until I'm married."

"Ruby, you have to get prenatal care. There must be vitamins you should be taking and things like that."

"I didn't realize I was pregnant until two months ago. I was so afraid to tell Walter, but of course he figured it out, and he's been so wonderful."

I pace, trying to think of any possible solution. "Have you told your father you want to marry Walter?"

"Goodness, no! Walter's Lutheran and I'm

Presbyterian. My father would never allow us to marry. And my stepmother, I can't imagine what she'd do, but it would be horrible." Ruby twists the fabric of her dress. "We have to marry without them knowing."

"What can I do?" I need to be useful. Standing by and doing nothing is like watching a train crash in slow motion over and over.

"If you could help me keep it a secret, that would be more than enough. If the head resident finds out, I'll be expelled and sent home."

I nod. We won't let that happen. I try to control my anger at the idea that a girl could get expelled from college just because she's pregnant.

"But suddenly, my stomach is too big to hide." The sadness in her eyes breaks my heart. "May I tell you something?"

"Of course."

Her face lights up for the first time since she walked into the room. "Sometimes I feel the baby move."

"Really? What does it feel like?"

"Little kicks from the inside." She rubs her hand over her baby bump and smiles. "At first I thought nothing of it, but they keep getting stronger."

Ruby grabs my hand. "Oh, Abbi, I can't wait to be a mother!"

I hug her tightly and wish, just this one time, that I could jump into the future to find out what happens to Ruby's beloved baby. I'm positive she doesn't raise it, but then it occurs to me that maybe the infant doesn't survive very long, and I worry even more for her.

Without warning, the door flies open and Mildred

appears. She stares at Ruby's stomach. Ruby pales and yanks her coat shut. Mildred glares at Ruby as if she's tainted. "You've ruined yourself!"

I step between them. "Mildred, this is none of your business. You aren't to say a word to anyone."

But Mildred ignores me and goes after Ruby. "And you've been parading around campus in that condition all this time? You're a disgrace!"

"Hey, back off." I get in Mildred's face. "They're getting married."

"Is that so? Where's her engagement ring?" Mildred says in a snotty tone.

"Walter is saving up for my hospital bill when the baby comes," Ruby says softly.

"This is what getting married looks like." Mildred shoves her hand in Ruby's face. She has a tiny diamond on her left ring finger. "Howard just asked me to marry him."

Ruby lowers her head, more miserable than ever, and I really want to smack Mildred. "Well, good for you, but it doesn't take a ring to make a family."

"Yes. It does. It takes a ring, a ceremony and a husband. You have none of that. You don't belong here."

"Mildred, stay out of it. This is none of your business."

"I'm on the dormitory judicial council. I'm bound by my oath of office to report her."

"No. You can't!" Ruby begs, jumping to her feet.

Mildred makes a beeline out of our room. I go after her, but Ruby grabs my arm.

"Don't bother. You'll never stop her. Everyone will know soon."

"You haven't done anything wrong. It was a mistake, but you can handle this."

"Abbi, she's off to tell Miss Peabody. I will be booted out. What am I to do?"

"Let's hide you." My mind races for a way to save her.

"And where would we possibly do that? The broom wardrobe?"

"No, but we'll think of something." But every thought I have is no good. In 1930, with no credit cards or cash, there aren't many options for a single, young, pregnant girl. And other than Will, I don't actually know anyone in this time who might help us.

"It's no use. I'm going to have to face my father, and then he'll disown me." Her shoulders slump. The fight has gone out of her.

I rush to her side. "No, he would never do that."

"Of course he will. He has no other choice. Mildred is right. I've disgraced him."

"There she is!" Mildred stands in the doorway pointing at Ruby.

Miss Peabody enters, her expression severe. "Miss Phelps, please open your coat."

Ruby looks at me in agony but obeys the head resident's command.

I hear the sharp intake of Miss Peabody's breath. "I see. Come along to my office."

"I'll come with you." I move to Ruby's side.

"No, Miss Thorp, you will not. Miss Phelps will be in my office while some difficult phone calls are made, and she will be staying in my suite of rooms so as not to upset the other residents with her condition."

"Are you kidding me? You're going to lock her up and hide her?"

Miss Peabody arches a sharply drawn eyebrow at me as if I'm an annoying gnat. "Come along, Miss Phelps."

Hanging her head, Ruby follows, leaving me alone with Mildred.

I turn on her. "You witch! How could you do that to her?"

Mildred snorts in reply.

"We're women. We're supposed to stick together, not throw each other under the bus!"

"Why would you want to associate with a girl like her? Perhaps there are flaws in your own character. I know you stay up late at night. What are *you* up to in the wee hours?"

If I don't watch myself, she'll be turning me in next. "I have insomnia, all right? No big deal. Sorry if I disturbed your *beauty* sleep."

"After tomorrow, it won't matter. I'm going home to plan my wedding."

"You're dropping out of school?"

"No, I'm getting married. I found my husband – that's what I came here to do." She holds out her hand and admires her engagement ring.

"Oh my God, you are so messed up." I raise my hands in the air.

"You shouldn't call the kettle black."

I storm out, so mad I could swear up a storm like these girls have never heard, but instead I escape to meet Will. I don't know if he can help, but at least he can be a shoulder to lean on.

* * *

I arrive at the library earlier than we had planned to meet and wait outside. Will rounds the corner with a blade of grass in his mouth and a smile on his lips, but the smile disappears the moment he sees my distraught face.

"What's wrong?" He rushes forward and takes hold of my shoulders.

"Everything. Walter has left and Ruby is definitely pregnant. Worse, she's been found out and the head resident is calling her father."

He pulls me away from the entrance to a spot where no one can overhear. "They're going to send her home," he says, matter-of-factly.

"Yes, and Walter isn't here to stand up for her. He's hours away in Sheboygan."

"He left?" Now Will is as shocked as I am.

I nod and explain why Walter had to leave.

Will tosses the blade of grass to the ground. "That's awful timing."

"I'm so worried. I'm sure all of this plays into what happens to Ruby's missing baby. Will, I have a very bad feeling."

"Come here." He pulls me into his embrace. His arms fold around me, and my head fits perfectly in the nook of his shoulder, providing a safe haven from the chaos around us. "It's going to be all right," he murmurs in my ear. I hope he's right, but I can't imagine how.

Still, I sigh and relax against him, my arms wrapped around his waist. He rubs my back and leans his cheek against my forehead. The closeness feels so good. I don't think I've ever felt so safe in my life. I never want this moment to end, but after a few minutes he slowly releases me. "You going to be okay?" he asks, pushing a fallen lock of hair off my face.

I nod.

Instead of trying to study, we walk until we end up at the Union. I lead the way upstairs to the grand rooms filled with fancy sofas and chairs, the place where I told Smitty that I'm a time traveller. It feels like so long ago.

Other students linger about, but we find a quiet spot in the corner that overlooks the terrace. We brainstorm ways of helping Ruby and Walter, but nothing seems possible.

"Do you realize it might be best to let this play out however it's supposed to?" Will asks, locking eyes.

"You're right. It's just so difficult to stand by and watch Ruby be treated so badly. She and Walter want to get married, but their families won't allow it."

"But they do end up married, and they have your grandmother, so all is not lost." Leave it to Will to remind me of the positive.

"I hate to know that Ruby has such a hard time ahead of her. Did I tell you that her mother died when she was only two years old?"

Will shakes his head sadly.

"She was shuffled around to different family members until her father remarried a truly evil woman. I wish I could bring Ruby some comfort in all of this turmoil."

"You have. In the short time you've known her, you've made a wonderful connection. Maybe you'll get to see her again after she leaves."

"I hope I do, but since I only seem to travel back in time, I don't think it's likely."

Will takes both my hands in his. I can't imagine being here without him.

We head back to the dorm so I won't miss curfew. "You know there's nothing you can do." Will looks at me through his long lashes.

I force a sad smile. "I know. Thank you for being with me tonight."

"My pleasure." He's so sweet, and I find myself wishing we didn't have to part.

"See you at the Carillon Tower at noon?"

"See you then."

* * *

Come morning Mildred is banging around making it impossible for me to get my normal dawn-till-eleven nap. Last night was horrible. All I could think about was poor Ruby being ostracized. Because she was on lockdown, I was afraid to walk the halls in case Miss Peabody was on high alert. I stayed stuck in my room, struggling to stay awake while nasty Mildred snored peacefully, dreaming of wedding cake and tea towels.

Mildred wasn't kidding when she said she was leaving school. Not only didn't she go to classes this morning, she's packing all her belongings for her trip home. She's not wasting another second at school now that she's achieved what she came for – her MRS degree.

Annoyed, I stomp out of the room to brush my teeth. On the way back, I take a detour to the third floor to see if Ruby might possibly be there. Her door is open and

Miss Peabody and another woman are watching over her like prison guards. Other girls look on curiously, but the head resident shoos them away.

As I walk by, I see Ruby inside packing her things.

"Move along, Miss Thorp," the head resident says in her nasal voice, as if I'm as tainted as she thinks Ruby is. Ruby glances up with red eyes. The prune-faced woman at Miss Peabody's side stares down her pointy nose at me.

But I can't abandon Ruby to these horrible women, so I slip past them into the room.

"Miss Thorp, I said move along!" Miss Peabody is out-raged, but I couldn't care less.

"Don't you think someone should help her? She's pregnant, not a leper." I turn my back on the women and join Ruby, helping her fold her clothes.

"Why, I never!" hisses the narrow-eyed stranger.

"Thank you," Ruby whispers under her breath.

"Anytime. I take it that's the evil stepmonster?" I mutter just loud enough for Ruby, which gets a giggle from her.

"Less talking and more packing," Miss Peabody chides.

"Ignore the ole battle-ax," I say. "What's she going to do? Kick you out?" Ruby smiles gratefully, and I'm so glad I can bring her a moment of relief. "Where are you going?" I ask.

"Back home to Lodi. I have to face my father." She frowns.

"Is there anything I can do to help?" This helplessness is frustrating as hell.

"If you hear from Walter, let him know I've gone

home," she whispers as she places a snapshot of him in the suitcase. "I've written him a letter, but in case he comes back before he receives it, I don't want him to worry about where I've gone."

"Maybe your father will force him to marry you. You know, shotgun wedding?"

Ruby sighs. "That would be wonderful, but Father will never permit it. We'll still have to elope. It's the only way."

"And you will be married. I'm positive," I say. It's one thing I know for sure. But I also know Ruby is facing a tough road ahead.

She places the last items in the suitcase, closes it and looks around the room. "I'll miss this place," she says sadly.

"And I'm going to miss you. I wish we had more time together."

I'll never know her later in life, and she dies so young. I fight back a tear and hug her, feeling her pregnant belly between us. "Would you write and let me know what happens?" I don't know if I'll be here to receive a letter, or if I will have travelled through time again, but I can hope.

She hugs me back. "Of course I will."

"And don't let those bullies get you down," I say loud enough to make sure they hear.

"Come along, Ruby," her stepmother snaps, taking one of the suitcases.

Ruby lifts the other, offers me a wistful smile and is gone.

CHAPTER 19

With Ruby gone, life sucks. On the bright side, I've got a lot more time to spend with Will.

The end of the semester is growing closer, and we don't know what we'll do when we're expected to move out of our dorms. Neither of us has ever been here during summer break.

We're sitting on the shore one Sunday afternoon. Will throws a stone into the lake, creating a ripple effect. "It's a shame we're both up all night, trying to stay here for each other, and yet we have to spend the whole night apart."

"Right? It'd be a lot more fun if we could be together. All I do is roam the halls, worrying about Ruby and hoping she sends me a letter soon."

Will stares out across the water. "And I worry about a future where I won't know a soul and everything will be so different." He flings another stone, this time further out into the lake.

I understand his fear. I feel it too. Being alone again in some other time is terrifying. "Will, what if I sneak you into my room? Mildred's gone, and I won't be getting a new roommate this late in the year. You can spend the night with me, and we can help each other stay awake."

A playful smile crosses his lips. "Spending the night in a girls' dormitory? Why didn't you think of it sooner?"

That night I wait a full hour past lights-out before tip-toeing down the back stairs. I push open the door, spilling light onto the walkway.

Within seconds Will appears out of the darkness, a blade of grass between his teeth and a grin on his face. "You realize if we get caught, I'll likely be expelled or arrested."

"Then be quiet," I whisper.

We sneak up the steps like burglars. My heart is pounding a million beats a minute. After I double-check that no one's around, we dart across to my room. Once inside I lock the door, lean against it and giggle nervously.

"Shh!" Will puts his fingers to my lips to shush me, which makes my heart pound even harder. I notice the curve of his mouth and the laughter in his eyes. I press my lips together to control myself.

"Well, that was easy," he says, glancing around the room at the dresses in my wardrobe and the hairbrush and makeup on my dresser. "So this is a ladies' dorm room."

"Yup."

"It's larger than my room and definitely smells nicer." He steps to my bed and touches the corner of the quilt. "Your grandmother made this?"

I nod, suddenly nervous to have Will here in my space, touching my few sacred belongings. It's one thing to see and talk to him every day, but with him here in the privacy of my dorm and a long night ahead of us, things just got a lot more intimate.

"And this is the magic – or should I say cursed – bed that you travel in? It seems rather ordinary, just like mine." He runs his hand along the headboard.

"It's nothing like a DeLorean," I say, though of course he doesn't get my *Back to the Future* reference. "I have wondered, though, if it's just this spot in the room, or if I moved the bed away from the wall, would I still travel?"

"Ever tried it?" He looks up.

"Nope. We could try, but I'm afraid it could somehow make matters worse."

Will indicates Mildred's empty bed. "May I?"

"Of course."

He sits on the edge, his long legs stretched out towards me, leaning back on his hands. "If it's okay, I'd like to stay with you in this time as long as possible. I'm not ready to face the future yet."

"I don't want to travel again either." I pause to gather my courage. "I won't see you after I leave this time." My eyes connect with his, pleading with him to understand how much I need him. "I'll be alone again." My voice trails off. I look away and pull my knees up into a hug. Every day that passes, I'm more terrified of what's next.

Will comes and sits on my bed, putting an arm around me. "Abbi. We can't let that happen. We have to find a way to fix this and get back to our rightful times."

I look at him, a little surprised. "You want to go back? Even though your family's gone?"

He considers it and nods. "I don't think there's any way I could prevent my family from getting sick and dying, but if I was back where I started, maybe I could save the farm and my father's legacy. I should at least try."

I relax into his side, the warmth of his body radiates through the soft fabric of his shirt. Everything about him feels strong, as if he could handle anything. He exudes masculinity. "I wonder ... if I ever make it home and tell people about this, will anyone believe me? Will my life be the same? Or will things have changed?"

"I don't know," Will says softly.

"Like, have I done something that changes the future? Or, have you? And did Professor Smith die in the bombing? Or did I save him?"

Will sighs. "I hope we find out." Despite his physical strength and the brave face he puts on, there's a vulnerability in his voice.

We settle in, Will on Mildred's bed, me on mine, and talk about anything and everything – our childhoods and friends, our wishes and dreams. Anything to avoid the reality of our situation.

As dawn breaks and the sun peaks over the horizon, I sneak Will out before any of the girls are awake. Then I crawl groggily back into bed for a few hours' sleep.

***

This becomes our new routine. Each night, we whisper in the dark, teasing and joking, making up stories about Mildred and the poor sap she found to marry her. But we also cover serious ground. I try to teach Will something

new about the future, like escalators, televisions, computers and mobile phones. Will, in turn, dials back and tells
me how to start a fire in a cookstove, how to hitch a horse
to a buggy and how to thread a kerosene lantern. The
fact that I may need this knowledge to survive is beyond
terrifying.

Each day forges our friendship more. I relax in the
safety Will brings, trying to ignore the fact that at some
point, I will leave him or he will leave me, against our will,
when we travel again.

Even though we catch a few hours of sleep each
morning, we're both exhausted. We stumble to classes,
nap through lectures and do the bare minimum to get by,
but Will, who also goes to rowing practice every day, is
especially tired.

"Why do you bother going rowing?" I ask one night as
we sit on the floor, leaning against my bed.

He looks down at his hands and rubs the callouses
with his thumb. "It's my one constant. Rowing is repeti-
tive and familiar, and the water helps me relax. I only have
to think about the strokes."

We yawn simultaneously, then look at each other and
laugh. We are both so tired and desperate to come up with
a solution. "What if we took turns sleeping at night?" I
suggest. "Then at least one of us would get some rest."

Will runs his hand through his hair, considering. "But
what if, by accident, the awake person drifts off? Or what
if the sleeping person somehow still travelled – right in
front of us?"

I consider those problems. "Or," I glance at my bed

and wonder how he'll react to my next idea. I bite my lip. "What if we both slept?"

His brow furrows as he waits for me to explain.

"I don't want to end up somewhere by myself. But if you're on my bed with me, if I travel, you'll come too," I explain, hoping that's actually true.

He gives me a crooked smile. "Are you inviting me into your bed?"

I shrug and nod the affirmative.

He flashes his eyes suggestively, and my stomach turns somersaults.

"There is logic to your idea – I can't argue with that. You've said that whatever is on the bed travels with you."

We stare at the narrow bed.

"Yeah, so far." I'm picturing us side by side, his lanky body stretched out beside me, us spending hours just inches apart, or even … touching.

Will clears his throat. "I know a gentleman would say no, but the idea of lying in bed next to a beautiful girl, well, I'm also human. And, I'm beyond exhausted," he says with a crooked smile.

I can't help wringing my hands. "So when do we start?"

"There's no time like the present." He lifts an eyebrow.

"Right. Tonight it is. So … how is this going to work?"

Will scrunches his face in thought. "First, we shouldn't go to bed with our shoes on."

"True."

We slip off our shoes. And for some reason, that simple act feels like I'm stripping off a whole lot more.

I pull back the covers and climb into the bed, moving

the hatbox to the corner. "This stays with me. And this."
I grab for my macramé bag, "Anything you need? Make
sure it's on the bed."

Will hooks his duffle bag over the post at the foot of
the bed and then stands grinning down at me. His devious
smile is adorable.

I shake my head. "Stop that. You're making me
nervous."

Will turns off the light and climbs in next to me, taking
up most of the space. Between the two of us, my hatbox
and my bag, there isn't an inch to spare. We lie side by
side, our heads sharing the same pillow. I realize I'm holding my breath.

After a few nervous seconds, I laugh. "This is going to
take some getting used to."

"I'm willing to put in the necessary practice to get
it right," he says in a serious tone as if this is a science
experiment.

"Oh, I bet you are."

The bed shakes from his chuckling. "At this rate, we'll
never be able to sleep."

As I stare at the dark ceiling, my body is pinging on
high alert because of the gorgeous guy beside me. His
forearm rests against mine, his blond arm hairs tickling
my skin, making it impossible to relax. And yet, there's a
sense of safety I feel when he's near, like we're in a cocoon
and nothing bad can happen. Having him in my bed, a
hair's breadth away, quiets the constant hum of fear that
has plagued me since my travels began.

Eventually, we must drift off, because when I wake, the
sun is streaming in. I'm smooshed between Will's warm

body and the wall. He's stretched out across the middle of the bed. His face is relaxed and unguarded. There's scruff on his chin, and his bare chest moves slowly with each breath. He must have taken his shirt off sometime in the night, I note with interest.

I could watch him all day, but I hear doors opening and closing in the hall. "Will," I say softly, looking around the room and seeing that it's unchanged. We didn't travel! But we overslept, and by this hour the dorm floor is crawling with girls.

I say his name again, but he doesn't even stir. I lightly touch his bare shoulder, well-muscled from all that rowing. He jerks awake, wondering where he is – something I often do these days.

"Did we make it?" He shoots up in alarm.

"We did." I smile.

"Well isn't that just the bee's knees," he relaxes back down and stretches like a cat. "I haven't slept so well in weeks."

"Goodie for you, ya bed hog," I tease.

He lifts his head off the pillow and sees that I'm squeezed against the wall. "That was horribly bad-mannered of me. I'll try to do better tonight," he says, making no effort to scoot over.

I laugh, filled with relief and even a little excitement that he'll be back to weather another night with me.

"Our next challenge is, how do we get you out of here without getting caught?"

He gets up, stretches and says, "Guess you're giving me the boot, eh?"

I shush him and check the hall while he slips his shirt

and shoes back on. When it's clear, he makes a dash for the stairs, turning at the last minute to tip an imaginary hat at me.

I grin in relief with the knowledge that I'll have Will by my side each night.

***

That night after dinner, Will and I meet at the library to research the effigy mounds. We discover that Sauk Indians were here before the land was turned into the university campus, and we dig into their story. After some help from a librarian, we have a number of history books, which are now spread out before us.

"Look here." Will places a book in front of me and points to a section. His face is inches from mine, and I'm having trouble focusing on the page. "It says here that after the Sauk Indians were pushed out of Madison, they travelled west."

His close proximity plays with my emotions. I dip my head and see the hollow of his cheek and the curve of his mouth. He angles his face towards mine, feigning a better look at the page. His breath tickles my neck.

I try to ignore it by reading the next section. "And then they were massacred in the Battle of Bad Axe. That's terrible," I say, turning to him.

Will looks at me and I lose focus, mesmerized by the flecks of gold in his blue eyes. "Poor souls," he murmurs.

I fight to keep my breath even, and not because of the book. My hands tremble, so I hide them on my lap and read on. "It says here that Elizabeth Waters dormitory was built on sacred burial grounds."

"And there's an effigy mound right outside my dorm." He gazes into my eyes. "We're cursed."

"Yes we are," I breathe.

He leans closer, his lips about to touch mine.

A door slams and voices sound.

Will moves away, and the moment is lost.

* * *

Later when I slip downstairs to let Will in, a shyness comes over me that I don't expect. There's no denying any more how much I like him, but I don't know if he feels the same. I know he cares about me, but is it only because we're stuck in this craziness together?

"Hi," I say with a nervous smile once we're safely behind my locked door.

"Hi." He twirls a blade of grass in his fingers. "Any word from Ruby?"

"Nothing yet." We have a long night alone together and I need to get my mind off hopping into bed, so I move across the room and rearrange the hairpins on my dresser. "How are you doing with giving up cigarettes?"

"I'd rather have a smoke, but you know what the future brings, so I'll have to trust you." He hooks his bag on the end of my bed.

"Even if I won't be there to nag you?"

"Especially because of that. It terrifies me to imagine a world where so much changes." Will sits on the extra bed and rubs his temples. "So many wars and disasters, not to mention those little boxes you say everyone holds that can tell you anything you want."

"Smart phones," I say, missing mine.

"My head can't comprehend much of what you've told me. I sincerely wish you could be there with me." When he looks at me, I see the fear he's trying to tamp down.

"I wish I could too."

"And what will you do if you keep going back?"

"I'd rather not think about it," I whisper and turn away. As each day passes, the stark reality weighs heavier on my mind. He's taught me what he can, but life in the early 1900s sounds difficult at best. How will I survive in times when women have even fewer rights than they do in 1930?

I take a deep breath and try to control my emotions, but when I exhale, my breath hitches on the edge of a cry.

Will appears at my side and pulls me close. I struggle to hold back my tears. It's getting harder to put on a brave face as the reality of my future becomes clearer ... or rather, completely unclear.

"I'm scared, Will." I admit, melting into his warmth.

"I know," he murmurs. "Abbi, I will move heaven and earth to be here for you. Even if it means travelling hundreds of years into the future, so that I can figure out how to come back in time and save you."

I look up at him, overwhelmed at the idea that he would do that for me. "Thank you."

Will kisses my forehead and I wish for more. I want to throw myself at him, but I must already seem brash and pushy compared to the women of his time, and I don't want to scare him away.

But then his lips move down to my cheek. He pulls back just enough to look at me with his deep blue eyes. He leans back in and lightly brushes his lips over mine, setting my nerve endings dancing.

He slides his hand to the small of my back and holds me slightly off balance, his strong arm holding my weight. He draws his hand through my hair, and angles his head down so that I have to tilt mine up, just enough that my neck is exposed to the light caress of his thumb. Finally, he lowers his lips to mine. This old-fashioned boy knows how to kiss.

When the kiss ends, I'm a misty-eyed puddle. He still holds me in his arms with that sexy confidence of his that I noticed the first day we met.

I murmur, "How the hell are we supposed to share the same bed now?"

Will laughs.

My hand flies to my mouth. "Did I say that out loud?"

He releases me and groans a bit. "You make an excellent point. I'm afraid I shouldn't have opened that can of worms, but there it is." He gives me a crooked smile.

I slip out to change into the T-shirt and sweat pants he gave me that first night in the boathouse. When I return, Will is studying the yearbook that Smitty gave me. I see he's looking at the photo of Ruby.

"I'm worried about her," I say. "Seems she should have gotten a letter to me by now."

"Maybe Walter was able to rescue her from her father's house." Will closes the book.

"Maybe, but wouldn't she have written to tell me? I wish I could go and see her."

"I don't have a car or know anyone who does. But, we could call," he suggests.

"That's a great idea. Do you think they have a phone?"

"Only one way to find out. We can try tomorrow."

When we prepare to crawl in for the night, Will is more polite than ever.

"I'll try not to hog the bed tonight."

"Don't worry, I'll just kick you out if you do," I tease.

We pull the quilt over us and lie facing each other. The hatbox and the rest of our things are in place. We're as set as we can be for whenever we might travel to, like the two souls on a raft in the open sea, with only each other to rely on.

Will curls his hand around mine. "Thank you for coming for me."

I revel in the touch of his skin on mine. "You're welcome, but it's not like I had any say in the matter."

"I don't know. Sometimes I wonder if there's more to us coming together than random time travel," he says thoughtfully.

"Because, heck, any ol' person can time travel."

We laugh, and I love the low rumble of his voice.

"That's right. All the kids are doing it now," he says. "But truthfully, I wonder if there's some sort of logic or pattern."

"You did introduce Ruby and Walter. If you hadn't, they wouldn't have my grandmother in a few years, and I wouldn't exist. That's ... epic."

"Very true. What are the other constants or coincidences that have happened?"

I think back. If I count days, it was about two months ago, but it seems like a lifetime. "Well, you. Grandma. Certainly the professor."

"Remind me. Did you meet him the first time you travelled?"

"No, I was freaking out too much. But I called my grandmother." My head drops. "She had no idea who I was."

"I'm sorry. But isn't it possible the professor was there and you didn't see him, because you didn't go to class?"

"True, and I did have physics on my schedule, but there's also the awful possibility that he died in the Sterling Hall bombing." I picture the professor through the years that I knew him, from a wise middle-aged man, to awkward young college student unsure of himself. "He was such a good person and was trying so hard to help me. I really hope he survived."

"I do too." He squeezes my hand.

"The first time I met Professor Smith, he seemed so hopeful about his theories."

"Good. So even if he did die, maybe his work was passed along to a colleague."

"He didn't mention anyone." I turn his hand over. "Your palms are all calloused."

He closes his hand and pulls it away. "I'm sorry. It's from rowing."

"Let me see." I open his fist for a closer look. I glance to see if I'm bothering him, but he's just watching my face. I move my fingertip lightly over his skin.

He laughs and his hand closes. "That tickles!"

"You're ticklish?"

"I am when you touch me like that." He shivers and says, "Okay, focus. What else? What are we missing?"

But focusing with Will holding my hand is nearly

impossible. I think back to what happened after the horrible bombing. "I met you."

He smiles.

I grin back. "And the professor. He toured my room and took pictures of everything in the hatbox to see if there's any connection."

"Good. All this supports your theory that he's the key to helping bring us home."

"And when I travelled again, I was with Grandma." I get quiet, thinking about how it felt to find her and then lose her again.

"I think that's a big key too. You were grieving and lonely and were drawn to the person you had such an emotional connection to. I was sad and melancholy too. Maybe that's why we found each other."

"I could believe that," I say. Will and I have only been together a short time, but already he means the world to me. "And that time with Grandma was the longest I've been anywhere, so far."

"That might be because you've figured out how to fight the system."

A lock of hair falls in my face. I tuck it behind my ear. "Maybe. And now that you mention that emotional pull, Grandma desperately wanted to find out what happened to Ruby's baby, and poof, here I am in Ruby's time and she's pregnant."

"And there's me. Don't forget that." He touches his nose to mine.

"I could never forget you." I touch his cheek and his eyes soften. "Heck, I wished on a star one night, 'Please send me back in time several decades to meet a cute farm boy,' and ta-da! Here we are."

"So it's *your* fault I'm travelling through time. You couldn't get a date, so you had to search this far back to find one?" He winks and kisses my hand.

"Hey, I don't believe you've ever technically asked me out."

"I broke into a bell tower for you. That's pretty original, if you ask me."

"That's breaking and entering, not a date."

He laughs. "Well, perhaps I'll have to do something about that."

"Perhaps you will."

Will leans forward and captures my mouth. He trails his fingers along my arm, giving me goose bumps. I place a hand on his chest and feel his heart beating powerfully. I curl my other hand around his back.

The touch of his mouth and taste of his kisses are like being transported to a home I never knew existed. Our legs brush and soon become linked when his knee slides between mine.

I lose all track of time as his fingers caress my shoulders and his lips lay kisses on my eyelids, my neck and my earlobes. His breath warms my skin, and we dissolve into a tangle of clothing and limbs, hands and lips exploring, yearning. I draw in his intoxicating scent and press my body closer, feeling happier and more content than ever before. It's as if he's opened up my soul and holds my future in his hands. Breathless, we finally force ourselves apart.

Will rolls onto his back and looks at the ceiling. "If I were a gentleman, I'd throw myself out. But considering our peculiar circumstances, I think the best I can do is try to keep my hands to myself for the remainder of the night." He crosses his arms against his chest.

I silently groan my protest as he moves a few inches further towards his side of the bed.

"We don't want to end up in the same situation as Ruby and Walter," he says, looking at me sideways.

"Oh my God! Can you imagine me showing up in the 1800s, alone and pregnant?" The thought is terrifying.

He turns to face me. "We can't let this get out of hand. I'm sorry I crossed the line. I won't let it happen again."

"The hell you won't!" I inch closer and curl into the crook between his arm and his side. With my mouth near his, I murmur, "We'll just be very good at self-control."

CHAPTER 20

Someone is smoothing my hair away from my face. My eyes flutter open to see Will gazing at me.

"Good mornin'." His voice is low and husky and hums through his chest where my hand rests.

I lift my head from his shoulder where I snuggled in last night. "Good morning." We ease away from each other.

"We made it another night," he says as if it's a triumph.

A knock sounds on the door. We freeze.

"What do we do?" I look at him stretched out contentedly on my bed in all his masculine glory.

"Ignore it?" he whispers.

The knock sounds again, louder. "Abigail, are you in there? I have some forms you need to sign."

"That's my resident advisor. I'd better answer. Quick hide."

"Where?"

My eyes dart around the room. Mildred's side is totally vacated, leaving few options for cover. "Wardrobe or under the bed. Pick your poison."

He dives for the tiny wardrobe, climbing behind the

hanging dresses. I push the clothes back together and tug the curtain closed, hoping his big feet don't peek out.

"I was just getting dressed," I say, opening the door to the RA peering back at me through thin wire-rimmed glasses.

She stares at the baggy T-shirt and sweatpants I'm wearing as if they're scandalous. Apparently girls don't wear guys' clothes too often in this era.

"You have something for me?" I prompt.

"Yes, of course. You never handed in your resident hall discharge papers, or are you staying for summer session? Paperwork was supposed to be turned in last week."

"I can stay for the summer session?" This will help solve the problem of having to move out at semester's end.

"Of course, but you need to fill out the attached card and return it to the office right away." She hands me the paperwork.

"Thanks. I'll get right on that." I close the door and go to the wardrobe, pushing back the hangers to reveal my handsome secret roommate with his hair all askew. "Did you hear that? We can stay for the summer session!"

* * *

Later that day we squeeze into a phone booth in the Memorial Union lobby. The tiny room is an oak cabinet with glass doors and a small built-in bench to sit on. It's a tight fit, but neither of us minds. I let Will take over since I have no idea how phones work in this time. To him these are modern, but at least still familiar.

"May I have the long distance operator, please?" He

holds the phone between us so we can both listen in.

"Please hold while I transfer your call," a woman with a pinched voice says. We wait nearly a minute, listening to different clicks before a new operator's voice sounds through the receiver. "What city, please?"

"Lodi, Wisconsin," Will says.

"One moment."

But it takes a lot longer than that. While we wait, I admire how Will's brows and lashes frame his eyes. I want to reach out and touch his narrow nose that leads to his mouth … that leads to his kisses.

He catches me staring and raises an eyebrow and the corner of his mouth into a knowing smirk.

"Does it always take this long to make a phone call?" I ask, blushing and pretending I wasn't caught checking him out.

"If it's long distance, it does. How does it work in your time?"

But before I have time to explain that the only phone booths I've seen lately were on *Doctor Who*, a new voice comes on the line. "What party, please?"

"The last name is Phelps. Miss Ruby Phelps."

After a pause, she replies, "There is no Ruby Phelps. I have a George Phelps."

Will looks at me for confirmation. I have no idea what her father's name is but nod anyway.

"Yes, George Phelps, please."

"That will be ten cents," the operator says.

Will hands me the receiver and fishes in his pocket for change. He drops a dime into the phone.

"Connecting you now."

We hear more clicking and then other strange ringing noises, which sound nothing like phone calls of my time. Suddenly I'm nervous and excited to talk to Ruby.

"Hello?" a woman answers.

Will urges me to talk. I suppose having a young man call for Ruby might not be the best idea. I lean in to the mouthpiece. "Hello, may I speak to Ruby, please?"

There's a long pause. "Ruby is away at school." The woman says guardedly. I'm sure it's her horrible stepmother.

I look at Will and he frowns. What can I say to convince her to put Ruby on the line? "Actually, I'm a friend of Ruby's from school. I've been worried about her, and I just want to hear how she's doing. I promise it won't take more than a minute."

"Ruby is not at home. Don't call here again," the voice is flat and unyielding, and my heart breaks to know that Ruby was raised by this awful woman.

"Wait! If she's not at home, where is she?"

There's another pause before the irritated voice responds. "She's taking care of her aunt, who's fallen ill."

"Please tell her that Abbi called – " The line goes dead before I can finish. Will takes the receiver and hangs up. We open the door and stumble out of the cramped booth.

"Do you believe she went to care for an aunt?" he asks.

I shake my head. "I think that's code for 'we sent her away so she won't shame our family.'"

"This is awful. I wonder if Walter knows what's happening?"

Oh, Ruby, where are you?

* * *

Will and I are nearly inseparable. It's like he's always been in my life. Because we're in summer school, each taking two classes, there's always homework. Will is a voracious learner, and while part of me wants to blow school off since my time here is temporary anyway, the other part embraces sharing this everyday college experience with him. This is what I'm meant to be doing … just not in this century.

Most days we settle a blanket on the grassy hill near the observatory and open our books. Will, with a blade of grass between his teeth, will lose himself in chemistry or calculus. He usually has his leg pressed against mine or one hand finding its way to my hair, winding his fingers through it while reading. Neither one of us seems willing to break the connection.

Sunny afternoons are spent overlooking the lake or borrowing bikes from Hoofers and pedalling down the cinder path to Picnic Point. Sometimes we hike, other times we wear swimsuits under our clothes and hang out on the beach. My swimsuit is a one-piece periwinkle number made of wool. It's not the most stylish, but Will loves to see me in it.

On a particularly gorgeous June day, we lie in the warm sun after playing in the water. Will moves a chunk of damp hair from my shoulder and kisses the tattooed star on my hot skin.

That's all the hint I need. I nudge him onto his back and plant light kisses on his bronzed skin, letting his chest hair tickle my cheek. I lay my hand on his flat stomach, his muscles tightening at my touch. "Guys in my time would die for abs like yours."

He raises an eyebrow. "Why's that?"

"It's all about having a six pack."

"A what?"

"Like a six pack of beer bottles lined up in two rows." I lightly tap each of his ab muscles. "Guys work out like crazy to get muscles like these."

"Hmm. I can't imagine why they'd care what their stomachs look like, but maybe they should try the rowing team," he says with amusement. "What else do guys in your time do?"

"Well, some of them pierce their ears and wear earrings."

"Like the women of your time do?" He pulls back, appalled.

I giggle. "Sort of, but it's a masculine thing. Some guys shave their chest hair." I run my fingers up over the sprinkle of blond hairs on his chest. "And some only shave their faces once in a while so it always has scruff."

"Let me assure you, I don't care what men do in the future, I will not be wearing earrings or shaving my chest. You're woman enough for me." He slips his arm around my waist and pulls me into a kiss.

* * *

One Saturday night, we catch a Marx Brothers movie called *Animal Crackers* at the Orpheum on State Street. It's a beautiful grand theatre with ornate decor. I didn't get a chance to see this place in my time and wonder if it still exists.

"Hey, look, there's a photo booth." A large box with a curtain and sign that says PHOTOMATON stands in the lobby. I drag Will over.

He examines the curtained box with fascination.

"Would you like your photo taken?" an attendant asks.

"I reckon we would. How does it work?" Will asks.

"Sir, you and your lady step inside and pose three different times. I'll capture your image and have it developed for you in a matter of minutes."

Will turns to me with an eager smile. "That sounds swell." He hands the attendant a few coins.

Inside we squish side by side on the small bench and give our biggest smiles. A flash pops brightly and we see stars. For the second picture, Will slides his arm around my waist and kisses me. For the last one, he tickles my side and we're laughing as the flash goes off.

When the attendant hands us our strip of pictures, we lean our heads together to see our images. I realize this is the picture that I found in the tobacco tin in 1948. We look like normal, happy college students. An outsider would never suspect we are time travellers.

The attendant cuts them apart so we can each have one.

"Which ones do you want?" Will asks.

I stare at the one of us right after he kissed me and realize with a jolt that we're looking at each other with undeniable love. I choose that one.

"I'll take the one of you laughing, because that's how I'll always remember you." He holds up the photo.

My smile disappears. He's already thinking of when we'll be apart.

"Oh, Abbi," he says. "I shouldn't have said that."

"No worries." I pretend it doesn't bother me.

After a moment he asks, "What about this one?" and holds up the third picture.

"You keep it." I know for a fact that he'll put it in the tobacco tin, because I saw it there. But I want to make sure that on this twisted journey, we leave a few things up to free will.

"Are you sure? Then you'll only have one and I'll have two."

"This is all I need." I kiss his cheek.

* * *

One night I walk into the room after changing in the bathroom to find Will on his stomach, studying something on the headboard.

"What are you doing?" I ask, locking the door behind me.

He turns around with a small jackknife in his hand and a guilty expression on his face.

"What?" I step closer to see what he's hiding. The window is open, and a warm breeze flutters the curtains.

"I thought I should leave a sign that we were here, for posterity."

There on the headboard he's carved the hands of a clock. I trace my finger over the fresh carving. "It was you!"

"What do you mean?"

"When I started school, I noticed this carving. It was worn down, but it was there." I sit next to him and let out a sigh. "It lasts more than eighty years." How have I not noticed that it was missing since I arrived in this time?

"Golly, that's a very old headboard by then. Do you mind that I did it?"

Leaning over, I give him a quick kiss. "I *love* that you did it."

He rolls over and sits up. "Abbi, it's such a beautiful night. It would be a shame to waste it cooped up in here."

"What did you have in mind?" I ask as I hang the day's dress back on its hanger.

"Let's go out on the roof and look at the stars."

I pull Grandma's quilt off the bed, and we sneak down the hallway, Will wearing the quilt over his head like a huge scarf, in case one of the girls makes a midnight bathroom run. Luckily we encounter no one as we make our way through the hall and fourth-floor study room. We unlock the latch to the door leading onto the flat roof and burst out laughing at our successful mission. I spread Grandma's quilt on the smooth surface, and we stretch out side by side to take in the night sky. The air is balmy, and the sky looks as if someone took a handful of glitter and tossed it into the night. The moon is nearly full, but still low in the east.

"The stars are incredible," I whisper, silently cursing the light pollution of my time that will dim these stars.

Will points out constellations I never learned. My knowledge only goes as far as the Big Dipper and Little Dipper. As he talks, I turn to gaze at him instead of the stars, never wanting this night to end.

I touch his arm. "I have a favour to ask."

He turns to me, his eyes sparkling in the moonlight. "Anything."

"When you see me again, in 1961, I don't want you to tell me about our time together."

Will props himself onto his elbow and takes my hand. "Why?"

"I've been thinking a lot about it. If I would have arrived knowing everything that happens, it might not have happened this way. I might have somehow messed things up, and this is too important to risk."

He caresses my cheek with his thumb. "Not even when we meet, or how?" he asks.

"Not even that," I say, shaking my head firmly. As hard as it is, I somehow feel this is how it needs to go. I cup his face with my hand. Will clutches it and brings my palm to his lips. I don't know how I'm going to survive being separated.

"Do you know how difficult it'll be not to tell you about our time together and what you mean to me?" he asks, serious now. "And when I see you again, all I'll want to do is hold you and pick up where we left off."

Leaning forward, I kiss his lips softly. "I know."

"So you're saying you think we can change what already happened? I mean, for you this already happened, but for me it hasn't. So I could botch it up if I were to tell you everything when I see you in the sixties?" he asks.

"That's what scares me. Is knowing the future or past helpful, or will it make us do things we wouldn't have otherwise done? And will that change the outcome? I don't want to risk it. That's what Professor Smith warned about."

"And, is the outcome of our futures already set? Or is it still to be determined?"

I roll onto my back and look again at the vast night sky, feeling like a meaningless speck in the scope of the universe. "That is the pretzel of our situation."

"It kills me to know that you'll be leaving." I hear the anxiety in his voice.

I face him. "Or maybe it's you who leaves me."

Will shakes his head and sighs. "Abbi, you are everything to me."

He kisses me, then says, "If this were just you and me, with no Carillon bells chiming, and no time travelling, I'd declare myself yours forever and always." He gazes at me so intently, my heart skips a beat. How could I be so lucky?

"I love you, Will."

"I know." He grins, and I laugh. "I love you too, and I've never been happier in my life than these past months with you."

I nod, because I feel exactly the same.

"And I'll carry this feeling through whatever time or troubles I must endure ahead. I'll always hold on to our love."

His words offer me hope for the future, but they also scare me. Each day I suspect I'm closer to leaving Will, and there's no reason to hope I'll be going home. My stomach clenches. I can't lose him.

Will sees my distress. "Come here." He opens his arms and I snuggle in. The touch of his body, his strength and his promise chase away my worries.

He brushes his jaw against my cheek but doesn't kiss me. His breath warms my skin. I close my eyes and graze my lips against his neck. His breathing changes and he's less reserved than before. He trails his hand from my hip, across my stomach until he cups my breast.

He nuzzles my neck and whispers, "There's nothing to worry about. Tonight there's only you and me."

I pull his mouth to mine, and we lose ourselves in long kisses that vow we will survive whatever time may bring.

After so many nights spent holding back, we lie under the blanket of stars, and do what we promised we never would.

CHAPTER 21

I jerk awake, startled from a dark dream. Will is sprawled next to me in bed. I breathe a sigh of relief and snuggle closer.

His eyes open and he smiles at me in his adorable way. I push his hair back to see him better. He holds my hand to his face and kisses it. I take a mental snapshot. I like to think of him this way. Relaxed. Happy. Mine.

"I love you, Will."

"I love you too." He nuzzles his nose against mine.

My smile falters.

He pulls back. "Abbi, is something wrong?"

"I don't know. Something is off and I'm not sure what."

"Did you have a bad dream?"

"Yeah, but I can't remember it." I get up, pull a brush through my hair and try to shake off the dark vibe.

"Is it because of last night?" he says with concern.

"God, no! Last night was perfect. I wouldn't change a thing. I don't know what it is."

He comes up behind me and puts his hands on my shoulders. "Promise you'll let me know if you feel worse."

I reach for his hand and give it a squeeze and force a reassuring smile. "I promise."

I go through the motions of the day, but something is different. I don't know what exactly it is, a sixth sense, a premonition, but something is changing.

In the late afternoon, I wait on the hillside and watch the rowing boats far in the distance, skimming across the lake like skating water beetles. I'm mesmerized by the delicate grace with which they move, all created from brute strength and perfect coordination. If one person is slightly out of rhythm, it upsets the flow of the whole team. Sort of like time.

Something in the universe has been out of sync and sending each of us hurtling through time, and we've been gaming the system, doing everything we can to cheat the clock from tearing us apart. But as I sit here with the Carillon Tower standing watch in the distance, I feel a rift like never before, as if there's pressure along the fault line of time, and it's building.

I try to imagine finding my way without Will, and I can't. He's been by my side practically every day and night since I arrived here months ago.

By the time the rowing boats return to the boathouse, I can barely keep from calling out to Will as the other teams pull up to the dock. Instead, I wait for the Wisconsin team, but they let the others go before them. When it's finally their turn to approach the pier, the visiting teams applaud the Badgers' victory.

There are cheers all around, and I find Will in his spot in the third seat, looking handsome, exuberant and worn out from the race. He laughs with his teammates. The guys raise their fists in the air in a cheer. I fight not to run to him. I wait as they shake hands with the other teams.

Will spots me, waves and pushes through the crowd of athletes to reach me.

"You're a sight for sore eyes." He kisses me quick, slides his arm around me and leads me away from the boathouse and the crush of people.

"Come here." He enfolds me in his arms and I press myself to his chest, strong and solid, his rowing uniform still damp from the spray of water during the race. He tilts my face up and I lift my eyes to his, so blue in the bright day. His nose and cheeks are sun-kissed.

"I love you, Abbi." He kisses me deeply, reminding me of our magical night on the roof, not that I'd easily forget. My heart clenches and I'm overwhelmed with emotion. I gaze at him, unable to avoid this sense of foreboding.

"Hey, what's the matter?"

I force a smile. "Nothing. Just still feeling kind of off."

He squeezes my hand. "We can't have that." He cups my hands in his and gazes into my troubled eyes.

I draw a deep breath and try to get a hold of myself. There's nothing I can do to explain this feeling. I don't want the poor guy to worry, so I say, "It's nothing. I'm just being silly."

"And that's okay. If you don't mind waiting while I finish up with the team, I'll walk you back."

"I'd like that."

I return to the boathouse with him and wait on the bank nearby as he works with his teammates on the boat. The guys are still happy about their victory, patting each other on the back. Will looks over often, checking on me.

When the work is done, he walks towards me with a few of the guys and waves them off. The guys see me sitting there with the top buttons of my blouse undone, my sleeves rolled up and my long hair flying in the breeze. I may wear the clothing of the time, but with a twenty-first century flair. I must look like a loose woman to them.

"Are you going to leave your girl long enough to join us at Eddie's stag party tonight?" one says.

"Yes, I'll come by for a bit, but trust me, fellas, Abbi isn't just any girl," he replies with a devilish grin and winks at me. "She's *the* girl." I feel warm and happy inside but bite back a proud smile, not wanting his rowdy teammates to see me blush.

The guys give teasing hoots and hollers as they wander down the path towards the dorms.

Will holds out his hand and helps me up from the grass. "Will you be okay if I go?"

I realize then, he'd cancel everything if I asked him to. "Absolutely, as long as you'll still be back tonight."

"Yes, of course," he says, then adds with a whisper into my ear, "A team of wild horses couldn't keep me away." He slides his arm around me and we walk, our steps in perfect sync.

"Have a great time, but don't get too crazy," I tease Will, squeezing his waist as we walk. It's 1930. How much trouble can a bunch of guys possibly get into?

* * *

On the way back to my room after dinner, I peek into my mailbox, expecting to see its hollow interior as usual. But this time, when I open it, I'm shocked to find a thin, pale blue envelope. I snatch it out and look at the return address.

"Ruby!"

Hugging the letter to my chest, I race back to my room and hop onto my bed to tear it open. Meticulous, graceful cursive loops cover the page.

Dear Abbi,

I hope this letter finds you well. You have probably left school by now, but it is my hope that your mail is forwarded.

My apologies for not having written sooner, but I wasn't permitted outside communications while at the convent. Yes, I said convent. My loathsome stepmother delivered me directly to a convent in Chicago that takes in girls like me.

As terrible as it sounds, most of the sisters were kind. The difficult part was not being able to reach Walter. Twice I tried to mail a letter to him, but the Mother Superior found out, which meant more penance time for me.

My son was born July 17th. He was the most beautiful sight I've ever seen. I was only allowed to hold him for a few minutes, but I'll cherish that time for the rest of my days. I begged the nuns to let me keep him, but they insisted that a child created in sin would forever carry a stain, and that I wasn't allowed to keep him under any circumstance. I wept when they took him away and have not stopped crying since.

The attending physician said that the baby will be placed in an orphanage until he's adopted, but he did allow me to name him. And so my son is named for his father, Walter Colton Smith.

I pray a loving family finds him soon and that he has a happier childhood than I had. Perhaps one day I'll be able to find him, or him me. But I suppose that won't be possible as his new parents will likely change his name.

I am heartbroken.

Walter's father has been slow in his recovery, but he is finally back on his feet. Walter is coming to fetch me in a few days, and we plan to be married regardless of what our parents say. But our lives will always have a void for the son we lost.

My apologies for this long communication, but I've had no one with whom to share my sorrows. Thank you for your kind friendship – I'll never forget it. I hope that you and Will finally had your date. He seems like a lovely chap.

Wishing you the best,

Ruby

I stare at the letter, torn between anger at the cruelty of her child being taken away and joy at the realization of what this means – *Grandma, this is your missing brother!* I want to shout.

I open the hatbox and pull out the picture of Grandma and her parents, Ruby and Walter. Then I dig further down and find the picture of the nun. I study the delicate features and sweet expression and realize the nun was Ruby all along, but with the habit and sad expression, she looked so different.

This is my family. I pick up the letter and read it again, stopping where she wrote the name of the baby. Walter Colton Smith. Why does this seem familiar?

I search my brain. Walter Colton Smith? I pace my room, repeating it over and over in my head. Smith is such a common name, but the only other Smith I can think of is ... the professor.

I freeze. He went by Smitty. That couldn't have been his real first name, though. It must be a nickname for

Smith. And then I recall the directory in Sterling Hall – WC Smith, and on the physics library plaque – WC Smith.

What the? I calculate the professor's age based on when I met him his freshman year. He definitely could have been born in 1930. And didn't he tell me, one of the first times we met, that he was raised in an orphanage, in Chicago?

Oh my God. Not only have I discovered Ruby's baby – but I know him! Smitty is Grandma's brother. I sink onto the edge of my bed in shock. And I introduced them that day in the lobby, right after Ruby's funeral.

I squeal and hug the letter. The professor, who has been with me from the start, is … he's … what to me? Not uncle, but great-uncle. I picture the first time I saw him with his kind, patient eyes, so determined to help me, and how he looked younger each time until he was the sweet and gawky freshman who seemed lost in the world.

And all that time, he was my family. Why couldn't we have known when I was with him? He would have loved it. I would have loved it!

I've finally solved the mystery of the missing baby. But now what do I do about it?

CHAPTER 22

The next few hours are torture as I pace my room waiting for Will. I think I've cracked the biggest mystery of my life, and he isn't here to share it with.

I trace the outline of Will's carving on the headboard. Is he also part of my destiny? It can't possibly be a coincidence that we found each other not once, but twice.

Starting at eleven o'clock, I look out of my bedroom window every few minutes in search of him, but he doesn't appear. By midnight, I'm tired. I'm not used to staying awake by myself any more. I struggle to stay alert as the ticking of the clock sounds like a metronome, threatening to lull me to sleep.

After checking the clock again, I tiptoe downstairs and open the back door to see if maybe he's waiting, but he's not. An uneasy dread creeps in. Something is wrong.

At one a.m. I'm sitting with my back against the cool wall to stay awake like I used to do, when I hear it. Not one, but a spray of pebbles hits my window like a hailstorm. I jump up to look out and see Will whipping another handful and hollering my name. I wave frantically for him to quieten down, but he yells again.

He's drunk! Laughing in relief, I rush down the back stairs and push the door open. Will is staring up at my window and yelling, "Abbi, I'm here!"

"Will!" I hiss frantically. "Get over here."

He spots me, drops the other pebbles and stumbles forward. "Abbi, I thought you forgot me," he slurs. His hair is messed up, and his shirt is half untucked as if he's been wrestling.

"You have a good time tonight?" I giggle. I've never seen Will drunk before.

"It was smashing!" he says loudly and sways on his feet.

"Shh. Come inside." I wave him over while holding the door open so we don't get locked out.

Will stumbles closer. "You're so beautiful. I love you."

"I love you too. Now come on, let's get you upstairs."

I reach for Will, but before I can grab his arm to haul him inside, someone says, "You, there. What's going on?"

Shit. It's a campus police officer.

Will makes to rush inside but trips on the step and falls to the concrete.

The officer approaches with a stern frown, looking all business.

"It's okay, officer. He's my boyfriend," I explain as Will tries to figure out how he ended up on the ground.

"It's well after curfew, girlie. Time for your boyfriend to go home."

"Will, get up," I beg. He crawls to his feet and straightens his torn dusty jacket.

I turn my pleading eyes on the stern-faced man. "Officer, he's had a little too much to drink. Do you think it would be okay, just this once, if I let him sleep it off here?"

The officer looks at me as if I've sprouted horns. "Absolutely not. That would be highly inappropriate, not to mention against university conduct rules."

Time to try another tactic. "Will, why don't you get back to your dorm, and I'll see you in the morning?" I nod and wink at him, hoping he'll get my drift that I want him to come back in a few minutes.

"I don't want to go to my dorm. I want to stay with you like I always – "

I clap my hand over Will's mouth and shrug at the officer as if Will is talking nonsense.

He's not amused. "Listen, son. It's time to say goodnight to the young lady. I'm sure she'll be here for you to woo again in the morning."

"Now see here, Mr. Officer," Will slurs, but I stop him again, before he makes things worse.

"It's okay," I say to Will. "Go back to your dorm. I'll see you later. Do you understand?"

He puts his forehead to mine and gazes at me with droopy eyes. "But, Abbi..."

Another officer appears from the shadows. Now I'm really worried. I need Will to get the hint.

"Come along, young man. Where's your dormitory? I'll walk you back." The first officer takes Will by the upper arm and tries to manoeuvre him away from the door I'm propping open.

Will tries to shrug him off, but the officer won't release him. "Let. Me. Go," Will says with a stubborn set to his jaw. Then out of nowhere, he jerks away, swings, and clocks the police officer with a right hook.

"Will, no!" I scream.

The other officer reacts and tackles Will, sending them both to the ground. The first officer joins the other and they pin him. "Boy, you just earned yourself a night in the slammer."

Will is pulled to his feet, with his hands secured behind his back. The reality of what he's done must be sinking in, because he mumbles, "Please, officer. I'm sorry. I'll behave. I promise."

"That's right. A few hours in the clink will give you a proper attitude adjustment."

Will looks at me in horror. "I'm so sorry," he moans.

"Please, let him go. He didn't mean it," I plead to the first officer, who's rubbing his sore jaw.

"Miss, I think you ought to reconsider the company you keep. Now get yourself back inside. You shouldn't be cavorting with men like this."

"Then I'm coming with him," I say even though I'm wearing Will's baggy shorts and T-shirt.

"What is it you don't understand about curfew on this campus? You will not be accompanying us, nor will you be leaving this dormitory before morning. If you'd like me to wake up the head resident, I'd be happy to do so."

I back off, defeated. "No, sir."

They each grab Will by an arm and haul him away.

"Will, don't go to sleep! Promise me!" I call out desperately.

He looks back at me in total despair, breaking my heart. "I'm sorry, Abbi!" And with that he's dragged up the hill and out of sight.

I trudge up the back stairwell and let myself into my

room. Tonight will be the first night I've spent alone in many weeks. I'm not prepared for this. And there's a painful ache in my heart as I resume my position against the cool wall and vow to stay awake.

CHAPTER 23

Bright sunlight streams across my face and the soft thump of distant country music coaxes me from the depths of slumber. I can't even open my eyes as my body slowly wakens, as if from a long hibernation or a coma. It's as if I've been sleeping like the dead. Gradually, bit by bit, I gain consciousness. My fingers caress the bumpy stitches of Grandma's quilt, and then I realize I'm hearing a Carrie Underwood song. Something about that strikes me as wrong.

I think of Will and my eyes spring open. I roll over and see Jada asleep with her Beyoncé poster over her bed.

"No!" I cry. This can't be happening.

Jada stirs. "What's wrong?"

Nothing. Everything. "Just a dream, never mind." I sit up, frantic, it's hard to breathe. This is my room as it was the day I first travelled. My mobile phone is on the bedside table, my laptop on the desk and my cheery matching storage bins are lined neatly on the bookcase.

I check out the headboard where Will carved the hands of a clock only days ago. The carving is worn down and faded from time. Oh, God, what have I done?

"What day is it?" I ask, my heart breaking. I've lost Will.

"Saturday," Jada mumbles still half asleep.

But what Saturday? How much time has passed? "No, what's the calendar date?"

"Um, September fourth?"

I've woken up the day after the bonfire, as if nothing happened. Did I dream everything?

That can't be possible. It was too real. It feels like a punch in the gut. I know it happened. All of it – Grandma, the professor, Ruby, Will – but what proof do I have?

I scan the room in a panic, searching for any evidence I travelled. Then I realize I'm still wearing Will's T-shirt and shorts. I nearly cry in relief and hug myself. I didn't imagine it. It was real. And yet, I've abandoned Will. I left him back in 1930. How could I have let that happen? My heart clenches. I've lost him. I close my eyes to block out the present.

I picture him searching for me the next morning, but finding me gone. *Oh, Will, I'm so sorry.*

Opening my eyes to reality, I look out of the window to where the Carillon Tower used to rise above the trees. My view of it is once again completely blocked by the barren, grey concrete walls of the Social Sciences Building.

This is what I wanted for so long, to return home, but now that I'm here without Will, I feel as if I left part of myself in the past. I don't just want my time any more. I want Will too.

I should have left a note in case this happened, but I didn't. I'm a fool. I just lost the most important person in my life. And then I remember that while I didn't leave him a note, maybe he's left one for me, letting me know what's happened to him?

Digging through my wardrobe, I scramble to pull on shorts, a T-shirt and my familiar old running shoes. After a quick glance in the mirror, I pull a brush through my hair a few times, grab my macramé bag and head out.

"Where are you going?" Jada mumbles when the door opens.

"For a walk. Go back to sleep."

I run the whole way, ignoring the cramp in my side. When I spot the smaller trail that leads to Will's treasure, I pause to catch my breath and say a silent prayer that I will find a new message.

After three more turns, the peaceful beauty of the woods is disrupted by orange tape marking off an area around Will's fallen tree. The decaying willow is now a decomposed mound on the forest floor. Three people are excavating inside the area.

I rush forward to confront the trespassers. The rock that covered Will's treasure has been rolled outside the cordoned-off area. Where his treasure should be is a deep empty hole. I'm gutted.

"What are you doing?" I bark, startling the people digging. They stare at me as if I'm the one intruding. I duck under the tape and come closer, seeing cameras, notebooks and computers in the area.

"Whoa!" A short guy with dirty hands stands. "Step out of the research area."

"What did you do with the tobacco tin?" I search the area hoping to find it on the ground.

He raises an eyebrow and glances at his cohorts.

"Where is it? It doesn't belong to you!"

"It belongs to the anthropology department."

"No, it doesn't. You need to put it back." My hands clench at my sides. "Someone buried it there for a reason."

The researcher wipes his hands on his work shorts. "The tin dates back to the 1920s. I'm sure that whoever buried it is long dead."

His words stab me in the heart. I must go pale, because now all three of them are staring at me.

He takes a step closer. "What do you know about the tin?"

I hold my ground. What can I say? *Everything?* I know the guy who buried it is somewhere out there, lost in time. I know that the pictures in it are of his family – and of me. I know Will left bank account numbers that no one should have access to except him. I put my hand to my forehead. Oh, God, what will happen if his things get into the wrong hands?

But I can't say any of those things. "Did you ever think maybe it's a legacy that's lasted decades? That there are people who know about it and use it as a means of communication? It doesn't belong to you."

Mr. Bossy narrows his eyes. "How do you know that?"

Now I take a step back. I can't say more. I just want it back.

The female researcher with them keeps staring at me, then the other guy stands and speaks up. "She's probably on the newspaper staff and saw pictures of all of those letters."

There are pictures? And how many letters did they find? It's not the same as holding Will's notes in my hand, but it may still be a way for me to see if he left any new messages.

The girl starts paging through a binder. "Hey, guys. Don't you think she looks a lot like the girl in one of the photos?" She holds up a page with an enlarged photocopy of the snapshot Will and I posed for in the photo booth.

Their faces screw up as they look at the picture and back to me.

"What's your name?" the first guy asks.

I panic. How would I ever explain? I duck under the ribbon and run.

"Wait! What do you know about the tin?" the girl asks.

I take off back down the trail. They've stolen Will's treasure. I'm out of breath, but not from running. The tin won't be there if he lands in this time or later. He'll need it. How can I help him?

On the long walk back, I try to come up with a plan. I need to look at those letters. Would someone on the newspaper staff let me see them? Who could help me? And then I think of Professor Smith.

Oh my God, I have to find out if he's alive. I bypass Liz Waters and go straight to Sterling Hall, which stands in all its glory and without the slightest sign of the horrible blast.

Inside I check the building directory. There is no WC Smith. I go through all the names twice more to make sure I haven't missed him. But of course he isn't there. Even if he survived the bombing, if he's alive today, he'd be an old man.

Deflated, I look around the empty hall. I've lost both

Will and the professor. I can't go back, but there are no answers here either.

As I'm heading out of the door, I see a newspaper rack filled with issues of the *Badger Herald*. The headline reads: BURIED TREASURE OR MODERN-DAY HOAX?

There's a large photo on the front page showing many of the things from Will's tin – the silver dollars, his father's pocket watch and a pile of the letters splayed out. I squint but can't read them.

The article continues inside. I'm relieved to see close-ups of the objects, including pictures of his family and the one of us. Tears brim in my eyes, and I hug the paper. Now at least I have a piece of him.

I step outside and sit on a ledge to spread the paper open. There is a close-up of Will's first letter to me, but not the others. I scan the article and find that they've transcribed some of them. I clench my jaw in frustration when I see our private words printed for all to see.

My dear Abbi,

I just saw you in 1961. It was glorious and made the waiting worthwhile, but then we quarreled, and you were gone.

My life is now empty. I go through the motions each day, but without you, none of it matters. My worry for your safety consumes me.

I'm so sorry about that night of the stag party. I am miserable with remorse and blame myself. If only I could have you back, I'd never let you slip away again. The future is frightening and uncertain with no promise of finding you. If ever you read this, and I pray you do, know my love for you is timeless.

Affectionately yours,

Will

I wipe my eyes, missing him desperately. Why has life been so cruel? Will is the best thing that's ever happened to me, and now he's gone. There's a deep chasm in my heart that will never heal. It was horrible to lose Grandma, but she had lived a good, long life. Will was young and full of potential ... and he was my soulmate. I scan the rest of the article and see one more letter.

Dear Abbi,

I saw you at Headliners in 1983. I was there! When that behemoth forced his kiss on you, I dragged him away and accidentally started a brawl. You looked around when I hollered your name, but I couldn't reach you. By the time the campus police released me, the next day had

dawned and you were gone. I can't believe you slipped

through my fingers.

I pray each day to find my way back to you.

Eternally yours,

Will

That was him! I think back to that night when Cheap Trick was playing. Will was the unknown guy trying to protect me! If only I had known then what I know now, I would have jumped into the brawl to reach him and never let him go. I trace my hands over his signature. We were so close and yet so far. *How will I find you now?*

I tuck the newspaper in my bag, dejected, and head back to Liz Waters. This whole ordeal has been exhausting. I have fewer answers and more questions than ever.

When I get to my room, I find Jada gone and a note on my pillow.

A cute guy was here looking for you! He wants you to

call him right away. He seemed desperate to talk to you.

Jada

A phone number is listed at the bottom.
Oh my God! Will!

I scramble for my phone and discover my battery is dead. "You have got to be kidding me!"

I dig in the drawer for my charger and plug it in, drumming my fingers till I see the first sign of life. The second it powers up, I madly tap out the phone number. It rings three times and just as I fear it's going to voicemail, a husky male voice answers, "Hey, it took you long enough."

My heart drops. This isn't Will. "Excuse me. Who is this?" I ask at a total loss.

"Colton. This *is* Abbi isn't it?"

I was positive it would be Will, but it's just Colton, the guy who walked me back from Picnic Point that night so long ago. Except to him, I suppose it would only be last night. Crazy.

"Yeah, how ya doing?" I try not to sound disappointed.

"Good, but I have a problem. This is going to sound really bizarre, so bear with me."

"My life is bizarre – go ahead." I plop down on my bed and notice Grandma's birth certificate and the picture of the two of us that slipped off my bed that first night. I pick them up and trace my finger around the tattered edges.

"I know it's really soon to cash in, but I sort of need a favour."

"Huh?"

"You know, the drunk guy I helped you kick to the curb … and you said you owed me… ?"

"Oh yeah," I say, feeling as if it was a long-ago dream.

"Okay, so there's this big Badger party my parents host every year for our entire family, and this morning my dad called and said I can't come without a date."

"That's the oddest thing I've ever heard. Why would they care if you brought a date?"

"I know, totally weird, but I was talking to my dad this morning and just happened to mention that I met a nice girl named Abbi last night, and he suddenly insisted that I bring you along. He said that I owed it to my mother to bring home a nice girl … for a change."

"Okay…" I'm trying to figure out how I got wrapped up in all of this, but I'm too exhausted to think straight about anything.

"Told you it was bizarre. But hey, you can help me make my mom happy and pay up your favour at the same time. Also I promise tons of awesome food!" Colton laughs. "And you know, when we talked yesterday you mentioned missing family, so, maybe it's fate."

My mind is spinning. I'm trying to figure out what happened to Will, find out if the professor is still alive and desperate to call my mom and hear her voice. But why did Colton use that word – fate? He's the last person I saw before I travelled, and he's practically the first person I've spoken to since I've been back. Could there be a clue here? But going to a party is about the last thing I want to do.

"I don't know," I say. I'm hedging. I don't want to leave campus, but something in his voice sways me. "If I were to say yes, where exactly are we going, and when would you pick me up?"

"You're the best! We're only going to Middleton, which is about fifteen minutes away. I'll pick you up in forty-five."

"I haven't even showered yet. I should say no and let

you abduct some girl off the street instead."

"Nice try." He laughs, and I remember what a nice guy he is. "Okay, I'll let you go so you can get ready. I'll be out front waiting. Thanks!" He hangs up before I can argue.

Crud. This is not how I planned to spend my day. I'm not even sure why I agreed. I could return that favour another time... but the fact that he mentioned fate caught my attention.

Forty-six minutes later, with my hair still wet, I grab the macramé bag that played ride-along during much of my travels, and head out. Colton is waiting, looking exactly as I remembered. Tall with brown eyes and a friendly smile that puts me at ease. It's a relief to see a familiar face.

"Worried I wasn't going to show?" I grin.

"No way. Girls never turn me down." He smirks as we head to a car at the curb.

"So then why'd you have to cash in a favour just to find a date?" I ask, poking his arm.

"You got me there," he says playfully.

I'm not much company on the ride over. Colton keeps up a steady stream of chatter and doesn't seem to notice my lack of conversation. He explains that the party is a big tradition in his family and that his parents usually host it, but this year his grandpa wanted to host it at his house. Colton pulls up in front of a large Victorian-style house with a wrap-around porch and hydrangea bushes bursting with colour. Beyond the house, the sun shimmers off Lake Mendota. Cars are parked up and down the street, the Badger fight song blares from speakers and the smell of barbecue fills the air. A handful of adults mill around on the porch, and a bunch of kids and teenagers play ladder golf in the garden.

"You *do* have a huge family," I say. I'm instantly intimidated. Leaving campus suddenly feels like a huge mistake. I should be at the newspaper demanding my letters back, or at the library trying to find out what happened to Professor Smith.

"They won't bite," Colton says. "My dad is the oldest of six. Everyone in our family tends to have a lot of kids."

"Is it just your grandparents in this big old house?"

"Yup. Gramps said he could never leave, that the only way he would move out was cold and in a box."

"He sounds like a live one." I say, thinking of my own feisty Grandma.

Colton leads the way through a group all wearing various styles of UW Badger red and white. I take a breath and brace myself for the onslaught of new people I'm about to meet.

"Tell me again why I agreed to this?"

"Because you owe me for rescuing you from that drooling bloodhound, Mitch," he says. "How could you forget?"

"Oh yeah, that." I laugh. My heart belongs to Will, but it's impossible not to like Colton as a friend. I realize that if I'd ever had a brother, I'd want him to be something like Colton.

He opens the screen door. I take a deep breath and enter. The energy inside is as boisterous as outside, with TVs tuned at top volume to the pre-game show and people laughing and talking even louder. Colton waves hello and whisks me down a wide hallway into a kitchen buzzing with more people, a huge punch bowl and platters of food.

"Colton, you made it." An elderly woman with salt and pepper hair steps forward and hugs him. "And this must be your friend," she says, looking at me with such affection that she could almost be my own grandma.

"Abbi, this is my grandma. Grandma, Abbi."

"Welcome to the madhouse." She hugs me as if I'm family. Colton smiles as I hug her back in surprise. "And this is Colton's mother, Joann."

A middle-aged woman with light-brown hair styled in a bob smiles and holds out a clear tumbler filled with a red beverage. "Hi, Abbi. Have some punch."

"Thank you. It's nice to meet you both." I accept the glass, glad to have something to hold on to.

"Drink slowly. It's my dad's recipe, and it has a killer 'punch'," Colton warns in my ear.

I take a sip and nearly choke. "Wow. You weren't kidding."

He sniggers.

"Did I hear Colton?" A man appears and I know immediately by his looks that he must be Colton's dad, but he reminds me of someone else too.

"Here and accounted for with a girl named Abbi from Liz Waters, exactly as requested. Abbi, this is my dad, Wally."

I turn to Colton in confusion. What's going on here? But before I can ask, his dad steps forward.

"It's nice to meet you, Abbi. I never thought this day would come." Wally shakes my hand vigorously.

"So, Dad, you going to tell me what this last-minute mystery about bringing Abbi is all about?"

"Yes, but first there's someone I need Abbi to meet. Please follow me." He beams with excitement.

Colton looks as confused as I am and shrugs. We follow his dad through a dining room, a living room and into a family room with thick carpeting, cosy sofas and French doors.

Something extremely odd is happening here, and I feel I'm trying to make sense of a nonsensical dream.

And then I spot an elderly man with snowy white hair and thick glasses sitting in a worn leather recliner. He peers up as we enter, and his brown eyes settle on me. Recognition flashes in his face.

I stagger back, bumping into Colton. My hands are shaking, I push my punch into his hands, hoping he takes the glass before I drop it.

Colton's dad speaks to the man. "Dad, is this the girl you've been waiting for?"

"Abbi." The old man's smile beams across the room and tears sparkle in his eyes.

I stumble forward and kneel at his side. Tears spring to my eyes too. He reaches for my trembling hand.

"Professor, you didn't die." I whisper, struggling to find my voice. Tears roll freely down my cheeks now, and I don't care.

"Dad, what's going on?" Colton asks, utterly confused.

His father shushes him. "It's okay," he says.

The professor's weary eyes never leave my face. "You warned me about that bombing, and I never forgot." His eyes are faded and crinkled with crow's feet but still shine with the level-headed stability that helped me at my darkest times.

I begin to weep in earnest and all my pent-up emotions of fear and loneliness pour out. He leans forward in his recliner and pats my back with his bony hand. It's as if the professor and I are the only ones in the room.

"It's all right, Abbi. You made it home."

"I was so scared." My voice hitches as I try to stop crying. "I never thought I'd be able to come back."

Professor Smith gazes at me with sombre relief. "You're safe now. No need for tears." He grips my hand as if he too barely believes I'm here. But I can't stop. I'm so relieved, and it's as if all my anxiety and stress flow out at once.

"Abbi, are you okay?" Colton kneels next to me, clearly wondering what the hell is going on.

"Yes. No. I don't know." I smile, taking the tissue he's holding out for me.

Colton looks to his grandfather. "Gramps?"

"It's a long story, Colton. Give them some time," Wally says.

The professor turns to his grandson. "Colton, you have no idea how happy you've made me. Abbi and I met a very long time ago." He pats my hand and I smile back. Colton is still as confused as ever but sits on the floor next to us as the professor begins.

"The first time she and I met, I was a frightened boy of seventeen starting college."

"Gramps? That's not possible…" Colton interrupts.

"Do you want to hear this or not, Colton?" the old man chides.

Colton looks to his dad as if to say his grandfather's gone bonkers, but his dad gestures for him to listen. "Okay, okay, go ahead," Colton says, casting me an uneasy look.

"Mom, why don't you sit down, so you can hear this too?" Colton's father suggests to his elderly mother.

Mrs. Smith takes a seat in the recliner next to the professor's with a spry energy that belies her age. "I've known this story for more than fifty years. I finally get to witness it first-hand."

The professor continues. "You see, Colton, Abbi was so kind to me and helped me gain my confidence when I was thinking of quitting school."

"And that was the last time I saw you," I say softly, remembering that day.

"But I saw you again three years later," he says, then addresses Colton. "That's when Abbi told me this ridiculous story that she travelled through time."

Colton looks at me with disbelief, as if I've been scamming his grandfather, but he holds his tongue.

"Of course, I didn't believe her, but Abbi was patient and eventually convinced me. I saw her several times over the years."

Someone yells "Game time!" from another room. Colton's mom closes the doors so we can have quiet, then takes a seat on the couch, soaking up the story.

The professor takes a drink from his glass and clears his throat. "It was during that time that I began work on my theories for time travel. I don't think I would have accomplished what I did in my career if I hadn't met you along the way. You believed in me before I believed in myself." He gives my hand a gentle squeeze.

"I was just a scared girl who needed a friend. You were always destined for greatness."

"And I was a lost young man with no direction and no family. The last time I saw Abbi was in my lecture hall in 1970. It's thanks to her that I didn't go to Sterling Hall the night of the bombing that August."

"Professor…" I say. As much as I want to rehash the whole story, I have to tell him who he is. "I have to ask you something. What do your initials WC stand for?"

He looks at me oddly, his brow creased.

Colton answers. "W is for Walter and C for Colton. All three of us are named Walter Colton Smith. I'm the third. Why?"

I sigh and smile wide with such relief. "I think you are the fourth."

"What?" the professor gasps. "Why do you say that?"

"You know how I was with my grandmother in 1951?"

He nods slowly, recalling the scene.

"If you recall, the note Grandma wrote that I received with the hatbox asked me to finish what I had promised. You see, she wanted me to help find the baby. She discovered that her mother – Ruby – had a baby before she was married. And now that I think of it, maybe that's what got this whole thing started. I think that near the end of Grandma's life, she realized that I had somehow, impossibly, been her roommate at Liz Waters."

I glance at Colton and the others in the room. They are silent, totally confused, but I can't stop to explain everything now.

The professor nods, hanging on my words.

"Soon after, I travelled to 1930."

"To Will."

I'm hit with a pang of sadness at losing him, but I need the professor to hear the rest of my story. I take a breath. "To Will, and also to Ruby, my great-grandmother."

"This is impossible," Colton says, getting frustrated and looking to his dad again to stop this nonsense, but his dad gives a simple shake of his head.

"I know it sounds crazy, but listen. Ruby was pregnant when I met her," I continue.

He stares at me.

"She was planning to marry the father, but her step-mother sent her to a convent to have the baby."

The professor goes still as a deer.

"The convent was in Chicago," I say softly.

The professor's wife takes his hand and says, "Abbi, what is it you're trying to tell us?"

"Ruby was dating, and later married … Wait! I think I put the letter here." I dig in my bag, filled with various things collected during my travels, and finally put my hands on it. "Ruby wrote to me in July of 1930." I unfold the letter and hand it to him. "See here, she was sent to the convent. And here, Ruby says her son was born July seventeenth, and she named him Walter Colton Smith … after his father."

There is an intake of breath from everyone in the room. The professor reads the letter and covers his mouth with a trembling hand to hide his emotion, but his eyes are brimming with tears. He hands the letter to his son, who quickly scans it.

"As soon as I read Ruby's letter, I finally put it together. Remember the picture of the nun we found in the hatbox? That was Ruby from her time at the convent. And your name is Walter Colton Smith, the same as my great-grandfather's, but I didn't know it was your name until that night."

"There were two other Walters at the orphanage, so Smitty was easier," he says, his voice breaking, and I wonder if all this is too much of a shock for him.

"You see, Professor, my grandmother, Sharon, was your sister." My voice shakes. "And Ruby, your mother, never wanted to give you up, but she was forced to. She and Walter always wanted you."

He pulls a tissue from the box and mops at his face. "I always hoped it might be something like that. But you know what this means?" He rests his weary eyes on me.

I nod, my eyes watering again.

"You and I are family." He reaches for me and I accept his bear-like hug.

"You're my great-uncle!" I laugh through my tears.

"And all my kids and their kids are your cousins." He gestures to the others in the room.

I beam. "I always wanted a big family."

"But, Abbi, why didn't Will tell me any of this?" the professor asks.

My gut tightens. "I never got a chance to tell him. He was caught sneaking in that night and was hauled off to jail."

"That's right. I recall it now. You see it was over fifty years ago he told me."

"And I travelled that very night, and woke up here, this morning."

Colton's eyes widen. "You're saying that you were in 1930, like, yesterday?"

I nod. "And I left Will all alone, trapped in time. As soon as I woke up today, I went to find his buried treasure, but they've taken it." And even though I've just gained a family and given the professor the knowledge of who his parents were, I'm filled with despair. I fulfilled my promise to Grandma, but I've lost Will.

The professor reaches for my hand. "Abbi–"

"Some grad students found Will's buried treasure, and now, if he ever travels this far forward in time, he'll never find his tin. I won't be able to get a message to him." I stare at the floor, miserable.

"Abbi," the professor begins again, this time his voice strong and direct.

I look up.

"Will is here."

"What?" My breath leaves me.

"I saw him last night."

CHAPTER 24

"He's here? Now? Today?"

He chuckles. "Yes, he was in this very room. I retired from the university years ago, but I told Will how to find me. That's why I've refused to move to a smaller house."

"But I've been here all day. Why didn't he come and find me?" Then I realize I was all over campus and never in my room for long.

Colton's brow furrows. "Abbi, what's this Will guy look like?"

"He's tall, has sandy-blond hair, he laughs a lot and has this dimple." I touch my cheek, picturing him perfectly with that sparkle in his eyes.

Colton's jaw drops open.

"What?"

"Does he row?"

I nod.

"That's my roommate! I invited him to the bonfire at Picnic Point last night, but he turned me down because he had someone to see. It was you!" Colton says, turning to his grandfather.

All of the sudden my sight narrows to tunnel vision

and nothing else registers. Will is here. I stand. I can't let Will slip away from me again. What if he travelled last night?

"Did you see him this morning?" I demand.

Colton nods. "Yeah, he's a night owl. He sleeps in."

"I have to go. I have to find him. Please, can someone drive me back to campus?" My eyes dart around the room in desperation.

Colton jumps up. "I'll take you."

"Thank you! Professor, I'm sorry, but I have to find Will. I promise I'll be back as soon as I do. There's so much more I want to tell you!"

"Hold on, I'm coming too." The professor strains to rise from his recliner.

Colton helps him. "Gramps, are you sure?"

"Damn straight, I am. I haven't had this much excitement since I met my first time traveller back in fifty-one!"

"Dad, I'll take you. You'd never be able to wrench yourself out of Colton's car," Wally says.

Together Colton and I help the professor to his feet.

"Professor, what if I can't find him? What if he's gone?" I can't keep the panic from my voice.

"Rest assured, Will is as desperate to see you as you are to see him." He chortles. "And to think how angry you were with him that first day!" I can see the professor thinking back to that time so long ago.

"Any idea where Will would be?" I ask.

"He was sleeping when I left my room a couple of hours ago," Colton says.

We hop into Colton's car and race towards campus.

"I know my Gramps won some prestigious awards for

his work in physics, but is all this actually true?" He looks at me sideways while taking a corner.

I pull the newspaper out of my bag. "You know that buried treasure discovered on Picnic Point? It's featured in the *Badger Herald*. There's a photo in there of Will and me that we took back in 1930. For me it was only weeks ago. Some of our letters are pictured, and see that gold watch? It belonged to Will's father."

He glances at the paper and the car veers towards a parked truck. "Eyes on the road! You can read this later. And would you please drive faster." If only I could zap us to wherever Will is right this very instant. Colton runs a yellow light and I grip the armrest. He speeds along, losing Wally and the professor in our fumes.

When we arrive on campus, students are everywhere, so it's difficult to get through. Once at Tripp Hall, Colton parks in front of his dorm and we jump out.

"Will must have been up all night, to make sure he stayed here." I say, imagining him pacing the halls.

We run into the dorm and down the first-floor corridor. My heart is pounding. When we arrive at his room, I see Will's name on the door and nearly hyperventilate.

"Hurry," I urge Colton, wanting to break down the door.

He swings it open, but the room is empty. The wind goes out of me. If Will isn't here, where is he?

I step into the room and recognize his bag hanging over the foot of the bed. I run to it and clutch it. The room even smells like Will. I sigh with relief. I'm getting close.

We run back to the car, and his dad and Professor Smith are waiting, their hopeful faces fall the moment they see us without Will.

"Now where?" Colton asks.

"Did Will tell you what he planned to do today?" I ask the professor.

"Only that he planned to see you, but we didn't know if you'd be missing from this time, or here, but unaware of the time travelling."

I glance over the surrounding trees and shrubs, willing him to step out of the shadows. "He could be anywhere, Picnic Point, at rowing practice, my dorm, maybe the Union Terrace."

Wally takes charge. "Let's split up. Colton, why don't you check out Picnic Point since it's too far for your grandfather. Abbi, try your dorm and see if he's been there. I'll take Dad to the Terrace where we'll keep an eye out and wait for you to meet up with us."

We take off in different directions. I take the path that cuts from Tripp Hall over to Liz Waters. The lawns are green and the bike racks are overflowing.

Inside my room, Jada looks up from painting her toe-nails. "You sure are popular today. Another guy stopped by to see you."

I nearly cry with relief.

"Are you okay?" Jada holds the tiny brush in mid-air.

"I'll be better soon. What did he look like? What did he say?" This has to be Will. I can't imagine anyone else who would come.

"He was tall, really cute. Oh, and he had this long

blade of grass in his hand. Kinda weird!"

Yes! "And what did he say?" I'm tense, like a spring wound too tight.

"That you should meet him at the bell tower."

Of course. "When was he here?"

"About two hours ago."

"He must have stopped by right after I left." I can't believe I missed him. "So you think he's there now?"

"Maybe. I asked if he wanted to leave his number, but he said he hadn't figured out how to use his phone yet. Isn't that odd?"

"No. That's Will."

"That's right. His name was Will. So you know him?"

Heading out the door I smile. "Yes, I definitely know him."

* * *

If Jada's right, Will is two minutes away. I hurry outside, where I can see the top of the Carillon Tower beyond the Social Sciences Building. I consider texting Colton that I may have found Will, but I want this moment for myself.

I follow Observatory Drive the short distance down the hill and then up to where the tower is. Other students on the pavement block my view of the tower's base. My heartbeat thumps against my chest and my hands perspire as I try to find Will in the crowd. *Please be there, please be there.*

A group of students cuts across the street, and finally, I see him. He's wearing cargo shorts, a grey Wisconsin T-shirt and leaning against the building with one foot braced on the stone wall. I grin at how perfectly he blends in with the other students.

Will stares into the distance, his hair blowing in the breeze and his mind seeming a million miles away. He's probably soaking up all the changes of the twenty-first century, with students buzzing by on mopeds or walking with their eyes glued to their mobile phones.

I stop about fifteen feet away, my heart bursting. He looks exactly the same as yesterday with his deep summer tan, sun-streaked hair and lean body.

Something causes him to turn and look in my direction, and he freezes. "Abbi," he gasps, and his expression morphs from casual indifference to shock and relief.

He tosses away the blade of grass and strides towards me. I run into his arms. He holds me tight, and I hug him back, releasing all the pain and anguish of losing him. Having him in my arms feels as if I've finally come home, and neither of us is willing to let go.

He nuzzles my neck and breathes in my ear. "I've missed you desperately."

I inhale his scent and melt in his arms. "I thought I'd never see you again," I whimper.

He pulls away to look at me, tears in his eyes. "My beautiful Abbi," he whispers. Then he lowers his mouth to mine.

When we part, he cups my face. "I can't believe you're really here. I hoped, I prayed, I wished on stars and here you are. It's a miracle."

"It's only been a day for me, but I was out of my mind worrying about you."

I spot a scar on his jawline. "What happened here?" I touch the mark gently and notice a fading bruise.

He smiles. "It's nothing. It doesn't matter now."

"How long has it been for you ... since we were last together?"

The light in his eyes dims. "A very long time, but we can talk about that later."

He alternates between hugging me, checking to make sure I'm real and planting kisses all over my face.

I laugh and pull him close, letting the touch of his body anchor me in the present. "You're really here."

"I am."

"Oh, Will." I pull away to look at him. "I have so much to tell you."

"And I, you." He weaves his fingers through my hair.

"First, why didn't you come and find me last night?" I ask.

"I did, but you looked right past me. It was devastating."

I rack my brain trying to think of when I might have seen him, but I have no memory of it. Then again it was months ago for me. And he would have been a stranger.

"I knew then you hadn't travelled yet. You'd have had no idea who I was. I couldn't take a chance that I'd change something, so I said nothing."

"I'm so sorry. I wish I could have talked to you."

"Last night was the longest of my life. I was terrified you wouldn't be here today, or if you were, that you still wouldn't know me."

"Of course I would know you." I trail my fingers over his arms.

"No, according to Professor Smith, it's possible you

might not have. But now that we're both here at the same time, we have to go and see if he can figure out how to keep us together." He links his fingers through mine. "I'm never leaving you again."

"You mean … you don't want to go back home? You want to stay with me?"

"Abbi, you are my home."

I give him another long kiss. "The professor is on the Terrace waiting for us."

"Right now?"

"Yes. Let me text him." I pull out my phone and text Colton and his dad.

Will watches intently. "I found a gizmo like that on my bedside table, but I can't begin to figure out what to do with it."

"That's all right. I'll teach you." I kiss his cheek. "Come on, we'll meet him and my new cousin there." I look up for his reaction.

"Who?" Will stops short and narrows his eyes. "Why do I get the feeling something else is going on here?"

I grip his hand in excitement. "I found Ruby's baby!"

"When?"

"While you were at the stag party, I got a letter from Ruby."

Will's eyes light up as I spill the whole story. "Professor Smith is Ruby's baby?"

I nod and he breaks into a huge smile. "That's amazing."

"Can you believe it? He is my grandmother's brother!"

He sweeps me into another hug and twirls me around as if we've just won the lottery, and I feel as if we have.

***

The modern-day familiarity of the Terrace is like an old friend, so much bigger than it was in my trips to the past. Music is playing and boats bob out on the water. Hundreds of bright tables and chairs are filled with students kicking back and enjoying the mild day.

"It's changed so much," Will says, giving a low whistle.

I hug his arm, fully intending to be here for him in this foreign era.

A group of girls takes turns posing for pictures in an oversized sunburst chair. There's an outside concession stand selling beer, and the scent of sausages and burgers on the grill fills the air.

"I could get used to it," he says, taking it all in.

"Abbi, Will! Over here." Wally waves from a round green table, where he sits with Professor Smith.

Will squeezes my hand and we join them.

"Hi. I'm Wally. It's incredible to finally meet you." He shakes Will's hand.

"My pleasure. Professor Smith has told me a lot about you over the years."

The professor smiles broadly. The fact is not lost on me that he and I have sat together on this same terrace at various times throughout my travels.

We take seats. "Colton is on his way," Wally says.

Misty eyed, the professor says, "I never thought I'd see this day."

Will and I, and our time travel, have been a part of his life since he started college. Now he's an old man, witnessing us finally back together. It's no wonder he's emotional.

"Me neither." Will looks at me and presses his knee to mine.

Colton appears, out of breath, as if he ran all the way from Picnic Point. "Hey, Gramps," he says, but his eyes dart to Will and me, studying us as if he can find some sign that we have truly travelled through time.

"Hi, Colton." Will stands. "I can't believe you're tied into this too."

"Dude, is it true? You're some sort of time traveller from, like, a century ago?"

Will laughs. "I'm afraid so."

Colton shakes his head, still struggling for it all to make sense.

"Relax, Colton. Give it some time to sink in," his grandfather says.

Colton drops into an empty chair, shaking his head in amazement.

Will and I grin.

I look around and sigh. I'm really back. "Professor–"

"You don't need to call me professor. I think we've known each other long enough, plus we're family now!" he says with delight. "How about Smitty, like back in my college days?"

I recall the awkward young boy I first met. "Uncle Smitty," I say fondly and lean over to peck him on the cheek. "So ... how did I get here?"

Smitty takes a deep breath. "You see, while I've cracked the why and how of your time travel, I never could determine how to control it. It's my firm belief that you and Will both landed back here of your own free will. Or, perhaps I should say, fate."

Will and I just stare at him blankly.

"Over the years, I've done a lot of research on sound waves, quantum theory of gravity, energy fields and string theory."

The rest of us look around the table at each other, already lost. Colton looks at his grandfather as if he's speaking Portuguese.

"Dumb it down, please, Grandpa. We aren't all geniuses," Colton says.

I notice a twinkle in the professor's eyes.

"All right. Let me see." He pauses and I can almost see the wheels turning in his brain. "Based on string theory, everything in the universe, from the tiniest particles to distant stars, is made from one thing: unimaginably small strands of vibrating energy called strings. It also theorizes there are many parallel universes similar to our own, connected by these strings."

"So there are all kinds of different versions of us sitting around a table eating lunch?" Colton asks, his mouth hanging open in shock.

"It's much more complex than that. While the theories I've mentioned have been around for decades, the idea of how one parallel universe might intersect with another has never been proven."

He takes a long sip of his beer and leans back in his chair. "I believe what happened to you and Will occurred due to several factors. One being the sound waves created by the bells ringing in the Carillon Tower."

"What are the other factors?" I ask.

"This is where things become a bit more sketchy. My

theory is that a vortex formed in your dorm room precisely where your bed is, which explains why everything on the bed travelled with you. The same type of vortex exists in Will's dorm room."

"And what caused this vortex?" Will asks.

"A number of occurrences. I've done extensive research on the effigy mounds located near the dorms. Native Americans understood unseen energies. I believe their mounds created some sort of magnetic field. In fact, at one time, an effigy mound was located exactly where Elizabeth Waters dorm is, and disturbing that mound stirred up another energy."

I look at Will with wide eyes. We were onto something back in 1930.

"In addition, I analyzed the dates both of you travelled, and it always occurred during a full moon, which affects gravity, tides and magnetic pull."

Around the table, we sit silently, trying to take this in.

"Do you think other people time travelled from our rooms?" Will asks.

"I can't say for certain, but I haven't found any such evidence."

"Then why us?" I ask, looking at Will, squeezing his hand.

He nods. "Now that I've learned that your grandmother was on her deathbed, longing for the identity of her lost sibling, I think that deep-seated emotional need was the final ingredient that brought all the factors together into the perfect storm for time travel."

He takes a breath and adjusts his glasses, seeming

to get a hold of his emotions. I can't imagine what he must be feeling right now to have learned that he is the lost sibling.

"Abbi, you were mourning the loss of your grand-mother so strongly. You were longing for family and whether you realized it or not, you needed to fulfill your promise to her. That, combined with the energy of the hatbox and the other factors, weakened the walls of the universe, transporting you to a parallel universe in a dif-ferent time. And Will was in a similar situation. He came to the university because of a deep-seated thirst for knowl-edge and to build a better life for himself. He's much like me in that way." The professor smiles fondly. "But then he lost his family and was left mourning and desperate for love. We must never underestimate the power of intense longing. I believe it's what brought you two together."

"Smitty," Will says, and I smile at his familiarity with the professor. "Now that Abbi and I are both finally here in this time, how do we stay?" He takes hold of my wrist, tethering me to him.

It's the only answer I'm looking for too. The odds of us finding each other in the randomness of time can't be a coincidence. We're meant for each other. I'm sure of it, and I know Will is too. And after everything we've been through, we can't risk being separated again.

Smitty leans back in his chair. "That should be rela-tively easy."

Will squeezes my hand. "Easy would be nice for a change."

"We need to get you away from the vortex," Smitty says with a serious set to his eyes.

"You mean they can't sleep in their dorm rooms?" Colton asks.

"Exactly. And I'd feel much safer if they were away from the effigy mounds and the Carillon Tower as well."

"So we need to find new dorms?" Will asks.

"More than that. You'll have to move off campus, and I suggest you do it immediately. Even though the circumstances have changed – you're both happy, and Abbi has resolved her grandmother's mystery – and mine! – I just don't want to risk having either of you anywhere near that vortex. In fact," he turns to Colton, "while I don't think you're likely to be going anywhere, I'd sleep better knowing you found a new room, perhaps one of the dorms far from the Carillon Tower."

I look to Will, then back to the professor. "But, where will we go?"

"I thought you might stay at my house. At least until you have time to find something closer to campus. I've been holding on to that big old house all these years in case you needed it. We have more bedrooms than we could ever use. Of course, I understand that two young kids like you might be mortified to move in with a couple of fossils like my wife and me."

Will and I smile and nod knowingly at each other. "We'd love to stay with you. At least while we make a plan," Will says, then adds, "And I could get some advanced physics tutoring from the best in the field."

"And you and I can make up for lost time," I say to Smitty. "Oh, and I'll have to get my mom to come to town so you can meet her. I'm not sure if we should tell her about the whole time travel thing right away. But she'll understand from the things Grandma sent in her hatbox how I looked into the past and found you."

I experience a twinge of sadness that I'll never get the chance to share the news with Grandma. Then I think back to the day I introduced Sharon and Smitty in the Liz Waters lobby, and I smile. There's a sense of peace in realizing that she's probably looking down on us, celebrating from above that I was able to tell Smitty in time. And I think that was the point all along.

"I would love to meet my sister's daughter. My niece." Smitty's face radiates happiness, and I catch a glimpse of the hopeful young man I met long ago.

* * *

That night Will and I stand on Smitty's back deck and look out over the water. The air is cool and the moon is full. Lights from campus twinkle from far across the lake. I shiver and Will slips his arm around me.

"Abbi, I know the reason I time travelled was to find you."

Turning to him, I place my hand on his chest. "Thank God you did."

He brushes a lock of hair from my face and gazes into my eyes. "You are my soulmate. I know we're too young to a make any permanent commitments, and we've shared the most life-altering experiences–"

I silence him with a kiss. "Will, I'm forever connected to you."

Joy spreads across his face. "I'm glad to hear that, because I've travelled a long time to find you." He grazes his lips over mine. "You look happy," he says in his low, husky voice.

"I am. I've gained a family, and now I have you."

"Until the end of time." He kisses me, and from across the lake, we hear the distant sound of a bell's chime.

Author's Note

Thank you for reading *Waking in Time*. There really was a Ruby and her life was the inspiration for this story. Unfortunately, very little is known about her. The clues to her life came to me as I was exploring genealogy. Any relatives who knew Ruby had long passed away, so all I had to work with was a birth certificate, a photo of a young nun and family lore.

When Ruby was two years old, her mother died suddenly. The story goes that her twenty-two-year-old mother received a fright from something outside the window and fell over dead while Ruby sat in her highchair. Little Ruby was shuffled around to different family members until her father remarried. Ruby referred to this woman as her wicked stepmother. Early pictures show the disdain on the stepmother's face and the apprehension on Ruby's.

As a teenager, Ruby was shipped off to boarding school, where she met a young man named Walter. I contacted the boarding school and they shared records showing Ruby's unexplained absence for one year, and then her sudden reappearance the next.

I also discovered that Walter went off to fight in World War I around that same time. It wasn't until later when I found a photo labelled, SISTER MARY RUBY, ME AT THE CONVENT, that I felt certain Ruby, who was not Catholic, was sent away to have her baby and give it up for adoption. While this may seem unlikely in today's world, it was quite common at that time and for decades to follow.

Walter eventually returned from the war, and he and Ruby were soon married and had three more children. Sadly, Ruby died from cancer at age forty-four while her daughter was away at college. Walter died of a heart attack three years later.

As I unravelled Ruby's story and the mysteries of her life, it broke my heart not to know what became of the baby she was forced to give up. Despite my best efforts, I was never able to discover what convent Ruby was sent to, ending all chance of finding Ruby's child.

Saddened and frustrated, I decided to write my own version of Ruby's story, giving her child a bright future and a loving family.

Here's to you, Ruby. You will never be forgotten.

For photos and more on *Waking in Time*, please go to:

www.AngieStanton.com.

Facebook.com/AngieStantonAuthor
Twitter.com/Angie_Stanton
Instagram.com/angiestanton_author

The Facts Behind
the Story

Many aspects of *Waking in Time* are factual, and great effort was made to bring a truthful representation of the fashions, buildings and events covered throughout the book. That said, creative license was taken when necessary to aid the story, so for any historians out there, my apologies for tweaking a couple of details.

Here are a few tidbits from the story that are true.

The Sterling Hall bombing is a devastating piece of the University of Wisconsin's history. One man died, four were injured, and years of research by teams of graduate students and professors was lost. Sterling Hall still stands today.

Many effigy mounds exist around campus, including on Observatory Hill and Picnic Point. It has been reported that there are more effigy mounds on the UW campus than any other place in the country. Unfortunately, several of the mounds have been destroyed over the years due to campus construction, notably one for the building of Elizabeth Waters dormitory.

The colourful Union Terrace chairs are an iconic symbol that date back to the 1920s in various styles.

Cheap Trick had a fondness for Madison and its supportive fans. They performed at Headliners throughout the seventies and after reaching fame, and occasionally snuck into town for a performance in the early 1980s.

The dates that Elizabeth Waters dormitory and the Carillon Tower were built have been altered to serve the story.

As a child, my family would occasionally trek to Picnic Point where I was fascinated by stories of buried treasure. Clearly that never left me.

Acknowledgements

Writing a book takes a village, but in this case, it also takes a team of University of Wisconsin alumni spanning more than seventy years to get a clear picture of life on campus throughout the decades.

Many thanks to the following for sharing their amazing stories:

WJ "Tip" Tyler, MS '42, PhD '45

Rex S Spiller, Sr., '43

Jo Ann Adams, '51

Patricia Green, '69

Sally Schlise, '71

Ryan J Herringa, '97, MD '06

Leslie Bellais, MA '09, PhD '16

Erin Zimmerman, x'18

Thank you to the University of Wisconsin Archives staff for allowing me countless hours to research the history of campus, page through ancient yearbooks and lose myself in sixty-year-old copies of the *Daily Cardinal*.

Special thanks go out to the people who answered crazy

research questions, provided critiques on early versions of the book or offered moral support when I'd hit the wall: Mary Kay Adams-Edgette, Deb Barkelar, Judy Bryan, Nichole Chase, Lynda Colton, Jolene Esterline, Mary Finnel, Alice Haley, Kris Hebl, Joanna Hinsey, Glenn Mullett, Elizabeth Reinhardt, Linda Schmalz, Claire Swinarski, Donna Van Keuren, Adam Weimerskirch, Kristi Weimerskirch and my Wednesday night Barriques YA writers' group. My apologies to the countless others who I've neglected to recall after the two-year journey of writing this book.

To my agent, Jane Dystel, for your steadfast support of *Waking in Time*. Working with you is always a pleasure. And to Miriam Goderich for your insightful suggestions and kindness. You ladies make a fabulous team.

To Kristen Mohn for falling in love with *Waking in Time*. Working with you has been a dream. And to the Capstone Publishing and Switch Press family, thank you for taking care of my baby.

Finally, to my family, who is everything to me. I will love you until the end of time.

Angie Stanton is a lifelong daydreamer who grew up with her hands on a book and her head in the clouds. As an adult, she's learned to put her talent to good use and writes contemporary fiction about life, love and the adventures they promise. She is the author of eight novels including *Rock and a Hard Place* and *Love 'em or Leave 'em*. Angie has a special place in her heart for the University of Wisconsin-Madison, where she earned a degree in journalism.